HOOKED ON YOU

K. EVAN COLES

D1714403

WICKED FINGERS PRESS

For information contact:

http://www.kevancoles.com

Book and Cover design by K. Evan Coles

Edited by Beth Greenberg

SUMMARY

*WHAT'S A STRAIGHT GUY TO DO WHEN HE FALLS FOR
HIS NEW FRIEND?*

Paramedic Connor Devlin is a stressed-out tower of a man. Hoping knitting will help him unwind, he visits a local craft shop, where he's overwhelmed by the yarn selection but more so by his feelings for shop owner Judah.

Judah Bissel is tired of falling for unavailable men. He can't help his crush on Connor, though, or wanting to get closer to the big, gentle bear. And that just might spell trouble because pining for straight guys is not Judah's style.

As a blizzard pummels the city, the men hunker down together to wait out the storm. When the spark between them ignites, will the revelation that Connor feels more than friendship for Judah bring them together or tear them apart?

Hooked On You is a 72.8K friends-to-lovers MM novel. It features a stressed-out paramedic who's figuring out he's not quite straight, a yarn shop owner with a bad habit of falling for unavailable guys, lots of knitting and snowdrifts, and a sweet, happy-sigh HEA.

For my son, who makes me laugh every single day.

Enormous thanks to Helena Stone, Randall Jussaume, Beth Greenberg, and Shelli Pates, who generously donated their time to help fix my words and improve my cover, and Barb Payne Ingram, proofreading ninja. You people give me life!

All you knit is love.

ONE

Thursday, January 3

YOU ARE in way over your head, buddy.

Connor Devlin had never seen so much yarn. Literal boxes of it, cubbies stacked floor to near ceiling on the walls of Hook Me, a knitting supply shop in Boston's North End and only a few blocks from Connor's apartment. He'd walked by the shop dozens of times on his way to work but had never been inside it until tonight. And he had very little idea of what he was looking at other than so. Much. Yarn.

Eyebrows drawn together, Connor peered into the cubby nearest him and its neat stacks of wooly bundles, vibrant hues ranging from deep rose to shocking pink. Movements tentative, he fingered one of the bundles, his frown growing deeper as he considered the colorful, organized chaos. Where the hell did he start?

"Do you have a particular pattern in mind?"

Connor almost jumped out of his skin. For a guy who stood

six-foot-four, he'd always been easy to startle, a personality flaw many of his co-workers exploited with great glee. Forcing himself to take a breath and peel his shoulders down from around his ears, Connor turned to the guy who had appeared at his side. Still, his surprise must have shown because the guy's face immediately scrunched up in a wince.

"I'm *so* sorry," he said to Connor. "I didn't mean to sneak up on you."

"You're fine," Connor murmured, blinking rapidly as the guy's lips quirked into a smile.

Oh, crap. Fine was an understatement.

This guy was nothing at all like the caftan-wearing ladies Connor had imagined working in this store. Mr. Hook Me was maybe five years younger than Connor's thirty-two, with striking gray-green eyes and a Pride pin attached to the collar of his black shirt. He'd been behind the counter when Connor had walked in and Connor's attention had been on the yarn. No chance of ignoring the guy now that they stood only a foot or two apart, however, especially with Mr. Hook Me smiling at him. Connor was abruptly glad he'd exchanged his Boston EMS uniform shirt and jacket for street clothes before leaving the station.

Wait, what? What difference did it make what Connor wore?

"I noticed you'd been standing here for a while," the guy said, then gestured toward the wall of cubbies. "I thought I'd check in, make sure you were finding everything you need."

"Thanks." Connor pushed his hair back over his shoulder, his cheeks on fire as he caught himself staring. He hoped his beard hid at least some of his blush. This guy looked like a film actor for crying out loud, all slim and sleek, his form graceful compared to Connor's meaty body. Not that Connor should be thinking about Mr. Hook Me's body. Or any man's. Except he was. And why?

Ugh.

Shifting his focus back to the wall of cubbies, Connor cleared his throat. "I'm, um, honestly not sure what I need."

"Is that why you were talking to yourself?"

"Say what now?"

Mr. Hook Me's smile grew a little wider when Connor glanced back, and his eyes crinkled at the corners. "You said 'Where the hell do I start?' A question I hear often, by the way. People talk to themselves all the time in this store. I suspect it's a knitter thing."

"Oh, I'm not a knitter," Connor said. He looked away again, his face blazing hotter. He was making himself sound awfully stupid. Not to mention talking out loud to no one in a public place. "Or at least not yet. I wasn't kidding when I said I have no idea what I need, though. I've never even held a pair of knitting hooks."

"They're called needles," Mr. Hook Me replied, his tone easy. "A hook is what you'd use for crochet, which is different from knitting entirely." An encouraging expression crossed his face when Connor met his gaze. "Or maybe that's what you want to do instead?"

"I'm ... not sure."

With a shake of his head, Connor glanced at the door. He could leave. Call this outing what it was—a mess—and go home and fix himself a sandwich for dinner. He'd only come in here because his coworker Olivia was convinced that a hobby would help wrangle some of Connor's anxiety. He could find a different yarn shop. Maybe do some googling before he ventured in, and hope it was staffed with safe, caftan-wearing ladies who didn't make Connor's insides go both tight and melty when they smiled.

"Don't worry about it," Mr. Hook Me said, his voice soothing. He cocked his head at Connor. "Can I ask what brought you in here tonight? That might help me understand what you're looking to do."

Connor gave a terse nod. "Right. Well, like I said, I've never knit or done crochet before, so I guess I'm more looking to get started than anything else."

"That makes sense." The guy's forehead puckered, and a thoughtful air came over him. "Is there a project you're looking to work toward once you understand stitches and the mechanics of needlework?"

"Yeah, actually. How did you know?"

"Lucky guess. A lot of people have an idea in mind when they decide they want to learn to knit, be it a scarf or socks, or even a winter hat."

"I want to knit a baby blanket," Connor blurted. He drew a rectangle in the air with his index fingers, then almost rolled his eyes at himself—what the hell was wrong with him tonight? "I'm not really sure what size would be best, though."

"No problem. We've got books of patterns that could be of help if you'd like to look through them." Mr. Hook Me tipped his head in the direction of the counter.

"That'd be great, thanks."

"Of course. Knowing what you'll need to create your final project may help me too, so I can direct you to the right yarn or recommend specific stitches. I also have plenty of suggestions about how to get started with the learning part. Oh, man." Bowing his head slightly, Mr. Hook Me set a hand over his heart. "I'm being super rude. I'm Judah and this is my place."

"Nice to meet you, Judah." Connor shook the hand Judah extended. This guy was something. Confident but genuine, too, and so good at not making Connor feel like a big oaf. "My name's Connor. I'll take any advice you can give me on the learning and the blanket and whatever else I might need to know about knitting. Or crochet. Hah." He huffed out a breath. "I'm sure I sound like a complete dope wandering in with zero idea of what I'm doing."

Judah gave a soft chuckle. "Not at all. People walk in here all the time with an idea of what they'd like to make and no concrete knowledge of what it will take to get there. It was a daily occurrence in the run up to Hanukkah and Christmas! That's where I come in." He gestured Connor toward the counter. "How about we get started with the patterns and go from there?"

Thirty minutes later, they'd come to the agreement that Connor wanted to learn to knit and not crochet, at least for the time being. Judah had settled Connor in a big, overstuffed chair near the counter at the back of the store and Connor was paging through a book of patterns. Glancing up, Connor caught sight of Judah talking quietly with a customer, his expression bright and interested.

It's nice in here.

Connor blinked, aware then of how heavy his eyelids had become. What the heck? Clearly, he was overtired, but he was in a yarn store, for crying out loud. While it might be cozy, what with the comfy chair and the chill house music, it was no place for a nap.

Sitting up straighter, Connor flipped the page of the pattern book and stopped, sure he'd found exactly what he wanted. He got to his feet and walked to the register, intent on showing Judah the pattern once the man was free to talk, when an abrupt increase in noise drew his attention to the door. Several women of varying ages trooped in, chatting among themselves. They waved cheerily at Judah, calling out greetings as they approached him and his customer, but the conversations stuttered when they spotted Connor. The women's eyes went wide then, and sudden smiles crossed their faces, two or three giving him a none-too-subtle once over. Connor quickly glued his gaze back on the book of patterns, heat licking along his cheeks again.

"Please go on in and make yourselves comfortable, everyone," Judah called out, much closer to Connor than he had been only moments before. "There is plenty of coffee and tea as well as some very nice cookies from our favorite bakery, and I'll be down in a few minutes. How are you doing over here, Connor?" he asked in a quieter tone as he walked behind the counter.

"Doing okay," Connor said over the chatter rising from the women once more. Glancing up, he watched them head through a door to the right of the register and disappear from sight. A quick look around told him the rest of the shop was now empty and Connor checked his watch. Quarter to six? He'd been in Hook Me for nearly an hour. "What time do you close?"

"Officially, we close at five-thirty," Judah said. "We host classes and social circles in the basement most evenings, however, including tonight from six to eight. That's what everyone who's come in for the last five minutes is here for—socializing while they knit or crochet." He raised his hand in greeting as another trio of women entered with a man just behind. The women did the same deer in the headlights upon noticing Connor, who turned his attention right back to the knitting pattern. "I'll be right with you," Judah said to the new arrivals.

"Damn, I didn't mean to stay so late." Connor could almost hear Judah's shrug as he replied.

"No worries. You couldn't have known and, obviously, other customers have been in. Besides, you were busy with your pattern hunting. Did you find one you like?"

"I think so, yeah. What do you think?" Spinning the book around, Connor nudged it closer to Judah and watched him eye the pages with a smile.

"This is an excellent choice. The garter stitch is not difficult to master at all—it's the first stitch you'd learn as a knitter and once you've got it down, this pattern will go quickly. That said, you'll be using two strands of yarn, so the blanket will be soft and squishy and super warm when it's finished. Perfect for a baby."

"Great. I really like all the colors." Connor ran his fingertip over the photo in the book, then pursed his lips. How the heck did you get purple, lilac, and pretty, soft green into one blanket? Before he could ask, the young man who'd just entered peeled off from the group and joined them, his eyes very like Judah's though more brown.

"Hey, bro," he said to Judah. "Just wanted to say hi. Who's your Viking friend here?"

The tips of Judah's ears turned pink. "This is Connor," he said in a tone that held a lightly chiding note. "He came in tonight to shop for knitting supplies." Judah looked almost abashed as he glanced back to Connor. "Connor, this is my brother Levi."

"Hello." Connor nodded but Levi surprised him by quickly pulling off his gloves and thrusting out a hand.

"Hiya." Levi gave Connor a firm shake before letting him go. He tipped his head toward the nearby door as the women he'd walked in with disappeared through it. "You going down to hang with the knitting nerds, Connor? I keep telling Judah it'd be nice to have some dudes around on these nights to break up the estrogen-fest."

Connor made himself return Levi's smile. "Uh, no. I don't actually know how to knit yet."

"Meh, that's okay. You could just join in for coffee, cookies, and gossip because, seriously, that is what the stitch-and-bitch is all about. You should sign up for the Knitting 101 class." Levi gave Connor a knowing look. "People come in here all the time who can't knit for crap, but once Judah and Molly get a hold of them, they find their inner skills."

Judah sighed. "I'm not sure you're doing a good job of selling it, bro."

"Says you." Levi made his eyebrows go up and down in an exaggerated manner that made Connor chuckle. "Anyway, I have homework and *you* should get down there before the circle goes all *Lord of the Flies*, Jude. You know what they can be like when you're not around to make sure everyone plays nice with the cookie platter."

Judah let out a laugh. "I do. I'll see you for dinner, okay?"

"You bet." Levi turned for the exit again but called back to Connor as he headed out. "Good meeting you, Connor—I'll see you around!"

"See ya, Levi." Connor watched him go, then set his hands on his hips with a small frown. "Judah? How many classes does a person have to take if they want to master Knitting 101?"

"There are four classes in the course, and each is two hours," Judah replied. "Most people can knit a garter stitch proficiently by the end of their first class, though, and I know plenty who've taught themselves to knit by watching YouTube."

Connor bit back a groan as the door opened once more, admitting a twosome of teenaged girls, one of whom let out a noisy "*damn*" as she ogled Connor.

"Jeez." Judah looked as though he was trying not to lose it laughing and waved them on. "I'm sorry about that," he said to Connor. "As Levi said, we don't get a lot of men in the circle, particularly not guys like you."

Connor pursed his lips, his stomach going tight. "Guys like me?"

Judah's expression softened. "You know you look a little like a real-life Thor, right? And the fact you might be even remotely interested in needlework ... well, you must see how that might make an impression on a group of crafting nerds." His small smile cut right through the awkwardness that threatened to overwhelm Connor.

"Fair." Connor said. "It's not the first time someone's ..."

"Admired you?" Now Judah smirked. "Yeah, that tracks."

Way to make yourself sound like a conceited ass.

Connor chewed the inside of his cheek. He knew he wasn't a bad-looking guy. He'd never understood why any woman would want to ogle him, though, and every time it happened, he just felt mystified and vaguely uncomfortable. Luckily, Judah seemed completely unfazed by the whole thing.

"Back to your question about knitting class," he said now to Connor. "New sessions start this week if you're really interested in attending."

"I'm interested. I think it'd be good for me. I want to finish the blanket *before* my partner's baby is born and I'm not sure I'll be able to do that by watching videos." Granted, Olivia wasn't due for another five months, but Connor had no idea how long it'd take him to knit a potholder, never mind an entire blanket.

"Got it," Judah said. "Not everyone likes to learn from a screen, and I respect that."

Heading past Connor, he rounded the counter so he could flip through a set of hanging folders. Plucking a sheet of blue paper from one, he turned back and laid it on the counter in front of Connor.

"Here we go." Judah tapped a calendar on the sheet with one finger. "Knitting 101 happens on Tuesday evening from six to eight, Saturday morning from ten to twelve, and Sunday afternoon from four to six. Most people sign up to come once a week, but if your schedule allows, you're welcome to attend multiple classes. They're held in the basement about ninety percent of the time, but now and then we'll have one up here in the store, just for a change of scene."

Connor nodded but couldn't help feeling something was off. Judah's demeanor had changed somehow, grown more closed off in just the few seconds it had taken him to find the class schedule, and damn if Connor knew why. What the heck had just happened?

"Okay," he said, rubbing his hands against his dark brown cargo pants. "And are you the teacher? Or would it be the person your brother mentioned?"

"Molly?" Judah's face relaxed a bit. "Most of the time I'm the instructor, yes, but Molly and I sometimes switch off when she's in town. Molly is my mom."

"Really?" Connor looked around the store again. "So, you run this place together?"

"Yep. We have a shop up in Stowe, too, and my mom and stepdad live there. My stepdad's an accountant, by the way, and he still can't tell the difference between a knitting needle and crochet hook, but my mom has never held it against him." He smiled. "They come down on Sundays for dinner with my brother and me, and Mom likes to teach class when she has time." Judah paused as a burst of loud laughter echoed through the door leading to the basement. "Um. I should make sure they're not doing anything too off the wall down there."

"The more I hear about this circle the more interested I get," Connor said. He picked up the class flyer. "Okay if I take this?"

"Absolutely." Judah walked back around the counter. "The class signup is online at hook me dot-com. Oh! I almost forgot."

He doubled back and grabbed a small, brown paper shopping bag from beside the cash register and handed it to Connor.

"This is a beginners' knitting kit. Needles, a small ball of soft yarn, and a sheet with lots of links for tutorials."

Connor peered down into the little bag, a warm buzz filtering through him. "Whoa, thanks. How much do I—?"

"Not a thing." Judah shook his head. "You can practice on your own and, if you do end up coming to class, just bring it along and I'll upgrade everything."

"Oh, I'll be back," Connor promised. "I still need the pattern for the baby blanket."

The corners of Judah's eyes crinkled as he laughed. "True! I'll make a copy for you and keep it here at the counter. Guess I'll see you around, Connor."

Connor sketched a wave as he headed for the door, but he carried the sparkle in Judah's eyes out of the shop right along with him.

TWO

Why does the universe hate me so much?

After closing up shop for the night, Judah Bissel dropped the shop's cash and credit earnings for the day in the night deposit box at the bank on the next block, then retraced his steps past Hook Me and around the corner to the residential entrance of the building. He climbed the stairs to the flat above the shop, still stewing about his bad luck.

Bad enough that cute-as-hell Connor had walked into his store and seemed genuinely interested in learning to knit. The big, bearded giant with the long hair had also been sweet, with earnest brown eyes and an accent too soft to be local with long, rounded 'o' sounds. He'd been adorably shy too, his cheeks flushing a gorgeous pink when he'd confessed to Judah that he didn't know where to start with his project.

Judah had just smiled at Connor's mention of the baby blanket, though most men in his place would have immediately taken it as a sign the guy was off limits. Judah had always been an optimistic soul, however, and quickly convinced himself the blanket could be a gift for a totally-not-romantic-kind-of-person in Connor's life. The whole effort had been for naught, of course, because that was how Judah's world worked, and Connor had been the one smiling when he'd talked about his partner and unknowingly squashed Judah's hopes.

Judah sighed. He really needed to get his head out of the clouds.

Letting himself into the apartment, he found his half-brother in the kitchen making salad. He instantly felt a little less sorry for himself when Levi's grin lit up the whole room.

"What up, creep?" Levi asked. "Did everybody make it out of the stitch-and-bitch in one piece?"

"Thankfully, yes." Judah went to the wine rack in the corner. "I thought I was going to have to hose some people down once the supply of raspberry bowties ran low, however. I swear, I've never seen people go so bananas for butter cookies." He gestured toward the bottles on the rack. "You want a glass?"

Levi laughed. "Uh, duh, of course. To be fair to the yarn nerds, butter cookies are yummy."

"Sure, but it's not like they're impossible to find. There are three bakeries that sell them on this street alone."

"Yes, but you're forgetting that the cookies at social circle nights are free which makes them extra delicious. People love a freebie and who can blame them?"

"True." Judah selected a bottle of pinot noir and carried it to the counter. "This is why I only put out two-thirds of every box I buy, because the platter would be empty before class even started. Hell, half of the cookies were gone by the time I made it downstairs tonight."

"Exactly how late were you to your own social circle?" Levi cocked an eyebrow Judah's way. "The social circle you host, one level down from the shop you own? What the hell took you so long?"

Judah worked a corkscrew into the bottle of wine. "I was

helping a customer," he said lightly, hoping against hope that Levi would let it go.

Something that was never going to happen of course, because Levi was far too sharp and knew Judah only too well.

"Yeah, that's a lie. Because you've got a face like a wet weekend right now and I want to know what the heck crawled up your butt and died."

Before he could stop himself, Judah snorted out a laugh. "I'm fine!"

"No, you're pouting." Levi's eyes got big. "Ohhh. Is this about the Norse god I met downstairs?"

"Yes."

"Uh-oh. But why? Is Tall, Blonde, and Viking already taken?"

"So taken. As in pregnant partner-with-a-baby-on-the-way kind of taken."

Levi grimaced and sprinkled the basil he'd been chopping into the salad bowl. "That really sucks. You didn't know when you started flirting with him?"

"I wasn't flirting." Judah pulled the cork from the bottle. "Or at least not purposely. A man wandered into my shop, project in mind but zero idea how to get there, and I took it upon myself to help him. That's my job, Levi. I sell people supplies so they can make their projects a reality."

"I know this." Clearly unfazed by Judah's dry tone, Levi carried the salad to the table. "You're also lying through your teeth about not flirting. I saw you with him, Jude. If you really think you weren't flirting with Connor, then I'm afraid our need to find you a man is a hundred times more urgent than I thought."

Judah rolled his eyes. "*We* don't need to do anything—my relationship status or lack thereof is my business, not yours."

"So you keep saying and so I keep ignoring." Moving to the

counter, Levi picked up a set of oven mitts. "I don't blame you for being flirty. The guy was a big cutie. Even I could see it."

Judah nodded. He'd always liked men who were taller and bigger than his own six feet and Connor fit that bill and then some, all broad shoulders and thick thighs, muscled build obvious even under his clothes. Connor had also carried a certain wild, lumbersexy vibe that a city-dwelling shop owner like Judah lacked, and had a smile that transformed his whole face, taking him from simply attractive to *damn.* Regardless, Judah liked men who weren't already in committed relationships and nothing was going to change that.

"He was cute but also still very unavailable and therefore not worthy of my flirting, real or imagined." Judah set a glass of wine for Levi on the counter. "Just as well. I promised myself I'd take time off from dating after Seb."

Levi's face fell. "Okay, but you guys split up two months ago."

As if Judah could forget—spending New Year's single had been *all* kinds of memorable in ways he'd rather forget.

"Yes, but I'm still working on getting my head on right. This is not about missing Seb, by the way," Judah hastened to add. "He's actually turned out to be a really decent friend. But I have to be realistic about what I want from a man and, honestly, I haven't been focused on getting there. Case in point, what happened with Connor tonight." Judah gestured toward the floor and the shop below. "The man told me he wanted to knit a baby blanket, but did I take those words for what they meant?"

"You did not."

"Nope. This is what I mean, Lee. I need to stop trying to wish the impossible things that I want into reality."

Impossible things like changing his ex's mind about getting married. Seb had been honest with Judah about not wanting a wedding from the very beginning of the two years they'd dated. And Judah had responded by doing his level best to change Seb's mind, an effort that had not only been deeply unfair to Seb but also broken Judah's heart almost in two.

"Fair." Levi pulled a baking dish from the oven. "Magical thinking can be fun, though."

"Only for as long as the fantasy lasts." Approaching the stove, Judah admired the vegetable lasagna his brother had prepared with sweet potato and zucchini. "This looks great."

Levi grinned. "Yes, it does. It's just for practice of course, and if neither of us dies, I'll bake one for Mom and Pops, too." He picked up his glass and tapped it gently against Judah's. "So, is this a drown your sorrows kind of evening?"

"No." Judah had to laugh. "It's only Thursday and I've got work to do after dinner. But while drowning isn't the word I'd use, I'm not averse to a gentle swim."

Levi pushed his lips into a pout. "That guy really got to you, huh?"

Judah frowned. "I guess he did. I'm not sure how to explain myself, either, and I *know* I sound ridiculous. Connor was different, though."

"Different how?"

"He was nice. Guys who look like him are generally very aware of their overall hotness and it's not always easy to get past that. A lot of the time, they're so busy being full of themselves it's like they forget how to behave around lesser beings."

Now Levi frowned. "Dude, you're not a lesser— "

"Connor wasn't like that at all," Judah said over him. "He was genuine and easy to talk to once I got him to open up, and he seemed honestly embarrassed by the attention he got from the social circle. Which was totally blatant, by the way—I thought a couple of the ladies were going to straight out wolf-whistle at the poor guy."

Levi let out a loud laugh. "Oh, shit."

"Right? Meanwhile, Connor was turning all shades of red."

And that took me off guard. Because I wasn't expecting a conversation with a guy who had at least four inches on me to be so stupidly adorable.

"Baw." Levi reached over and patted Judah's shoulder. "I don't blame you for being bummed. But hey, look at it this way —if someone like Connor is making *someone's* fairytale come true, your dreamboat is out there too, right?"

Judah couldn't help smiling past the ache in his chest. "That's a surprisingly optimistic way of looking at things."

"Especially coming from me!" Levi straightened up. "Clearly a sign I need food, so let's get this pasta and cheese into our faces as soon as possible."

IT WAS past ten by the time Judah opened his laptop, but he'd barely gotten his email open when a shadow fell over him. Though a part of him wanted to groan at the interruption, he immediately glanced up at his brother, whose expression was tense.

"What's up?" he asked Levi. "Everything okay?"

"I think so." Levi settled beside Judah on the sofa. "You're not mad, are you?"

"Mad? About what?"

"About me giving you crap for staying single so long."

"Oh. No, I'm not mad. I think it'd be great if you'd mind your own business when it comes to my personal life but we both know that's not going to happen."

"You're right." Levi rubbed a hand over his head. "You know I just want you to be happy, right? Because it's not like other guys aren't interested. A dude hit on you while we were grocery shopping last weekend, for crying out loud, and it was like I wasn't even there."

"That man asked my opinion about an avocado's ripeness," Judah replied, "which is hardly the same thing as hitting on me. Besides, what was he supposed to do—ask your permission to speak to me first?"

"Maybe. Avocado Man had no way of knowing you and I were related or that I was straight, which makes his hitting on you in front of me flat out disrespectful. For all he knew, I could have been your boyfriend!"

"Please, stop."

Levi smiled. "Okay. I'm just trying to figure out ways to get you back out there, you know?"

"I do, and a part of me thanks you for looking out." Warmth went all through Judah. "I might complain, but I appreciate it."

"Good." A crease lingered on Levi's brow. "I've seen how hard you're working at the shop and at your editing and sometimes I wonder. Like, when do you get to relax and have a good time, Judah? Because I feel like you've hardly been out since things went south with Seb."

Judah frowned slightly as he considered the truth in those words. He *hadn't* been socializing much in the last couple of months, at least beyond chatting with friends online. He and Seb had lunch on occasion, but Judah didn't meet up with anyone else, be it for coffee or yoga class or a walk along the city streets. He hadn't been out on any nights just cutting loose either, not even on New Year's Eve, or gone on a single, bona fide date. And while Judah really was okay with holding off on the dating for a while longer, not going out at all was unusual for him.

"You're right," he said, his voice quiet. "I haven't been out in a long time just for fun. I can change that. But I haven't *wanted* to date and I'm still not feeling much of an urge to get out there." Judah pushed down the voice in his head that reminded him those words weren't entirely true. He'd certainly felt an urge to get out there with Connor and they hardly knew each other at all.

Leaning forward, Judah set the laptop on the low coffee table and rested his elbows against his knees. He sighed. "I wanted a break after Seb, and I took it. Then things got hectic in the store because of the holidays, and maybe I let myself get sucked into it more so than usual. Doesn't mean I have to *keep* acting like a hermit now that I'm aware of it."

"There you go." Levi beamed. "You're twenty-seven, Jude —way too young to swear off fun just yet."

"I haven't. I'm just recommitting myself to figuring my shit out before I jump into dating with anyone else. And maybe making sure they'd be okay with tying the knot somewhere down the line." Judah shared a grimace with his brother. "A question I'm sure ranks high on the list of things not to ask your date."

"It tops the list, dude, at least until you get to know each other better." Standing, Levi slipped his hands in his pockets. "This is probably an appropriate time to let you know Mom's been asking me about you." He chuckled when Judah sat back with a grunt. "I did my best to put her off, but you know how she can be when she's got an idea stuck in her craw."

"Relentless as the tides, yes." Judah lolled his head against the seat back. "Thanks for the heads up."

He turned back to his work after Levi had gone, trying hard to ignore how raw he felt in the wake of their talk. His instant infatuation with Connor had clearly been a sign that Judah needed to make some changes. Have fun with his friends. Get out of the shop and this apartment occasionally, and out of the rut he'd clearly gotten too comfortable in. And yeah, Judah really *should* work his way back into dating and stop his dumb heart from yearning after guys who were just plain wrong for him.

That determination wavered the second Judah glimpsed an email in his inbox, though, because it had come in after one 'Connor Devlin' had signed up for the following Sunday's Knitting 101 class. Apparently, Judah was going to be spending more time around that big, shy guy. Which gave him just over two days to squash his silly crush for good.

THREE

Brown paper bag in hand, Connor headed for Hook Me on Sunday, his insides knotted as tight as the woolly tangle he'd produced with the needles and ball of wool Judah had given him for practice. Because no matter how many videos he watched or how often he watched them, teaching himself to knit was not going well. He'd tried every evening after his shift on the ambulance, usually in between dinner and sleeping, but each time he worked at what his brain told him were basic moves, Connor just ended up more stressed than before and that was the opposite of what he wanted to happen.

Jeez.

Pausing on the sidewalk outside the shop, he forced himself to haul in a deep breath then slowly blow it out. *Be chill*, he reminded himself. There was nothing to stress about, not when he was moments away from spending time with someone who knew what they were doing. That's why Connor had signed up for Knitting 101. So someone could help him unsnarl his yarn and straighten his stitches, and maybe help him form habits to keep his thoughts from getting tangled up around each other, too. Whether any of that was possible remained to be seen, of course. Especially since the someone would be Judah Bissell of the big eyes and wide smile, who'd been so welcoming and patient the other night while Connor hemmed and hawed his way through talking about his project.

Okay, so maybe there was something to be stressed about. Connor knew a good-looking guy when he saw one, but he wasn't into dudes, so why was he thinking about Judah's eyes again? Better yet, why had he checked out Judah's bio on the Hook Me website when they'd already met in person?

Because I like to know who I'm talking to, Connor told himself. If those words didn't feel quite right, it didn't really matter. He had a baby blanket to knit and that was not going to happen if he didn't get his happy ass inside for his lesson, so, with another deep breath, he reached for the door.

"Hello!"

The voice that rang out as the door closed behind Connor was cheerful and warm. It didn't belong to Judah, however, but to an attractive, middle-aged woman. She smiled at Connor from the counter, the corners of her eyes crinkling in a very familiar way, and Connor found himself doing the same without even meaning to, despite a sinking feeling in his gut.

This had to be Molly. Judah had said his mother sometimes taught Sunday classes and, heck, Connor was glad he'd tied his long hair back before leaving his apartment today. Meeting someone's mom with his hair all wild wasn't the best way to make a good impression. Not that Connor was ready to examine any reason he might have for wanting to make a good impression, either.

"Are you Molly?" He smiled wider when the woman practically beamed.

"I am indeed." Molly set down a handful of wooly bundles

and clasped her hands in front of her. "And are you a friend of Judah's?"

"Um, not exactly. I met him the other night when I came in to ask about yarn," Connor said. "Judah helped me figure a few things out and we got to talking, and he mentioned that you like to travel down for class on Sunday."

"Oh, I come back to Boston on Sundays to have dinner with my boys," Molly replied. "If I end up teaching a class here and there, it's just for fun." She gestured to the bag in Connor's hand. "Are you here to do more shopping?"

"No, ma'am. I signed up for the knitting class, actually." Connor glanced toward the door on his right. "Should I just go on down?"

Molly nodded. "Absolutely. You're in luck, too, because the class will be on the smaller side today, which means more one-on-one with your instructor." She checked her watch. "We'll get started in about five minutes, so please, go ahead and make yourself comfortable along with the others."

Others? Ugh.

Well, of course. Connor hadn't really expected he'd be the only person in class. But he hadn't thought about other people actually being present or that they'd be watching him either. And he certainly hadn't considered that someone *other* than Judah might be instructing him how to get his knitting needles to behave, all of which made Connor feel foolish and very much like hightailing it out of Knitting 101 before class even started.

Connor didn't flee, though. Keeping his gaze lowered, he descended into the basement and found himself a seat at the only remaining empty table, which also happened to be closest to the stairs and furthest from the front of the room. Only then did he glance around, avoiding eye contact as he took in the four other worktables and his fellow would-be knitters, all of whom were female and had small brown paper bags of their own.

The workspace was well lit with walls painted creamy beige behind yet more stacks of cubbies, each holding the now familiar bundles. The scent of coffee hung in the air and, as Connor watched, a woman from one of the other tables approached the counter near the front of the room where she poured herself a cup, then sampled from a platter of cookies that had been set out.

Connor hid a smile as he recalled the comments Judah's brother had made about the stitch-and-bitch and just how much its members enjoyed Hook Me's coffee, cookies, and gossip.

Footsteps on the stairs drew Connor's attention and this time his smile slipped free because there was Judah, looking just as put together in head-to-toe black as he had on Thursday night. He flashed a grin at Connor as he stepped off the last stair, his mother just behind him. Molly immediately walked to the front of the room, but Judah paused by Connor's chair and bent at the waist just slightly, his voice low and honeyed when he spoke.

"Nice to see you, Connor. You want to grab a snack before we get started?"

A cozy warmth settled in Connor's chest. "I should probably keep my whole brain on the yarn and needles today," he replied. "Besides, your brother put the fear of God in me the other night when he talked about the games people play down here just to get hold of some cookies."

"That's fair." Judah didn't laugh, but the sparkle in his eyes as he stood straight made Connor feel even warmer. Damn, was it hot in here or what?

"Welcome to Knitting 101, everyone," Judah said to the room at large. "I'm Judah and this is Molly." He gestured to his mother with a flourish. "We're going to show you some basics today and give you the foundation you'll need to start knitting like pros."

The next several minutes flew by in a blur as Judah walked the class through casting stitches onto their needles, a process covered in every video Connor had watched and one he didn't have any better luck following now. He worked as best he could while Judah and Molly made their rounds, providing instruction to students as needed. Unfortunately, Connor's seat at the back of the room made him Judah's last stop and though Connor really did try, he couldn't get the yarn, the needle, or even his fingers to behave. Then again, he probably shouldn't have used the same mess of wool he'd been practicing with for the past couple of nights.

Judah's brow furrowed when he caught a glimpse of the tangle in front of Connor. "Oh, hang on one sec, Connor. I'll get you some fresh wool."

Grabbing a bundle from a nearby cubby, Judah tore off the paper label and untwisted the coil of yarn. "If everyone feels comfortable, go ahead and cast twelve stitches onto your needles," he said to the rest of the class. "And don't be afraid to flag down Molly if you get stuck or have a question."

Heat flashed across Connor's cheeks. "Sorry," he murmured as Judah sat down. "Turns out I was right about how-to videos not working for me."

"You have nothing to be sorry about," Judah said, his voice just as quiet. "I certainly didn't learn from watching someone knit on a screen and, like I told you on Thursday, not everyone wants to. I'm glad you showed up today so we can help you learn in a way that *does* work for you."

Judah picked up one end of the yarn. "I'm going to show you another way to cast on. It's called a reverse loop and some people find it easier than the method Mom and I just demonstrated."

He wore his Pride flag on his wrist today, embossed on a black leather cuff, and its vibrant colors flashed as he worked. Movements smooth and unhurried, Judah made a simple overhand tie about a foot from the end of the yarn, then tightened the loop around Connor's knitting needle.

"Take this in your dominant hand," he said and held the needle out to Connor, who grasped it with his right hand. "Good. Now, we make a finger gun with your other hand."

Leaning over, Judah shaped Connor's left index finger so it stood straight, then tucked the remaining three fingers against Connor's palm. Connor couldn't help noticing how soft Judah's skin was against his own and how nice he smelled, like coffee and soap and fresh hewn wood.

Stop.

Connor frowned.

"We wrap the yarn around your gun barrel," Judah said. Taking the loose end of the yarn, he did exactly that, then tucked the trailing piece under Connor's other three fingers. He gave them a gentle squeeze. "Hang on to this but keep your grip light so you still have room to move."

A beat passed before Connor remembered to speak. "I can do that."

"Of course, you can. Now insert your needle under the loop on your gun and slip the whole thing up and over and onto the needle to cast on the stitch."

Connor followed the motions Judah guided him through, his brow furrowed as, together, they slid the yarn over his fingertip then pulled it taut. Connor's eyes went wide when the stitch appeared as if by magic.

"Whoa. How the ... what the heck did you just do?"

"*You* did it," Judah said with a chuckle. "Let's get a couple more on there and then maybe you'll believe me."

Still working in tandem, they cast on several more stitches, each repetition growing smoother as the muscle memory settled into Connor's fingers. By the time Judah moved his own hands away, Connor was confident enough to keep going on his own, and he couldn't help his burst of pride at Judah's smile.

"This looks excellent." Judah tapped the yarn still wrapped around Connor's index finger. "Just remember to keep the tension fairly loose so that when we start working with the other needle, you still have room to move."

"Oh, God." Connor gave a quiet groan. "I sort of forgot we had to do stuff with a second needle." His frown faded at Judah's gentle laughter, though, and before Connor knew what had happened, he was laughing too.

"You're going to be just fine, Connor," Judah said as he got to his feet. "You just need to trust me and yourself to get there."

AN HOUR LATER, Connor's hands were tired, but his head felt *great*, clear and calm and grounded in ways it hadn't in way too long. Once he understood how his fingers should be positioned, he'd caught on quickly and cranked out stitches with a speed that had genuinely surprised him. Connor had liked watching the yarn move between the blunted points of the needles and found their muted click-clacks and the murmurs of the class around him strangely soothing.

Judah's expression was more than a little smug as he approached Connor's table. "You look a lot happier than you did when I first walked in here."

"I feel it." Connor ignored the fire in his cheeks. "A lot of that is down to you."

"Eh, I was just doing my job."

Though Connor didn't argue, he meant what he'd said. Every time he'd run into a wall during class, Judah had been there, his voice easy and his touch light as he'd guided Connor's hands. Not that he'd even needed to get close; there were times when just looking at Judah had made the rest of the world grow fuzzy and indistinct for Connor, with Molly, the classroom, and the rest of Knitting 101 nearly fading away.

Connor glanced down at the long, narrow strip he'd managed to produce. "I'm starting to get why some people say knitting is relaxing. If only I knew someone who owned a chihuahua that needed a winter scarf."

Judah's laugh rang out against the basement walls. "Well, that would be adorable. You could also unravel your project and start over, but this time make sure the scarf was human sized."

"Not sure I feel up to starting anything over tonight, but maybe by the time next Sunday rolls around." Connor frowned. "Do you think I could start the baby blanket project in the meantime?"

"Absolutely. Speaking of which, I put aside some wools you might use for your blanket."

Connor worried his bottom lip with his teeth. Was it his imagination or had the light in Judah's eyes dimmed just the slightest bit? "You did?"

"Uh-huh. Stop by the counter on your way out and I'll show you. You sure you don't want some coffee or a snack?"

"Thanks, but it's late for me to be having coffee and I'm not really one for sweets." Quickly, Connor packed his needles and the chihuahua scarf into his paper bag. "I have enough trouble getting in and out of the rig as it is. I'm a medic with Boston EMS," he added when he saw one of Judah's eyebrows go up in a silent question. "Ambulances aren't always friendly spaces for a guy as big as me."

A softness passed over Judah's face. "I can only imagine."

The journey back upstairs was quiet but not uncomfortable, and Judah went to the counter at once where he withdrew a square basket piled high with bundles of yarn. *Hanks*, Connor reminded himself as he smiled down at the collection. Judah and Molly had walked the class through the differences between skeins, hanks, and balls of yarn during class and Connor now knew the twisted bundles before him were hanks.

"Oh, wow. This is great, Judah. Thank you." He spied a set of knitting needles too, thinner than the ones he'd been using for practice and connected to one another by a slim plastic cable. "What's this about?" he asked, his fingers already around the cord, testing its strength.

"These are circular needles," Judah replied. "Technically, they enable a person to knit a 360-degree tube. Like if you wanted to knit the neck of a sweater or a hat, for instance."

"Damn, that's clever. Not something I'd be doing, though, right?"

"Maybe not yet." Judah made his eyebrows move in a funny little waggle. "Doesn't mean you're not far off from sweaters and hats, though. Until then, the cable will make it easy to cast on a lot of stitches and knit a blanket without having to use needles the size of yardsticks."

A laugh bubbled out of Connor before he could stop it. "Okay, I get what you're saying."

They talked needles and yarn for a while, Judah's focus less on wool color than texture, a factor Connor now saw as critical considering the blanket needed to be kind to delicate baby skin. He considered the pattern he'd chosen with new eyes then, particularly as it was laid out in broad stripes of color.

"Is it hard to do the color switching thing?" he asked Judah.

"Not once you've learned how. But these variegated yarns will give you a range of colors without having to switch at all." Judah ran a hand over a hank dyed pretty shades of purple, green, and blue. "I kind of assumed you'd want to use unisex colors, but there are plenty of blues and pinks in the shop to choose from if that's what you'd like."

"No, these are perfect." Connor ran a hand over the yarns. "Even if I did know the baby's gender, my partner thinks the gender binary is crap, so I want to stay away from the usual shades. I like the stripes, though."

"Me, too." Judah smiled. "This wool won't give you stripes exactly, but you'll get some very nice color shading, almost like an ombré where the hues gradually go from light to dark. And, like I was saying the other night, it'll be really snug and soft since you'll be working with two strands of yarn at a time."

Two strands? At the same time?

"I'd forgotten about that." All the good feelings Connor's lesson had conjured inside him quickly drained away. Knitting with two strands sounded tricky. Certainly for a guy with only a single class under his belt. Now Judah was frowning too.

"What's wrong?" he asked Connor.

Connor rubbed the back of his neck with one hand. "I'm not sure about this, Judah. What if four classes aren't enough to get me on track so the things I knit don't look like doggy chew toys?"

"Hey, you're going to be fine. From what I saw tonight, you'll be more than capable of creating gorgeous things, including that baby blanket for your partner." Pausing, Judah glanced around the shop, his lips pursed as if he were trying to decide something. "I'm sure you've figured out that I'm here every day," he said at last. "Come by anytime we're open, and I'd be happy to help you if you get stuck."

"Really? I wouldn't be imposing?" Connor swallowed again

at the expression that flashed over Judah's face, sweet but also wistful, though a smile quickly replaced it.

"Not at all. But keep coming to the regular classes too," Judah said, "especially since you paid for them in advance." He narrowed his eyes as if daring Connor to refuse, but there was humor in his face and Connor couldn't help smiling back.

"I will, I promise."

"Good." Judah walked back around the counter and went to one of the cubbies, gathering more hanks of yarn. "I can tell you still don't believe me, but I will make a knitter out of you yet, Connor Devlin."

FOUR

Though Connor's lips parted as if he were about to reply, he pressed them together again as Judah's mother bustled back in, the rest of the Knitting 101 class trailing in her wake.

"Hello, boys!" Molly practically chirped. "Have you been talking *all this time* while the rest of us ate our weight in cookies?"

Her eyes gleamed as she looked from Judah to Connor and back and oh, boy, Judah could see where this was headed. His heart squeezed a little at the flush that immediately rose in Connor's cheeks.

Damn.

Judah had never met a man as bashful as Connor. And though he'd tried to be all casual and cool during the knitting lesson, his mom had clearly picked up on *something* between Connor and himself. She'd given them the hairy eyeball several times during class and the fact that she hadn't gone anywhere near Connor and instead left him to Judah had been very telling. Her gaze was sharp as she watched them now and expecting her to act subtle when she clearly thought she was on to something was very much out of the question. Molly was terrible with boundaries and always had been.

"We were just getting some supplies together for a project," Judah said quickly, and made sure to enunciate each word he spoke next with care. "Connor wants to knit a baby blanket for his partner."

He knew the penny had dropped when Molly raised her eyebrows ever so slightly. Her smile changed then, still warm and infinitely kind, but colored with a disappointment that only someone who knew her well would recognize.

"Oh, how nice," she said to Connor. "That's a wonderful idea, and practical in a truly special way. My heartfelt congratulations to you and your partner!"

To Judah's surprise, Connor's forehead puckered.

"Congratula—*oh*." He rubbed a hand across the back of his neck again, his cheeks flushing an even deeper crimson. Connor gave Molly a helpless grin. "I'm sorry. When I said *partner*, I meant the person I ride with on the ambulance. I'm a paramedic, ma'am, and Olivia is my co-worker. She's having a baby with her husband, not me. I don't have the, um, romantic kind of ... partner."

Sweet, fancy Moses.

The thrill those words—and that tiny pause!—set off in Judah almost sent the hanks of yarn in his hands cascading to the floor. Connor was *not* about to have a baby with someone else. The man didn't even have a partner for fuck's sake, and it was all Judah could do to keep a straight face and simply nod. He didn't dare look at his mom, though, or the smirk he was certain she'd be wearing.

"This is on me, too," Judah said. He gave Connor what he hoped was an easy smile. "I shouldn't have assumed anything when you told me about wanting to knit a baby blanket the other night, so, I'm sorry as well."

"Pfft, neither of you should be apologizing." Unmistakable glee filled Molly's face when Judah and Connor turned her way. "It was a simple misunderstanding and it's been cleared up just like that!" she said with a snap of her fingers that Judah thought sounded very loud.

That was the moment he noticed the exchange among Connor, Molly, and himself had drawn the attention of the other students from knitting class, all of whom were watching the interplay from their positions around the shop, expressions ranging from amused to curious. Fighting off an impulse to retreat to the basement himself, Judah hoped with all his might that Connor didn't catch on because the big guy might die of embarrassment.

"Do you have everything you need to make your blanket, Connor?" Molly asked.

"Err." Connor glanced down at the wool and needles he'd chosen from Judah's stash. "I think so?"

"Yep, you should be good." Moving quickly, Judah walked out from behind the counter to one of the cubbies hanging on the wall. "I just want to grab a few more hanks before I ring it all up."

"Excellent." Molly beamed at him. "After you do that, Jude, I'm going to need a favor, if you don't mind."

"Of course," Judah said on his way to the counter. "What can I do for you, Ms. Abrams?" he asked, purposely drawing out the 'z' sound in Ms.

His mom rolled her eyes and laughed. "Oh, you. I made the mistake of putting out the whole box of pastry for class," she said, "including the cookies your pops and I can eat. That leaves us with nothing for dessert tonight, so would you mind running over to the Public Market and grabbing another box?"

Judah wagged a finger at her. "That was a rookie move, Mom, especially after all this time. But sure, I'd be happy to.

Let me just get Connor's stuff straightened out and I'll be on my way."

"Thank you, sweetie. And instead of cookies, how about cupcakes instead? Your pops' birthday is in a few days and I thought we'd celebrate while we're all together.

"Have you tried the treats at the vegan bakery in Boston Public Market?" she asked Connor. "They're really quite delicious. Judah can point you toward the ones that taste best," she added, "including a lemon raspberry creme cookie that I swear is one of the best things I've ever eaten."

Relentless as the tides.

Caught between amusement and exasperation at his mother's blatant matchmaking, Judah bit back a smile, though he felt tremendous sympathy for the shy man who'd become the object of her attention. As Molly's son, Judah was accustomed to her cheerfully bulldozing into social situations as she saw fit. Connor was a virtual stranger, however, not to mention a customer, a combination that made Judah hurry as he rang up the yarn and needles, intent on rescuing the poor guy before he decided to take his business elsewhere.

Or so Judah told himself, anyway.

"I'm sorry," Judah said as he and Connor finally emerged from Hook Me a long ten minutes later. "My mother is sort of a force of nature. I've learned to just kind of roll with whatever wave she throws out, even when it might not make a whole lot of sense."

"I really didn't mind." Connor glanced back at the shop's door with a half-smile, his obvious bemusement tempered with something more mellow and almost pleased. "Your mom's nice and fun to talk to."

Judah swallowed a sigh. What a sweetheart.

"Be careful how loudly you say that," he teased. "Pretty

sure Mom would set her mind on adopting you if she thought you'd let her."

Connor hummed. "Worse things could happen." He gestured to the bright, rainbow-striped gloves and scarf Judah had pulled from his pocket. "Did you make those?"

"I did!" Judah wound the scarf around his neck. "There's a matching hat, of course, but it's nice enough today that I don't need it. Which way are you headed?" he asked.

A crease appeared between Connor's eyebrows. "No way at all, really—this is my day off. You mind if I tag along with you? I didn't get a chance to go grocery shopping this week and I figure I can pick up some food at one of the stalls in the Market and save it for dinner."

"I don't mind at all." Hope leaped inside Judah again, though he did his best to shove it down as they began walking. Connor might be unattached but that didn't mean he was interested. Especially in men, Judah reminded himself; Connor could very well be straight. Which just made the words Judah spoke next even more surprising, at least to himself.

"We could grab some hot mulled cider if you like," he said, "since you've already said you're not up for coffee."

Connor's eyes went wide for a second before he smiled. "Cider sounds nice."

"Great! There's also a kickass Vietnamese counter with some of the hottest chili sauce on the planet if you're in the mood to set fire to your face." His breath stuttered a little as Connor let out a belly laugh, the loudest noise he'd made around Judah yet.

"Spicy food and I do not mix." Connor said. "I keep telling myself to try new things though, so maybe I can find something that won't make my stomach angry."

"'Atta boy. So, you drive an ambulance, huh?"

"Yup. Though 'drive' can be a relative term when you up to your eyeballs in rush hour traffic."

Judah chuckled at Judah's dry tone. "Oh, man, I can't even imagine!"

Chatting, they moved along Hanover Street, eventually leaving the North End neighborhood and crossing into Haymarket. The Public Market building was busy with tourists and locals alike, shopping at the artisan stalls as well as those selling prepared food and baked goods, and locally grown produce, meats, and fish. Connor bought a turkey sandwich for dinner and, after they'd picked up his hot cider and a coffee for Judah, they fell to window shopping as they talked.

Judah learned Connor was originally from a suburban area outside of Baltimore where his brother and sister-in-law still lived. He'd been in New England for five years total, having relocated first to Connecticut where he'd worked as an EMT for a private company while completing a course in paramedi-cine. Degree in hand, Connor had then applied to train with Boston EMS and moved to the area after being accepted by the academy.

"I got really lucky with a shot at a medic position after just two years," Connor said. "Some EMTs have to wait a lot longer for a position to open up. The job kicks my ass every day, though, and I still feel like I'm figuring out how the city works, even now."

"How so?" Judah asked.

"Well, Bostonians aren't super friendly, and every day of the year is basically damp. And then there's the sports thing, which states that if you're not cheering for the home team, you may as well get lost. I actually get that a little because everyone I grew up with was a rabid Orioles fan."

Amusement filtered through Judah. "I understand what you're saying. I think it's easy to find a place in this city, though, no matter what you might like. Well, unless you're politically conservative, because this state votes pretty blue overall and I'm sure that gets aggravating."

"Oh, I knew that before I'd even packed up my stuff. My brother James went *off* when I told him I'd be moving here." Connor chuckled. "He doesn't swear much, but he had some choice words for me about steering clear of crazy liberal Yankees who want to wreck our great American values. Seemed sure my moral compass would get all messed up purely by association."

Oy.

Judah found himself wondering if Connor's brother voted red as they stepped into the bakery line, and maybe if Connor did, too. And shit, he dreaded the answer so much, he couldn't bring himself to ask. Besides, Connor had been nothing but friendly toward Judah despite his Pride pins (and awkward non-flirting).

"Another thing is that I've been in New England going on five years and haven't experienced a blizzard," Connor said then.

"Dude, this is not a thing to be sad about," Judah replied, "though I'm not sure how that is possible? We got smacked with a storm right before St. Patrick's Day last year and I swear it was like the shoveling was never going to end."

"I was out of the town—went to see James and his wife." Connor shrugged. "The snow piles were more than halfway melted by the time I got back, and there hasn't been a big storm since. It's been the same every year. Any time there's a blizzard, I'm somehow out of town."

Judah eyed him askance. "Again, with the tone of disappointment. Honestly, being stuck inside gets old pretty quick, especially when you find yourself rationing coffee creamer because you don't know when you'll be able to get out again."

"Hah, point taken."

"Now that you're learning to knit, you'll have a hobby to fall back on when the time comes and you do get snowed in, though. What made you want to try knitting, anyway?"

"It was Olivia's suggestion," Connor said. "I've been working on being less stressed and she read somewhere that needlework can be helpful. She thought it'd be good for me."

Judah nodded. This man really was full of surprises. "My mom swears the same," he said. "She started the social circle to give people a chance to enjoy the combination of crafting and community because it's a fantastic way to get your brain producing the hormones that make you cheerful." He smiled at Connor's raised eyebrow. "I'm sure it sounds hokey to a medical professional, but people seem so relaxed after the classes and social circles. Provided we don't run out of cookies, of course."

A thoughtful look crossed Connor's face and Judah thought he was probably examining his own reactions to his first knitting lesson. Connor didn't say anything more on the subject though, and simply glanced over the bake shop's display case as he and Judah approached the head of the line.

"Does your whole family eat vegan or is it just your mom?" he asked. "I noticed you ordered a latte with cow's milk, so I wasn't sure if maybe you were cheating or what."

"I can't even imagine what that woman would do to me if she caught me cheating at anything." Judah sipped the last of his coffee. "But no, none of us is actually vegan. My mom and stepdad keep kosher, though, which means they're not allowed to have dairy and meat together. So, we usually just buy or make a good vegan dessert they *can* eat." He watched Connor nod, his eyebrows drawn together again as if he were puzzling out a problem.

Oh, hell. Maybe I should have clued him in on the

Jewishness.

Judah huffed to himself. Before he could speak again, however, a familiar voice rose above the crowd.

"Judah!"

And suddenly Judah had an armful of man and cello case, Seb's eyes looking extra dark in contrast with his ice blue hair and megawatt smile.

"Hey, player." Judah exchanged cheek kisses with his friend and leaned into the hug for a second before he let Seb go. "Are you on your way to rehearsal? And how the hell do you look even more tan than the last time I saw you?"

"I was born tan, you dork," Seb said with a laugh, "thanks to my Filipino parents, of course. And yeah, I'm headed there now. I just stopped in for a bite on my way across town." A subtle movement from Connor caught Seb's attention and he did a totally obvious double-take when he realized just how tall the man beside Judah stood. "Holy hot Christmas cake, wow."

Oh, man.

Judah pressed his lips together against a laugh, but Seb had already recovered his composure and grinned as he stuck a hand out toward Connor.

"Hi!" he said, voice a shade too loud. "I'm Seb, Judah's friend and still favorite pain in the ass."

Connor took the hand and shook it just once. "Connor," he replied in a tone so clipped Judah literally blinked.

Who the hell was this surly stranger?

"Um. Connor lives in the North End," Judah said to Seb, who eyed Connor with blatant interest. "I roped him into sitting through a Knitting 101 class today."

Seb rolled his eyes at Judah. "Ugh. You just made a stupid yarn pun, didn't you?" An impish air fell over him as he looked back to Connor. "Don't let this guy talk shop, big Con, because *nothing* says unromantic like business chatter on a date and once Judah starts in on hanks and skeins and Amazon ads, good luck getting him to stop."

Judah stifled a groan. Connor's spine had gone ramrod straight and his demeanor even more stony and at the very idea he and Judah might be *together,* and hot damn if that didn't sting Judah more than he'd ever admit.

Smile serene, Seb hiked his cello case a bit higher onto his shoulders. "I've gotta go, babe," he said to Judah, "but let's catch up sometime this week over foods, yes?" He leaned in for another kiss then headed off, his cheery "Give my love to the fam!" trailing into the strange, charged silence that hung over the men he'd left behind at the bakery counter.

The depth of dejection that Judah felt honestly surprised him. Who the hell was Connor to him anyway? A customer, sure, and perhaps a nascent friend. But it was way too soon to call him anything more, so why did Judah feel like the floor had dropped out from beneath his feet?

Judah placed his cupcake order, then turned and faced Connor head on.

"Seb and I were together for two years," he said, his tone even. "We broke up not long ago but stayed friends and my family is still very fond of him. He's actually a really standup guy. I knew it while we were dating, of course, but I've come to appreciate him even more since we broke up. Like when Seb broke it off with a new guy he'd been seeing because the guy told him that having a Jewish friend was, and I quote, 'deeply problematic.'"

Judah drew out his wallet as a bright purple bakery box was set in front of him. "I think everyone hopes their friends will rise to the occasion when you really need them, but it was still nice to get confirmation that Seb supports me, no questions asked."

"Friends are important," Connor said at last, his voice

much quieter than Judah had expected. "And family. I'm glad you have them in your life, Judah."

"Me too."

After paying for the cupcakes, Judah picked up the box and headed for home, not sure what to make of the fact that Connor continued to walk beside him in silence. They'd made it all the way outside and halfway back to the North End before Judah found his tongue again, but he didn't get a chance to ask Connor what the hell was going on because Connor stopped walking and faced Judah, his expression troubled.

"Do you ... are you still in love with him?" Connor asked. "With Seb?"

"No. I loved him when we were together, though. Sometimes I even thought we'd make it long term." Judah managed a smile. "Flowers and rings and kids—the big, romantic story with the happily ever after, et cetera. But Seb doesn't want any of that. And I knew he didn't. He was always candid with me about it and we tried to make it work, but finally decided to go back to being just friends. It was hard at first, but it's been good for both of us."

Judah swallowed past the butterflies that suddenly rose in his throat. "Does it bother you, Connor? Me being gay or Jewish? Because ..." He huffed a breath through his nose. "I know we haven't known each other long, but if you're going to be in my shop once a week, I think I have a right to know if anything about who I am is going to be a problem for you."

His head shake almost violent, Connor stepped closer. "No. Nothing about who you are is a problem for me, Judah. I'm not ... I'm not *that* guy and I like you just fine."

"Okay." Judah frowned. "Then what was going on with you back there? Because, if you don't mind me saying, the vibes coming off you when we were talking to Seb were the opposite of friendly."

"I don't ... Damn it." Connor hauled in a deep breath, his face twisting in the unforgiving glow of the streetlights. "I don't *know* what that was. I don't even know what was going through my head when Seb— God, this is so embarrassing."

Judah had no idea what to make of how rattled Connor appeared. Without a second thought, he reached out and caught hold of Connor's wrist, his stomach tumbling when he realized the big guy was trembling. "Whoa. Connor, come here for a minute."

He led Connor through the park, his grasp firm around Connor's wrist. Connor stayed silent. He pulled his arm free after a few steps, but then quickly took hold of Judah's hand, his grip almost too tight. A knot formed in Judah's chest.

What the hell had just happened?

They reached one of the long bench swings that hung along the edge of the park and only then did Connor let go of Judah's hand. They sat, bakery box on the bench between them, and without a word, each pushed into the ground with their feet, setting the swing into lazy motion.

The longer Connor stayed quiet, the more concerned Judah became. Connor's eyes had been blazing when they'd faced off outside the market building, emotions changing too rapidly for Judah to interpret, but he knew confusion and distress when he saw them, along with a healthy amount of fear. Connor had mentioned he was looking for ways to manage his stress, but this was something else entirely. Panic, maybe? And over what?

"Do you want to talk about it?" Judah asked and though Connor's headshake didn't surprise him, the words he spoke next did.

"I'm not sure I know how." Connor took his bottom lip between his teeth for a beat. "The stress I mentioned before— it's more than the usual everyday worrying." He sighed, his voice strained when he continued. "I'm sure you figured that out on your own."

Despite the low light, Judah was almost sure he could see the red in Connor's cheeks. He decided to be honest anyway because dancing around the subject when Connor had brought it up just seemed stupid. "I wondered, yes. How are you feeling now?"

"Better than five minutes ago." Connor winced. "It's GAD, a generalized anxiety disorder."

Judah nodded. "One of my good friends from college has GAD, so I'm somewhat familiar with it. I know every person is different though, and what you feel when you're anxious isn't the same as what my friend feels."

"Right. With my job, I can't take anything that would slow my reaction time, so I'm lucky my symptoms are mild enough that I can function on duty without them. I've actually been off all meds for a couple of years, but I still have trouble turning my brain off which makes it hard to sleep. That and the fussy stomach can make anything else I'm feeling worse."

"I'll bet. Is there anything we can do at the moment to help you feel better?"

"This." Connor gestured at the swing beneath them. Though he didn't exactly appear relaxed, he seemed much more settled. "I'd really like to keep sitting for a while, if you don't mind."

"Sure. Doing more of this isn't exactly a hardship." Judah smiled and was pleased when Connor returned it.

"Thanks."

This guy needs a friend, Judah thought with sudden clarity. Whatever had set Connor off back there in the market, he had to be ready to talk about it first. Judah could do that for him— act as a sounding board if Connor needed and, even more importantly, make sure he knew someone was there to listen.

"Of course," Judah said. "Mom's not expecting me for at least another hour, and until then, we can do this for as long as you want." He paused, then made his tone as dry as he could. "I'm going to blame you if my ass winds up frozen to this swing, though, so you should be ready for that."

He grinned even bigger when Connor's face truly relaxed for the first time since they'd run into Seb. They stayed there, swinging gently as they chatted about the shop and Judah's family, until Judah's phone chimed with a message from his mom that made him snort.

"She asked if I'm lost or trapped under something heavy." Judah smiled at Connor's soft chuckle. "I should get back before she sends Levi and Pops out to search. Are you feeling okay or—?"

"I'm good, thanks. Sorry if I made you late, though." Connor frowned as they stood, and Judah quickly shook his head.

"You didn't. That's just Mom being Mom—you know how it is."

Connor simply hummed in response and though Judah wasn't sure what to make of that, he decided not to push; the last thing he wanted to see was the big guy's anxiety ramp up again.

"Are you going to start the baby blanket tonight?" he asked as they crossed into the North End, soft warmth unfolding in his chest at Connor's smile.

"I might. But first, I have to figure out how to keep the yarn you sold me neat, because I already know that the one thing I am *awesome* at is making tangles."

"Wind the hanks into balls before you start. That'll make it way easier to keep your yarn neat, especially if you're carrying them to the shop for class or when you need a hand with your project." He nodded when Connor looked at him askance. "I meant it when I said you were welcome anytime."

"Really?" Connor's smile was equal parts shy and pleased and ugh, Judah kind of wanted to hug him. "I appreciate that, Judah, I really do. I wasn't sure if you'd still want to after—" he waved a hand in the direction of Haymarket "—that."

Judah licked his lips. "Yeah, well. I wasn't sure you'd still want to either. You said you're cool with me being gay and Jewish, but—"

"No buts," Connor rushed in, his tone fervent. "I am *absolutely* cool with both of those things and more sorry than I can say if I made you think I'm not, even a second."

"Okay. Thanks for saying that." Judah gave him a small smile. "You know I'm out and proud, but I'm also proud to be a Jew."

"I know. And I'm *glad*. Glad you have good things in your life." Connor chewed the inside of his cheek. "I'm sorry I was an ass to your ex."

Judah smirked. "Don't worry about it. I'm pretty sure Seb was way too busy absorbing the overall Thor vibe to notice. Besides, Seb may come off as flighty, but the guy is tough as nails. He wouldn't have hesitated to call you out if he'd thought you'd needed it."

Connor rubbed a hand over his face, but he was clearly fighting a smile. "Okay. If you're sure I wouldn't be in the way, I'll come by the shop. I really would appreciate your help if I get stuck. Or when I get stuck, rather, because I'm one-hundred percent sure that is going to happen."

"Come by anytime," Judah said, just as they arrived at Hook Me's front door. "That big chair by the counter is a great spot for knitting." He grinned at the gleam that lit Connor's eyes. "It's popular with the rest of my customers too, so I'm going to leave it to you to show up and claim it for your own."

FIVE

"What's got you so smiley?"

Taking his eyes from the road for a moment, Connor furrowed his eyebrows, honestly taken off guard by his partner's question. Olivia squinted at him, suspicion clear in her gaze.

"Who, me?" he asked. "What are you talking about?"

"This," she said, and waved at his face. "This goofy-happy smirk you've been wearing all shift. You actually look relaxed for once in your goddamned life, Connor, and I want to know what the heck that's about." Olivia grunted. "Don't think I haven't noticed the new accessories, too. Since when do you wear jewelry?"

"Since I bought some new stuff." Connor glanced at the slim leather bracelets he'd started wearing a few days before.

"Jesus. You're doing the smirky-smile again."

"Sorry."

Connor wasn't sorry at all though; not that he was smiling or feeling relaxed, or that Olivia had noticed. He flipped the left turn signal and steered Ambulance P1 through lightly falling snow onto Purchase Street.

"I took your advice." He felt positively giddy as he shot another glance at his partner. "I signed up for a knitting class at the shop in my neighborhood and I've been going every Sunday for the past few weeks." He had time to see her eyes go wide before he turned back to the task of driving.

"Get out," Olivia said, her voice hushed. "Do you like it?"

Connor didn't hesitate to nod. "Uh-huh."

He *loved* it. The knitting, the lessons, the quiet camaraderie he'd built with his fellow classmates—all of it was good. After sailing through the first three weeks of Knitting 101, he was more than half finished with the baby blanket he'd agonized over even starting. He'd signed up for a second class and started planning new projects, too, because as big as he was, Connor had *skills* with needles and wool.

For that, he had Judah to thank. Judah, who was patient and encouraging during lessons, and welcomed Connor anytime he stopped by Hook Me with his needles and balls of yarn. Which, to be fair, was every day and not only because Connor needed help with his stitches. Connor really enjoyed hanging out with Judah, even though the friendship they had built had started off with Connor acting like a total jackass over a blue-haired cello player named Seb.

Connor was still at a loss to explain the behavior he'd shown that night. His rudeness toward Seb. His own distress at seeing confusion and hurt in Judah's expression. The fear that stole his confidence to make himself heard until Judah had led Connor to a bench swing in the park, sat him down, and kept him talking.

Judah had been making space in his schedule for Connor ever since. Sometimes they ventured out for lunch and Connor worked on expanding his palate beyond the five sandwiches he liked most in the world. Other days saw them shopping, browsing stores around the downtown area where Connor discovered things like the leather bracelets Judah had insisted he buy or a grey fleece pullover that was so soft, he could have happily used it as a pillow. It wasn't unusual he and Judah stayed in the yarn shop though, particularly if Connor stopped by in the evening after his shift. He was tired enough by then to welcome some downtime and more than content to work in peace on his blanket while Judah handled the customers or taught class.

Connor had spent several hours in the overstuffed chair by the counter last night in fact, nursing a travel mug of the peppermint tea Judah had started stocking in the workroom downstairs and knitting away while Judah had led a Crochet 102 lesson below. He'd gotten so comfortable he'd been close to dozing off by the time the students had trooped back in and while Connor's face had gone hot, Judah's wink had immediately set him at ease. The simple gesture let Connor know he'd have been welcomed to a short nap if he'd needed it, no questions asked.

Connor didn't know how—or even if—he could explain any of that to Olivia, though, so he smiled at the road instead. "It's been great. Like, really great and thank you for pushing me to do it."

Olivia clapped her hands together. "I knew it'd be good for you!" she exclaimed. "Are you making lots of good stuff? Did you bring your needles with you? When can I see your projects, Connor, when, when, when?"

Connor's laughter bounced around the cab. "Would you stop? You're worse than a kid on Christmas Eve."

Both fell silent as the radio on the dash squawked, followed by the measured voice of the EMS dispatcher.

"Ambulance P1, woman experiencing difficulty breathing

at 32 Fleet Street, Unit 3. Thirty-three-year-old pregnant female in second trimester, history of asthma. 6-D-2, difficulty speaking between breaths. 911 call placed by six-year-old child in the residence."

Olivia straightened in her seat. "Shit, I was really looking forward to using the bathroom." Her growing baby bump played havoc with her bladder control, a development that sometimes ended in a sprint for the nearest restroom in between calls. "I can't believe we're only two blocks from the station and now this."

"Sorry, girl." After checking the rearview mirror, Connor flipped on the lights and siren. He raised his voice over the wail. "Think you can hold it?"

"We'd better hope so!" Olivia said through a laugh.

They found their patient alert and responsive upon entering the apartment, which Connor knew went a long way toward calming the tiny girl who had answered the door.

"Hi, ladies." Olivia immediately approached the woman seated on the sofa. "My name is Olivia, and this is Connor. Can you tell me your names?"

"Felice," the woman squeaked out, face pale and one hand over her sternum as she struggled to breathe. She nodded toward the child who was busy scrambling up onto the sofa beside her mom. "This is—Ellen."

Connor sent a wink in Ellen's direction as he and Olivia squatted down in front of Felice. "Hiya, Ellen."

"Hi. I'm six," Ellen said. Her big eyes moved from Olivia to Connor before she held up her right hand and waved, her fingers spread wide. All five were covered in something green and sparkly and sticky looking, and Connor might have been grossed out if the kid hadn't looked so pleased with herself.

"That's awesome. Six-years-old is my favorite age." Curling his fingers into a fist, Connor held it out for the little girl to bump with her own. "Did you call for help when your mom needed it?"

"Yup." Ellen bobbed her head, ginger curls bouncing against her cheeks. "Sometimes she can't breathe so good."

"Think my—inhaler's bad." Felice pulled a blue plastic case from her pocket, then shook and pumped it, another wheeze squeaking past her lips when nothing came out. "Just opened today. Nothing—else in the house."

"Okay." Connor took the inhaler from her outstretched hand. He examined it while Olivia checked their patient's vitals, and he quickly found the metering valve inside it cracked. Grabbing the oxygen tank and handheld nebulizer he'd brought from the rig, he got an Albuterol-oxygen mist going for Felice, steadying her hands on the mask as she breathed, and he chatted with Ellen to keep the child from worrying.

"Your badge is wicked shiny," Ellen said to him, her eyes bright and admiring as she stared at the silver badge affixed to the right breast pocket of Connor's jacket. "And wow, your hairs are way longer 'n mine!" She bounced out of her seat so she could get a better look at the braid he wore down his back and made a suitably impressed 'ooh'. "You look like a Thor elf!"

"My husband loves comics and *The Lord of the Rings*." Felice's voice was much stronger now that her breathing had evened out, and the gaze she turned on her daughter was loving. "He's raising Miss Ellen to be a major fan too, especially of Legolas."

Turning his attention to his tablet, Connor felt a tug that told him the little girl was playing with his braid. "Can't say I blame her," he said to Felice. "Middle Earth is full of heroes, but Legolas is the s-h-i-t."

"Connor! You spelled shit!" Ellen's shout of laughter cut through the air. "You are in trouble!"

She stepped around in front of him again, hands on his jacket sleeve as she lost herself in hilarity, and Connor was so amused by her antics, he almost missed Felice's pained noise.

"What's wrong?" Olivia immediately reached for Felice's hand. "Are you hurting, honey?"

"No." A grimace twisted Felice's features. "We were making a potion in the kitchen before I started having trouble breathing and when I came in here for the inhaler, Ellen stayed behind and kept mixing." She gestured to Connor's jacket sleeve, which was smudged with bright green, visible even against his dark brown jacket. "I've been so busy trying not to freak out, I didn't even notice until now."

Dismayed, Connor cast his gaze around the room. He hadn't noticed when they'd walked in either because his attention had been on his patient, but green handprints like the ones on his jacket were *everywhere*. The sofa and rug. Felice's and Ellen's clothes. All over the wall by the door and, of course, on the door itself.

Crap.

He caught Olivia's eye, unsure whether to laugh or groan. "Liv? Is there green stuff in my hair?"

Olivia licked her lips, then slowly craned her head back enough to get a look at Connor's braid. He knew from the way she wrinkled her nose that the news she was about to give him was very bad indeed.

"There sure is, Con. Your braid looks like a giant asparagus stalk and I swear to God, it's sparkling."

JUDAH WAS ORGANIZING knitting needles at the counter when Connor walked into Hook Me that night, clothes crusted with what had developed into a much heavier snowfall.

"Hey, stranger," Judah said with a smile. "Wasn't sure you'd be in here tonight."

Connor frowned. "Because of the snow?"

"Mmm-hmm. I figured you'd go straight home and hunker down with a pizza and celebrate what could be your first wicked New England snowfall."

"That sounds pretty excellent, actually." Connor brushed snow from his jacket sleeves, then pulled off his black stocking cap. "The pizza part most of all since I didn't have time to eat a real lunch."

The needles in Judah's hands clattered onto the counter. "Whoa."

"Yeah." It took everything in Connor to resist the urge he felt to slip the hat right back on to his now *very* short hair. He stuffed his hands in his pockets instead and waited as Judah simply stared at him, eyes wide and his task clearly forgotten.

"What happened?" Judah asked at last.

Connor pursed his lips "Accident at work today."

Judah came out from around the counter then, his mouth turning down at the corners. "What kind of accident?" he asked, sweeping his gaze over Connor from head to toe. "You weren't hurt, were you?"

"Oh. No, not all." Cheeks warm, Connor hung his head. He really needed to think before he spoke. "Nothing physical beyond weird stuff ending up in my hair and my ego being slightly dented."

"Yikes, Connor. I'm sorry." Judah's bearing had softened considerably when Connor looked up again. "Glad you're otherwise okay, though." He cocked his head then and looked even more intently at Connor. "If you really are okay, I mean."

"I am, thanks." Connor couldn't help but chuckle. Because suddenly, after a long and much weirder than usual day, he really was okay.

Yes, he felt off kilter. His uniform jacket and shirt were a mess and would probably need to be replaced. Making the decision to cut off his hair had sucked hard too, especially after his barber Will had spent almost an hour coaxing the glittery slime out of Connor's hair only to discover that the dark blond had turned a uniquely ugly shade of green, the streaks uneven thanks to Connor's braid. Will had been gentle as he'd snipped and trimmed, sympathy for Connor's predicament pouring off him in waves. Connor had still kept his eyes closed for most of it though, unable to watch as the long locks had fallen to the floor.

His nerves had been a vicious tangle as he'd walked to Hook Me and he was tired and hungry and totally over doing double-takes every time he saw his own reflection. His anxiety had melted the moment he'd walked into the shop and seen Judah though, a realization that would have weirded the ever-living crap out of him just a few weeks ago.

So ... why wasn't he weirded out now?

Connor breathed in deeply through his nose and hiked the strap of his duffle bag higher on his shoulder. "Okay if I hang out for a while?"

"Of course. You know you're always welcome." Judah glanced out the window. "The social circle is canceled on account of the storm though, and I was about to close up shop, even though it's not even eight." He focused on Connor again. "You're the first person I've talked to in over an hour."

"Right." Disappointment curled through Connor like a tide. "I should have thought of that."

"No worries. We can just bring the knitting upstairs. Levi's up in Stowe with Mom and Pops, so the place will be peaceful for once."

Connor could feel himself beaming. He really didn't care where he hung out, so long as Judah was there. "I like that idea. Want me to grab a pizza from the place across the street first?"

Judah waved Connor off. "Not unless you *really* want pizza. I have a whole crockpot full of beef stew upstairs. Plenty enough for both of us if you're in the mood for something meaty."

"Dude, I ate turkey jerky and an apple at noon so I'm in the mood for a-a-anything."

"Okay, yikes again. Lucky for you, I baked up some really good bread with my pops over the weekend, too."

Connor's stomach growled loud and proud and it was all he could do to keep from laughing. "Sounds amazing. But I didn't expect you to feed me, Judah. You sure you don't mind me butting in?"

"No way, man. You have to tell me what happened to make you cut off your hair, though." Judah walked back around to the register, then shot a sly smile Connor's way. "I had plans to binge watch *The Mandalorian* tonight, too, so I'll expect that story before we finish eating."

———

TWO HOURS LATER, snow fell fast and furious on the world outside, but it all seemed quite distant to Connor who was settled on a cushy sofa in front of Judah's TV, his knitting in hand. He was full of tasty food and beer, and the stress of his bonkers day had completely disappeared.

He felt grounded. Content. Heck, maybe even happy, despite missing his hair, sensations that deepened further as he worked on his blanket, his needles clicking softly. Even better, Judah was knitting too, spinning out rows of tiny, knotted loops in a beautiful sky-blue wool, his hands moving with a deftness Connor hoped he'd one day attain.

This is nice, Connor thought, a second before wind rattled the windowpanes.

"Jeez." Judah glanced outside, a small frown on his face. "Would it be weird if I said I thought you should stay here instead of going home?"

Connor set his knitting down. He turned his attention to the windows too, a funny, trembly feeling going through him. "I ... don't think so?" Judah was laughing when Connor met his gaze.

"Sorry, that came out kind of weird," Judah said. "It just seems silly to send you out in a snowstorm when Levi's room is empty, especially since I'd just end up worrying the whole time that you'd ended up in a snowdrift."

"I'm sure I'd be okay," Connor said, his words coming slow. "But sure, I can stay if it would make you feel better."

"It would." Each turned back to his needles, but Connor knew his friend was pleased. "Levi's room is the door to the left of the bathroom, by the way, in case I pass out and forget to tell you."

"Do you pass out a lot?"

"More than I like to admit. This sofa is deceptively comfortable, and I'll bet you'd fall under its spell too. By the way, are you having second thoughts about being snowbound yet? Because I'm pretty sure it's about to happen."

"As long as I have access to coffee in the morning, I'll be fine." Connor laughed at Judah's snort. "Luckily, I'm off for the next couple of days, 'cause I'm not big on the idea of driving around in this much snow after the day I had." He sighed. "I still can't believe I ended up with green hair. And then *no* hair."

"Dude." Judah's eyes were wide when Connor glanced his way. "I was so sure I was hallucinating when you pulled off that hat."

"You and me both."

"Aw. Do you miss it?"

"Honestly, I'm not sure how I feel—I think my brain is still processing." Connor shrugged. "Had to be done, though. We were so busy today, I couldn't deal with it until after my shift ended and my barber said he'd never seen quite that combo of slime, glue, and glitter all in one place. The food coloring really sealed the deal. Even after the sticky parts were washed out, it was still freaking green and it was *not* cute."

Judah laughed. "I'll bet you're wrong."

"Trust me, I'm not." Connor tried to smile. "I couldn't go on duty like that, either. The long hair was fine provided I kept it off my face and out of the way, but green? No." He sighed. "Anyway, it'll grow back."

"True." Leaning over slightly, Judah set a hand on Connor's arm. "Your face tells me you're not excited about having to start over though, and I'm sorry about that." His expression turned fond as he moved the hand from Connor's arm to his hair, and suddenly Connor had to fight not to let his eyes slip shut under the gentle touch. "You were sweet to let that little girl play with your braid."

"It made her happy," Connor murmured. "And as long as she was happy, her mom was too, which made Liv's and my job easier."

"I get that. And you honestly look great, you know. I mean, yes, your hair is beautiful when it's long, but this big chop suits you, too. It makes those gorgeous eyes of yours look even bigger. Oh, *damn*."

Face pinched, Judah dropped his hand away from Connor's hair as if he'd been burned, leaving Connor blinking at the sudden change in the air.

"What happened?"

Judah grimaced, the tips of his ears going red. "I'm sorry,

Connor. I didn't mean to ... I was *way* in your space, and I didn't even ask if—"

"Hey, you're fine." Connor only just caught himself from reaching for Judah. *To do what?* a little voice in his head wondered even as Connor kept talking. "You didn't hear me complaining, did you?"

The tension in Judah's face relaxed a tiny bit. "No. But I've always been a touchy-feely kind of guy and there are times I have to remind myself that not everyone's boundaries are the same. Some people don't want to be petted."

I would if you were the one doing the petting.

Lips pressed into a firm line, Connor dropped his attention to his project, sure that little voice in his head was going to be the death of him. But before long, he found himself drawn to looking at Judah again or at least at the yarn he'd been working with, which he'd formed into what looked very much like an oversized tube.

"What're you making?" Connor asked. "And don't tell me it's a sweater neck or a hat because it looks big enough to fit an elephant's trunk."

"Hey, I could be making an elephant trunk sweater," Judah replied. "Stranger things have happened." The way he waggled his eyebrows told Connor he might be fibbing, though, and now Connor was the one to roll his eyes.

"Fine, don't tell me. I'll get the secret out of you one way or another."

———

THE WIND WAS POSITIVELY HOWLING against the windows when Connor blinked awake and, for a second, he had no idea where he was. The room he glimpsed wasn't entirely familiar, nor were the soft cushions beneath him because nothing in Connor's own apartment was anywhere near this comfortable. He felt at ease despite his strange surroundings, and for several moments he simply lay still, soaking up the warmth of the person lying beside him.

Wait.

Every cozy impulse in Connor's body evaporated as the full understanding of exactly who he was cuddled up against came over him.

Judah.

Face on fire, Connor carefully lifted his head. Yeah, that was Judah all right, features relaxed in the flickering light of the television, despite Connor lying half on top of him. Connor didn't remember falling asleep of course, though he'd felt his eyelids growing heavy the longer they'd watched TV. Still, he'd put off saying goodnight, enjoying talking to Judah too much to end the evening. It seemed Judah had put off going to bed too, because Connor's knitting was nowhere in sight and Judah's legs were stretched out alongside Connor's. Though Judah was still mostly upright, he bore the weight of Connor's upper torso against his own and his arm lay loose over Connor's shoulder.

Connor hardly dared breathe. Shifting, he moved enough so he could study the man beside him, his pulse speeding faster the longer he stared. Judah looked even younger in sleep, eyelashes thick and dark against his fair skin. His eyes moved behind his closed lids and Connor knew then that Judah was dreaming, his grip on Connor growing firmer before it relaxed again, his lips parting just so on a whisper-soft sigh.

The air around Connor practically hummed, the buzz strengthening as it filled him head to toe and he closed his eyes, a thought sliding into place with a nearly audible click. He wanted to touch Judah. And he had no idea where the impulse had come from.

You sure about that?

Connor ignored the murmur in his head. Opening his eyes again, he slowly raised a hand, then held it over Judah's face, his head spinning at the implications of what he wanted to do. Which was what, exactly?

You want to know if that mouth is as soft as it looks and kiss him until neither of you can breathe, his brain supplied once more.

Connor closed his hand in a fist. This ... couldn't be. He dated women. A lot of women actually, at least when he had energy for dating. He'd had a few girlfriends too, though none had been serious. And maybe being preoccupied with his career over the last couple of years had put a serious dent in his social life, but it didn't change the fact that Connor was a straight guy who liked girls.

You sure about that? the internal voice asked again, sharper and more insistent. *'Cause I don't think you've never wanted to kiss a woman the way you want to kiss Judah.*

Heart in his throat, Connor pulled his now shaking hand away from Judah's face, cringing when the motion jostled Judah awake. Blinking, Judah turned sleepy eyes on Connor, the corners of his mouth turning down. Connor's heart tumbled right along with them because oh, man this was about to get awkward. No way in hell was he going to be able to explain why he'd been staring at Judah like he'd never seen him before. He tried not to flinch when Judah moved his hand from Connor's arm and rested it between Connor's shoulders instead.

"Okay?" Judah asked, voice low and scratchy as he rubbed his palm in a circle that heated Connor's skin.

Connor nodded without a second thought. "Okay," he whispered back, the ache inside him going both deeper and softer when Judah gave him a small smile.

Judah held Connor's gaze. His eyes were already at half-mast though, and his body seemed to sink lower into the sofa cushion as he closed them once more. He was out again between one breath and the next, slipping back under into sleep without another sound, though his hand stayed between Connor's shoulder blades, his touch even warmer.

Judah had never really been awake, Connor understood then, but hovering in the soft space between slumber and awareness, even as he'd met Connor's eyes and spoken. He probably wouldn't remember any of it, especially the part where he'd woken up to find Connor gaping at him, which meant Connor could absolutely get out of this. Get up right now and head for Levi's empty bedroom where he could finish out the night, while Judah slept on, and pretend nothing had ever happened.

Connor didn't move, however. He was cozy and comfortable here, not to mention so very, very tired. Almost as if he hadn't really been awake either or had a small but totally needless freak out. But if he was honest, Connor didn't want to move or tiptoe off and sleep alone in Levi's room. Connor liked Judah's warmth against him. The weight of that hand between his shoulders. Judah's quiet breaths just audible over the sound of the storm outside. So, Connor closed his eyes and rested his head against Judah's chest again. He listened to the low thump-thump of the big, generous heart beneath his ear and followed it down into sleep.

SIX

Judah didn't dare move. He was almost afraid to breathe, in fact, for fear that his very favorite dream of all time would break apart and disappear in a puff of smoke.

In the dream, Connor was cuddled up against Judah's ribs like a big, sleeping bear, one heavy arm laying across Judah's belly. They were in Judah's apartment too, stretched out together on the sectional sofa where Judah spent most nights seated beside his brother, each working while images flickered on the TV screen.

And then Connor snored softly in his sleep and burrowed closer, his grip on Judah tightening enough that Judah knew without a doubt he wasn't dreaming at all.

Holy shitballs.

Judah tilted his head enough to glimpse his friend's blond hair. Connor had dozed off at some point while they'd been watching TV, but he'd done it so quietly it was as if he'd blinked out like a bulb, there one minute and gone the next. He hadn't woken when Judah had gently pulled the knitting project from his hands but leaned over instead and settled his head against Judah's shoulder. Unsure if he should wake his friend or not, Judah had sat frozen as Connor's breaths evened out, and their slow, steady rhythm persuaded him to stay still. He knew Connor sometimes had trouble sleeping. Knew he'd had an ass kicker of a day, too, and that he'd been wiped out even before they'd come up to the apartment from Hook Me. No harm in letting the big guy sleep for a while, especially since Judah didn't see why he couldn't catch a quick nap himself.

Some nap, Judah thought. The whole night had passed if the weak gray light outside the windows was anything to go by. Connor was still deep under too, his snores growing softer as Judah carefully shifted his weight so he could see Connor's face.

Reaching up, he smoothed a stray lock of hair back from Connor's forehead, silently marveling again at how different his friend looked now. Though still shocking at first glance, the haircut opened up Connor's face and highlighted the elegant lines of his nose, jaw, and cheekbones in a very pleasing way. His looks held an edge the long hair had masked, making Connor look tougher than the sweet-natured man Judah had come to know. His strong brows came together now, and he murmured sleepily before settling again, breaths puffing past his full lips.

Judah's already half-hard dick perked up a bit more. Tenderness mixed with the lust in his core, along with a healthy dose of regret. As much as Judah loved being close to Connor like this, it made him melancholy, too. Connor was never going to be more than a friend to Judah. The trouble was, Judah *liked* being friends with him, so much he wished he could stamp out the attraction he felt, if only to make his life simpler. Pining for a straight guy was not Judah's thing and, at the moment, it honestly made him feel like a goddamned creeper, too.

Carefully, carefully, he eased himself out from under Connor's arm. He bit back a grunt as his body protested the hours he'd spent sleeping in a mostly upright position but managed to grab the knitted afghan that lay across the back of the sofa. It was one of his mom's projects and fashioned from a cream-colored velour yarn so gorgeously soft that just being wrapped up in it felt like a hug. Connor seemed to think so, too, even in his sleep, because he buried his nose in its folds after Judah had covered him with it and made a muted noise of pleasure.

Fucking A.

Judah's desire leaped even higher. This man was going to wreck his sanity, no question about it, particularly if Judah kept putting himself in situations like this.

Forcing himself to turn away, he headed for the bathroom, dick aching as he locked the door behind him. His hand shook as he fumbled at the fly on his jeans, and he barely got a hand inside his boxers before he had to close his eyes, his head full of images of a beautiful, sleepy Connor, staring into Judah's eyes with an intensity that set his blood on fire. Judah's lust coiled tight.

Wrapping his fingers around himself, he bit his lip hard, imagining how it would feel to settle over Connor, those thick thighs wrapping Judah up while their cocks slid together. He'd push inside Connor, their breaths mixing when their mouths met, and before Judah could even process how fucking much he needed that in his life, pleasure melted his bones. He grunted and pumped himself, mouth falling open and his hand flying until cum pulsed over his hand.

Jeez.

It took a few minutes before he was able to stagger toward

the sink. He couldn't help smiling at his own sex-mussed reflection in the mirror too, all sparkling eyes and pink cheeks, because whether or not it was wrong to get off thinking about his totally not gay friend, he sure felt fucking good right now.

"You need to get laid," Judah told his reflection, then vowed he'd download some dating apps as soon as he had time to devote to picking and swiping.

Thirty minutes later, he was standing at the kitchen stove and frying up some breakfast when Connor ambled in, looking cute as fuck with his t-shirt and brown cargos all rumpled and eyes heavy lidded. Judah flashed him a big grin.

"Good morning, sleepy! Did you find the toothbrush I left for you on the sink?"

"I did, thanks."

"Cool." Judah tipped his chin toward the counter. "There's coffee in the French press if you want it. I hope you're hungry by the way, because I made a fuckton of eggs and sausage and will need your help eating them."

"I could get behind that," Connor said. "Anything I can do to help?"

"There are some bagels warming in the oven if you want to grab them. I already put out butter and cream cheese and all that jazz."

They chatted as Judah finished cooking, but only after they'd sat down did he notice Connor wasn't truly looking at him. He stole glances instead, as if afraid to meet Judah's gaze directly, and though Judah doubted Connor would admit it, he suspected the night they'd shared on the sofa was the reason. That had to loom larger for a shy guy like Connor than it ever would for Judah, who was very accustomed to being physically affectionate with men whether they were his lovers or not.

Big talk coming from the guy who jerked off thinking about how hot it would be to fuck his straight friend.

Judah swallowed a mouthful of eggs before he could choke on it, then seized upon the first thing that sprang to mind that would keep his brain off thinking about Connor in *that* way.

"I don't think I've ever asked what made you decide to become a paramedic," he said. "Does that make me a bad friend?"

The line of Connor's shoulders relaxed by several degrees. "No." He sounded amused. "Although I never asked you why you decided to open a craft store, so maybe I'm a bad friend, too."

Judah laughed. "We suck. For the record, I didn't decide to open the store—it was Mom's idea and she just looped the rest of us into her plan."

At last, Connor looked directly at Judah. "You didn't want to own your own business?"

"It wasn't a question of wanting so much as having never considered it," Judah said. "I have a journalism degree and, in a past life, I was a book editor."

"Really? And you liked it?"

"Yes, I did. I mostly quit after Mom asked me to go into business with her, but I still do some editing on the side to keep a hand in."

Connor cocked an eyebrow at him. "What kind of books do you edit?"

"Anything that comes along. I usually stick to fiction, but I've edited non-fiction books in the past. I use a web platform that allows writers to request quotes for services. If an author and I match up and it feels like a good fit, they can engage my services."

"I had no idea you worked two jobs. When the heck do you sleep?"

Judah chuckled. "I manage okay. I do some editing when I have down time at the store, but it's still a business that needs to be run. I have to limit myself to two or three manuscripts every couple of weeks, otherwise, I really wouldn't sleep at all."

"Cool." The smile on Connor's face quickly faded. "Is that what you meant when you said you pass out in front of the TV more often than you like to admit?"

"Pretty much. I have a bad habit of pushing myself even when I know I should call it a night and that sofa is like quicksand when I'm tired–I'm basically helpless against the power it holds over me." Judah made sure his voice held a teasing note as he said, "You too, from what I saw last night and this morning."

"Ugh, yeah." Connor put a hand over his eyes, but he was laughing too. "I'm sorry about that. I like to ... I usually grab a pillow when I'm sleeping. Been doing it since I was a kid."

"Being used as the world's biggest teddy bear didn't bother me. And you're not the only one who fell asleep," Judah reminded him.

Connor rolled his eyes but though his cheeks flamed, he seemed less uptight than he had only a few minutes ago.

"My gram was the one who suggested I go into paramedicine," he said, finally circling back to Judah's question. "I really wanted to apply for the Fire Academy in Baltimore, but I have mild asthma." He shrugged at Judah's immediate frown. "It's only triggered by cat dander, so I just avoid them and don't even think about it ninety-nine percent of my life. The asthma probably wouldn't have stopped me getting into the Academy, to be honest, but I couldn't do that to Gram. She raised my brother and me and spent more time than was right worrying about us, and I didn't want to stress her out any more than I had to."

Judah simply nodded and wondered at Connor's openness this morning. While they spent lots of time together, their conversations typically revolved around work and knitting, or Judah's life in Boston.

Connor knew Judah had lost his dad at age seven. That he'd adopted a more agnostic point of view toward religion in his twenties but still attended synagogue, particularly when he wanted a place to gain focus. He knew Judah had been happy when his mom had remarried yet worried about his place in his new family after Levi's birth, and that he preferred working in Boston because staying in Vermont made Judah feel lonely in ways he never felt otherwise.

In comparison, Judah knew relatively little of Connor's history. There was the brother named James and a sister-in-law Ally, and Connor had talked a little about his journey from Maryland to Massachusetts. Judah knew about Connor's GAD of course, and about his efforts to manage his symptoms, and that the guy never used curse words, a habit Judah found oddly endearing. He also knew Connor was passionate about his job with Boston EMS, though scrambling in and out of the back of the ambulance was a challenge for someone so tall.

"My parents weren't around much," Connor said now. "They had problems of their own, mostly drugs and drinking." His tone and demeanor were so even, Judah didn't know what to think.

"Damn, I'm sorry, Connor. I had no idea."

"Thanks. James and I were lucky to have Gram, and she took us in around the time I turned seven."

"You didn't live with your parents at all after that?"

"No." Connor paused, then dropped his gaze to his plate. "My parents ... they wanted to party more than raise a family and having two little kids got in the way of that. James did his best to take care of us both but he's only three years older than me, and he didn't deserve that."

Sorrow crept over Judah. His mom, dad, and stepdad were key pieces in the foundation of his world and without them, he wouldn't have become the man he was today. He couldn't imagine having lived Connor's life. "Neither of you deserved that," he said quietly, chest going tight when Connor gave a small shrug.

"That's true. Anyway, they took off one day and didn't come back and that was when Gram stepped in and took us to live in River Hill. The GAD diagnosis came around the same time," Connor said. "Could be I'm just wired to worry, but James thinks it stems from our home life being chaotic for so many years."

Judah set his hand over Connor's, new respect for the guy washing through him. Connor had been through a lot in his life and endured more turmoil than Judah could even begin to conceive. But somehow, he'd come out of it more than okay. He'd matured into a gentle, generous soul who was driven to give of himself to the people around him and if Judah had to guess, Connor's brother was cut much from the same cloth.

"What does James do for a living?" he smiled at the raised eyebrow Connor showed him. "You said you became an EMT out of deference to your grandmother so ..."

"You wondered if maybe there was more to the decision?" Connor grinned. "You're right, there was. James is the one who became a firefighter."

"Oh, shit." Judah laughed. "I had a feeling! Did he give you crap for not following in his footsteps?"

"Not at all. He'd been on the job a couple of years by the time I was ready to start my own career and it opened his eyes quite a bit to the dangers of the job. He didn't like the idea of me running into burning buildings any more than Gram did."

Judah hummed. "Okay, I get that. EMTs are still first responders, Connor, and the odds you'd have to enter a burning building or someplace equally unsafe aren't exactly low."

"Oh, I know. It can be a dangerous job for all kinds of reasons and even a quiet day is tons more dynamic than your typical corporate gig. I liked it from day one, though. It felt *good* doing my job, and there was always so much more I could learn." Connor's brow creased. "The more experience I got, the more I wanted to know, so Gram started poking at me to get a degree to further my career. She even left me an inheritance when she passed to help me make it happen."

"She sounds wonderful." Judah set his hand over Connor's, his heart doing a little flip when Connor turned his own over and clasped Judah's fingers. "I'm sorry to hear that she died."

"Thanks. I miss her every day, you know? I think she'd be over the moon with the way things are turning out for me, too, though I *know* she'd never have imagined I'd end up on a rig here in Boston."

"Or that you'd have to chop off all your hair after some kid turned it green with a bucket full of glitter slime."

Connor belted out a laugh. Pulling his hand out from under Judah's he reached for a bowl of fruit salad. "You don't know the half of it, dude."

They continued talking over their meal and, apart from that moment of handholding, the energy between them was easy, just like always. Judah wasn't surprised that Connor didn't initiate more contact, but he couldn't help feeling disappointed about it too, even as he did his best to hide it.

"I've got to get up to the garden and take a look around," he said once they'd loaded the dishwasher. "I want to make sure the snow isn't piling up too deep."

Connor drew his eyebrows together. "How does a person go 'up' to a garden? And I thought you said it was too windy to go anywhere?"

An odd, flustered feeling came over Judah, scratching at him like wool fibers that had broken and gone coarse and rough. Did Connor think he'd lied about the weather conditions last night to keep him from leaving?

"Sorry—I didn't think about how it would sound without some context." Judah licked his lips, then headed out of the kitchen and toward the front closet and the boot tray by the door. "We have a garden on the roof," he said over his shoulder as Connor followed behind. "Nothing's growing right now of course, but snow this deep gets heavy and I should check that the drifts aren't too large."

"What will you do if they are?"

"We have a service to help with removal if it gets really bad, but usually I just shovel some of it over the edge of the roof and onto the street. It probably won't come to that," Judah added when Connor's eyes went round. He slid his feet into his boots then faced Connor beside the closet door. "One good thing about high winds is that they blow a lot of the snow back into the air."

Almost as if on cue, a big gust rattled the windowpanes and Connor shook his head.

"Judah, I don't know if this is such a good idea. It sounds freaking dangerous to be walking out onto a roof in that," he said with a wave at the windows.

"I've done this a hundred times before—it'll be fine, I promise." Judah opened the closet, then paused, his stomach dipping when he saw that Connor had started pulling on his own heavy boots. "Oh. Are you heading home?"

Already tying his boot laces, Connor gave Judah a look that said, '*What the heck have you been smoking, Bissell?*'

"Do you want me to?"

"No, it's not that." Judah jammed his hat onto his head. "I just thought—"

"Well, I guess you thought wrong," Connor shot back through a grin. Straightening, he reached past Judah into the closet for his own coat. "I'm coming up to the garden with you, because someone's got to make sure you don't turn into Mary Poppins and disappear into the storm altogether."

Judah snorted. "Not gonna happen," he said. "I may be shorter than you but I'm pretty sure it'd literally take a tornado to blast a guy my size off the roof." He opened the front door and gestured Connor through with a flourish. "We'll be out there for fewer than five minutes if everything looks okay, ten minutes tops if I actually have to shovel."

SEVEN

"Okay, that was definitely more than ten minutes." Judah huffed as Connor half-hauled him back into the apartment, both dripping snow with every step.

"I'll take your word for it," Connor muttered. "Where do you keep your First Aid Kit? In the bathroom?"

"Uh-huh. But wait."

"Judah— "

"Boots and coats stay here." Gently, Judah shrugged Connor off. He gestured at his wet clothes with one hand, the other wrapped around a big ass drone that had dive bombed them out of nowhere and smacked Judah in the head as he'd shoveled. "I don't want to step in a puddle later, dude, or wipe a million little water stains up off the floors."

"Better than cleaning up bloodstains, *dude*."

The acid in Connor's tone surprised him, and he knew from the way Judah's posture tensed that he'd been equally taken off guard. Judah's mouth was a thin line and his face pale as he looked up at Connor, which made the mix of blood and melted snow trickling from the cut on his right temple even brighter.

"Hey, I'm good, Connor. You don't have to baby me over a teeny, weeny scratch."

"I know I don't have to." Connor forced a calmness he didn't feel at all into his voice. The strength of the howling winds around the roof had been scary but knowing Judah would have been out there *alone* if Connor hadn't followed him was downright terrifying. Whatever Judah said, Connor knew a person could easily be blown over the roof's edge if they lost their footing or became dazed, and now his brain was serving up all kinds of awful images he didn't need to see, no matter that because Judah was *safe* and whole and standing right here in front of him. Connor gave himself a hard internal shake.

"I'd still like to help," he said, voice sounding tight to his own ears and damn, he needed to get it together. "Both because I'm good at my job and because I'm worried about my friend." He paused for a beat, hating the wariness clouding Judah's eyes. "I'm sorry I snapped at you," he said quietly, "but I don't think you can blame me for being more than a little freaked out that a hunk of plastic legit fell out of the sky and sliced open your head."

The rigid line of Judah's shoulders sagged. "Yeah, that sucked. First time I've been that close to a drone drive by, y'know." He pulled the rainbow striped hat from his head and grimaced when he saw it was smudged with blood. "Or was it a fly by?"

New concern trickled through Connor at Judah's snicker. Rambling after being hit in the head wasn't exactly a good sign. The poor guy was shivering too, though Connor put it down to adrenaline rather than being truly cold and quickly took the drone from Judah.

"C'mon," he said and set it on the floor. "Let's get you cleaned up."

They stripped off their coats, Judah's laughter quickly fading, leaving him looking exhausted by the time he bent over to remove his boots. He grumbled a bit when Connor made him sit on the bench by the door, but it gave Connor a chance to dash to the kitchen for a wad of paper towels and some ice which he fashioned into a quick compress.

"Do you feel dizzy or sick to your stomach at all?" he asked as walked back to Judah.

"No." Judah sighed. He'd gotten his right boot off and was working at untangling the wet laces on the left. He paused when Connor handed him the compress. "Just cold and wet and epically embarrassed."

Connor waited for Judah to press the ice pack against his face, then squatted down so he could work on the remaining boot. He'd never seen his friend look so down. "What are you embarrassed about?" he asked, chest pinching as Judah hunched in on himself slightly.

"I got hit by a drone in the middle of a snowstorm which rates high on my Weird-O-Meter, if you know what I mean." Judah sounded drained. "Being knocked on my ass in front of a cute guy wasn't much fun either, and if you tell me this cut needs stitches, I swear I am going to crawl into bed and stay there until spring."

"Well, dang." Setting Judah's boots aside, Connor levered himself up and settled onto the bench, where he used his hand to carefully smooth back the damp hair that had fallen onto Judah's forehead. His heart squeezed a little when Judah closed his eyes.

"I hope you don't mean that," Connor said. "I think I'd miss seeing your face around the neighborhood. Not to mention I'd have to find someone else to help me finish the baby blanket."

The way Judah's lips quirked up at the corners made Connor smile too, and he let go of some of his worry. "As far as sutures go, I'll need a better look at the cut, but we'll figure it out one way or the other."

Helping Judah stand, Connor led him toward the bathroom, each trailing wet sock prints behind them. Judah insisted they change into dry clothes before doing anything else, which was how Connor wound up tending to the cut on Judah's forehead clad in borrowed thermal leggings, thick, handknitted socks, and a soft flannel bathrobe at least two sizes too small.

"Sorry I can't offer you anything better," Judah said, as Connor checked him over. "Levi's the tallest person in the house so we got lucky with a pants option, but no way his shirts would work. He probably weighs a buck-eighty and I'm quite sure you'd bust right out of his shirts like the Hulk. Are you warm enough? I can turn the heat up if you like."

Connor used another butterfly closure to seal the edges of Judah's cut. "I'm fine."

That was a lie because Connor was kind of a mess. He was ... distracted standing in this bathroom, his torso mere inches from Judah's. Judah smelled so good, like coffee and whatever soap he used, along with a healthy tang of sweat from hauling snow around on the roof. He looked sort of sweet and sleepy right now too, a small smile on his lips as he stood with his butt braced against the bathroom sink, legs stretched out on either side of Connor's and his eyes heavy lidded.

Why. Are. You. Thinking. This?

Connor pursed his lips. "You're lucky that thing didn't knock out your teeth," he said to Judah, almost desperate to distract himself. "Do you have any idea who it belongs to?"

"Maybe." Judah sniffed. "A group of college guys live down the block and I'm about ninety-nine percent sure the drone is theirs. There's a roof deck on their building too, and everyone knows they like to fly in inclement weather and post the footage on their blog." He laughed then, his shoulders shaking enough that Connor had to laugh too.

"What now?"

"I really hope they got a shot of you charging across the roof after that thing dropped out of the sky. You must have looked terrifying!"

With the butterfly closures in place and the bleeding stopped, Connor covered the wound with a larger bandage. He swept his gaze over Judah's face once more, noting that while he still looked slightly tired, he'd been alert and lucid since they'd gotten their coats off, good signs he hadn't suffered a concussion.

"That should do it." Connor set his hands on Judah's shoulders and turned him around so they both faced the mirror. He met Judah's eyes in the reflection. "The cut isn't deep enough to require sutures, and I think you'll be just fine with the ointment and bandages. Change them tomorrow or if they get wet, and make sure the wound stays covered to help speed up the healing. I can write all this down if you think it would be helpful."

"Thanks." Judah sniffed again. "Your clothes should be ready to go in the dryer soon. Are you sure you don't want to do another load with your uniform coat and shirt? We might be able to get the green out if we run them through a couple of times."

"I dropped them at the dry cleaner on my way here last night. The shirt's probably toast, but we'll see. And I'm not in any big rush to get changed again, unless your family is about to walk through the door." Connor glanced down at himself. "I might actually crawl into a hole if that happens."

"Why?" A chuckle bubbled up out of Judah. "You look very sharp in blue and green plaid, Mr. Devlin."

Connor smiled through the heat flashing over his face. "Thanks. It's been a while since I walked around in thermal underwear though, and I feel kinda naked."

Judah made his eyebrows go up and down. "All according to my master plan, you see."

"Oh?" Amusement followed by a flush of heat Connor didn't expect *at all* wound its way through him as Judah spun around. The look on Judah's face just then hit Connor right in the chest and suddenly, he didn't feel like laughing at all. "What plan would that be?" he asked more quietly.

"The one where I keep you here in my apartment by withholding your clothes and we take the rest of the day off."

"Does it count if I already had the day off?"

"Of course. We can camp out on the sofa and binge more TV. Maybe do outrageous things like eat cookies and *nap*."

Connor's insides quaked in a really excellent way at the idea of being that close to Judah again, but he frowned as Judah raised a hand to the bandage, his face screwed up in a scowl.

"Are you sore?" Connor asked. "Or is this more of a real headache?"

"Just sore," Judah replied. "But, honestly, I ache all over. Nothing a hot shower won't fix."

The word 'shower' reverberated through Connor's head like a shot. He glanced at the old fashioned clawfoot tub on his left, mouth going dry at the possibility Judah might mean they'd climb into it *together*. Now that the thought had settled into Connor's brain though ...

"You want to go first?" Judah asked, his voice breezy. "I'll get the laundry into the dryer in the meantime and maybe find some snacks for later."

Connor swallowed hard; he really needed to get a grip. "Okay. But are you sure you don't want help? You've done all the cooking since I walked through the door and I'm starting to feel guilty."

"The snacks I have in mind don't exactly require much in the way of cooking, but I'll try to find something reasonably healthy for you." Judah aimed a sassy look in Connor's direction. "Except for the cookies, of course. You're on your own there, big guy."

They spent the day just as Judah had promised, lounging around and doing nothing more strenuous than knitting and comparing notes on their favorite streaming shows. Connor could have changed back into his own clothes once they were dry but found he didn't want to give up the soft flannel robe and socks, and when he felt himself growing drowsy as the afternoon lengthened, he didn't fight it.

The light in the room was dimmer when he woke, the TV's volume low, and he wasn't surprised to find himself once more curled into Judah's side. He tried not to feel embarrassed about it. Judah had seemed utterly blasé about Connor's pillow hugging habit when he'd heard about it that morning. Plus, something was different for Connor now and had been since last night. He felt so close to Judah, like they'd known each other years instead of mere weeks. Being near him felt *right* in ways Connor really wasn't ready to examine, especially just now when they were sprawled out together on the world's most comfortable sectional sofa and Connor's brain was still muddled with sleep.

Several seconds passed before he realized Judah was not only awake but reading on his tablet, a slim white stylus held between the index and middle fingers of his right hand. He drew his eyebrows together slightly as Connor watched him, then used the stylus to make a note on the tablet's screen.

"Thought you were taking the day off," Connor murmured, smiling at the way Judah's ears immediately pinked up.

"Caught me." Judah didn't look away from his work. "I thought I'd do some catching up while my partner in crime was zonked out."

"You shaming me for sleeping, Judah?"

"Absolutely not."

"Good, because it sounds to me like you were cheating."

"I wasn't," Judah said, then gasped as Connor snatched the stylus from his hand. "Hey!" Despite the outrage written on his face, he laughed and quickly held the tablet over his head when Connor reached for it too. "Quit it!"

"Make me."

Shifting his weight, Connor grabbed onto Judah's shoulders with both hands and simply dragged until Judah lay flat on the sofa cushions beside him. Their laughter echoed through the apartment as Judah fought Connor, twisting and squirming as best he could to hold the tablet out of Connor's reach. He was no match for Connor's greater height and wingspan though, and he squawked when Connor rolled half on top of him, using his weight to immobilize Judah. Grabbing hold of Judah's free hand by his wrist, Connor pinned it down and it was hardly any effort from there to catch a corner of the tablet and pry it from Judah's grasp, while Judah cursed Connor through his laughter, cackling the whole time.

"You're such a pain," Judah grumbled, struggling to free himself. "And no fair using a wrestling move!"

Connor laughed too. "I never said I played fair." He made a big show of setting the tablet on the table, then faked a glare at Judah, who was red-faced and giggling and so very beautiful, Connor hurt just looking at him.

Wait.

Connor's breath caught. He could hear Judah joking about being squashed like a bug, but the words were fuzzy and hardly made sense. The buzz Connor had felt when he'd woken in

Judah's arms last night was back, much more intense this time, crawling under his skin and into his blood. He stared into Judah's gray-green eyes and at his mouth, so lush and pink, and Connor's breath shook when Judah's smile faded.

"Connor?" His whisper cut through the noise in Connor's head. "Are you all right? You look like you've seen a ghost."

"I'm okay."

Connor was sure he'd never spoken truer words. He liked being here with Judah so much. He felt ... safe, somehow, and wanted. Cared for in a way he'd never known before. A need to get even closer stirred inside him, filling Connor up just as surely as it knocked him for a loop because he honestly had no idea where any of it was coming from. He was sure he needed Judah's touch, however, more than anything he could remember needing in a very long time.

His hand wasn't quite steady as he lifted it to Judah's cheek. Judah watched, eyes huge as Connor leaned in. He inhaled sharply under the slow brush of Connor's lips, and Connor's whole body thrilled at the electricity flashing under his skin.

Oh, Jesus.

Judah's expression was dazed. He didn't move a muscle as Connor kissed him again, though his eyelids fluttered for a second before sliding closed and he kept them shut even after Connor drew back.

"Connor," he whispered, his voice so small. He sounded spooked and vulnerable, feelings Connor knew well but had never seen in his friend. He ached at the apprehension he sensed coming off Judah in big waves. "What are you—?"

Judah broke off as Connor took his mouth a third time and though he still didn't move, he kissed Connor back, lips pursed in a slow movement both gentle and chaste, yet still the best thing Connor had ever felt. And despite the strangeness of it all

—the red alert screaming in Connor's brain, warning him away from something he absolutely didn't know—he threw himself headlong into it. He closed his own eyes at Judah's soft sigh and swore something vital inside him clicked when Judah brought his hands up to frame Connor's face.

Yes.

Want spun up inside Connor, so heady he felt instantly drunk, and left him helpless to do anything but sink into it and Judah. The contrast of beard stubble and soft skin shook him inside and out, the intensity of the sensation unlike anything he'd ever known. Judah kissed Connor deeper, slow and lazy like they had all the time in the world, and the heat that rose in Connor's core turned him to goo. He groaned as Judah gently pushed him onto his back, wonder running all through him.

"Mmm, Connor."

Connor's breath stuttered at Judah's low purr. He slid his hands into Judah's soft hair, his heart trembling at Judah's hum, and he moaned outright as Judah arranged himself over Connor, his body an absolutely intoxicating weight. Connor's whole being caught fire. Jeez, he was *hard,* and he couldn't remember ever feeling so good, like every part of him was alive and burning for more.

Except ...

He didn't know what he was doing. Connor had never kissed a man. Touched a man this way, with intimacy and passion. The way Connor usually touched women. The way Judah was touching Connor now.

This was more than Connor could handle. And he didn't ever want to stop.

His throat locked up when Judah suddenly pulled away, leaving Connor shaking. God, he was a mess.

"Hey." Judah's voice was hushed. "You're okay, Connor. If you don't want to do this—"

"I do want it. But I don't know why. Never been with a guy before." Even speaking those few words made Connor feel raw and the shock in Judah's face hurt him to see. Connor clenched his eyes shut but when Judah shifted like he was going to pull away, Connor grabbed on to him even tighter. "*Sorry.*"

"No, don't." Judah dropped a small kiss on Connor's cheek. "You've got nothing to apologize for, Connor. You surprised me in the nicest way possible."

The knot behind Connor's sternum loosened. "Yeah?" He peeled his eyes open and managed a smile when Judah nodded, his movements vigorous.

"Oh, yes. I've been wondering what it'd be like to kiss you for weeks and it was every bit as excellent as I'd imagined."

Connor relaxed more under Judah's gentle laugh. He always knew how to set Connor at ease. To make it so much easier to talk about ... whatever the heck was happening between them right now. "How come you didn't tell me?"

"Well, I thought you were with someone else at first, what with the baby blanket and 'my partner' and all that." His expression fond, Judah slid his fingers into Connor's hair, petting him gently. "Even after I found out you were single, it didn't mean you were into guys. Or me. Still not sure how right or wrong I am about that," he added in a wry tone that made Connor take Judah's hand.

"I'm not sure I know either."

"What do you mean?"

Connor frowned and wound his fingers around Judah's. "I've always gone with girls."

"I wondered," Judah murmured, his mouth quirking up in a crooked smile when Connor looked at him askance. "I've seen the way women act around you, Connor, but I could never tell if you were interested."

"Oh." Connor huffed a breath through his nose. "Honestly,

I've been so busy with my studying and work since moving up here, it's like I don't have energy for any of that. But I like women just fine. Never really looked at guys in the same way. Or ... not until recently."

Judah raised his eyebrows. "Yeah?"

"I've had thoughts," Connor said, words coming slowly. "Thinking that a man is good looking. Sexy, even."

"That's not all that strange. Lots of straight people can look at someone their own gender and think 'that's hot.'"

"I know. I never really did, though. Or ... sure, that a man could be handsome, but not hot. And then I *did* have those thoughts and that was new. But it was always fleeting. I'd realize the ideas were in my head, but they'd disappear before I could really get a bead on them. Then I met you." Connor hated the way Judah's gaze instantly shuttered.

"And was meeting me a bad thing?" Judah asked, his tone so, so careful.

"No, not at all. Just the opposite, Judah. Meeting you, getting to know you these past few weeks, has been great. Like, *really* great and I'm not even sure I could explain how." Another piece fell into place for Connor. "I changed. Like I blinked and the whole world shifted. Except ... I think it was shifting all along, every day I've known you, and I just didn't realize it until now."

"Hell, Connor." Regret flashed in Judah's eyes. "This can't be easy for you. I'm sorry if—"

"Don't." Leaning up, Connor pressed his forehead to Judah's, then carefully slid his arms around Judah's waist. He hauled in a deep breath before he spoke again. "You've got nothing to apologize for either," he said, his voice rough. "You're right, this isn't easy. I'm not even sure I know what this is yet, to be honest. But I'm more myself and happier knowing you than I have been in a long while."

The sorrow faded from Judah's face, and when he pressed his lips to Connor's again, the kisses were sweet. A lovely, comforting warmth fell over Connor, further easing the fear that had been gathering inside him. Gladness thrummed through him as Judah laid him out on the cushions again. They curled up together like that for a long time, simply exchanging nuzzles and soft touches, while the wind railed against the windows and the snow fell on the city beyond.

EIGHT

"When did you first know you were gay?"

Judah had answered that question many times in his life. And though there were myriad instances he could count as lightbulbs that illuminated his attraction to men, Judah thought a different question was more crucial for him and, perhaps, for any person who identified as LGBTQ+.

"When did you first realize the implications of being queer?"

That moment, when a sixteen-year-old Judah had truly understood how his life would change—even become dangerous—over a thing he couldn't control, had been a crossroads. As a Jew, Judah had already been aware of people's capacity for hate. He'd wept at the knowledge his sexuality could add fuel to that fire. He'd considered the possibility of his parents turning their backs on him. That he was different from everyone else in his life. That people he might love could scorn him. And Judah had known without a doubt that denying he was gay would make everything so much easier. If only he could bring himself to lie.

Judah hadn't lied, of course. While his big gay life hadn't

been totally free of angst, he'd tried never to expect it would be. And he'd been lucky. His family hadn't turned their backs and he'd found people who didn't judge him for who he loved. Judah had never looked back or second guessed the decision his teenage self had made to come out. He couldn't help wondering now, though, if Connor had even begun to approach the same kind of understanding, and what might happen when he did.

The question tumbled around Judah's head as he and Connor worked side-by-side to make dinner. They'd stumbled up from the sofa at last, Judah's whole body practically vibrating—a marathon petting session with one of the hottest guys he'd ever met would do that to a man. He hadn't made a big deal about it though, because the last thing he wanted was to make Connor feel bad. Not when it was clear Connor was gobsmacked by a facet of his sexuality he'd never known existed.

The emotion—the *fear*—rolling off him when he'd kissed Judah then held on for dear life. That push and pull had been almost painful to witness, particularly since there wasn't much Judah could do beyond just being there for his friend. Judah had made up his mind to do exactly that, however, no matter how much his body told him he needed more than some light petting. Hot as he was, Connor had a lot going on in his head and heart, and he deserved time to find his feet without being rushed by Judah's hormones.

That brought Judah's swirling thoughts full circle. Connor seemed to accept he was attracted to men as well as women. Or, attracted to Judah, at least. Less clear was whether Connor had considered how being bi or pan might affect his life, and particularly when it came to his family or job.

That uncertainty made Judah worry for his friend, who was navigating a brand new world. If he was honest, Judah worried for himself, too. He liked Connor more than he should. Yeah, he'd put the guy in the friendzone soon after they'd met but the sudden discovery Connor might want him as more than a friend was seriously rocking Judah's world, too.

Even so, you're his friend first, Judah reminded himself as he opened the oven, squinting against the blast of heat. He could do it. Put friendship before hormones because he valued this bond with Connor so much. Judah cared for the guy, if he were being honest, and if that seemed a little over the top given they'd only known each other for about a month, too bad—he wasn't about to talk himself out of a friendship that made him happy. He wished this friendship came without the sexual frustration though, because no way in hell was Judah going to forget how good Connor tasted.

Quickly, he swallowed down a sigh. Lifting a casserole dish from the oven, he set it on the stove, then followed with a cast iron skillet of cornbread, executing a little bow as Connor ooh'd and ahh'd.

"Dang, that this all looks dangerously good," Connor said. "Never had mac and cheese with apple before. I'm sort of looking forward to telling my sister-in-law about it."

"Oh?" Judah closed the oven door. "Is it going to be an epiphany or blasphemy when you mention there was chicken sausage in it, too?"

Connor grinned. "I honestly don't know. Ally's more adventurous than James or me when it comes to cooking but she knows better than to mess with one of James's favorite dinners. I think she'd have to bribe him to try it."

"Sounds like your brother is more conservative than you, at least when it comes to dining."

Damn. Judah had meant it as a joke, but the shadow crossing Connor's face told him it'd fallen flat.

"I found this mac and cheese recipe on Facebook, if you

can believe it." He grabbed a serving spoon up from the counter. "My pops hates most fruits and vegetables unless you disguise them, so I try to find creative ways to sneak them into the Sunday dinners. I figured I'd try this out on you, his fellow picky eater, and see how you like it."

"I've liked everything you've cooked for me, actually, and those are not words I'd say to a lot of people." Connor sounded amused. "You were right about James, though—he's probably on par with your pops as far as being picky. Ally's got all kinds of recipes with undercover vegetables in them and every one tastes so good my brother never has a clue. She always tells him what he ate afterward so he gets a chance to pretend to be outraged."

Judah laughed. "Ally sounds fun. And a lot like she and my Mom would get along like a house on fire."

They carried bowls of pasta to the table along with a plate of the cornbread, chatting lightly about Connor's brother and sister-in-law.

"Amazing that they met in high school," Judah said. "My parents did too. Mom always says she knew they'd be married, even after my dad went to live in Israel for a year."

Connor cocked his head. "What was he doing there?"

"Volunteering but also just living." He shrugged. "My grandparents wanted Dad to understand how to live independently outside of the family bubble before he went to college and Dad thought it would be better for my mom to keep her options open. A year is a long time to be separated, especially at seventeen. They got back together two days after Dad flew home to Boston and never looked back." Judah laughed. "Which he should have known was always going to happen given my mother is the most determined person on the planet."

"Ally, too. Says she knew she was destined to be a Devlin and was going to find a way to make it happen. Mind you, we've been tight since third grade, so I know what I'm talking about. She was even after me for a bit, too, before she set her sights on James."

It took a second for the words to make sense in Judah's head. "Wait, what? Your brother was Ally's second choice to *you*?"

"Uh-huh." Connor's expression was tickled. "Though it all sounds way dramatic when you say it like that."

"So, no Lifetime-style movie about star-crossed lovers in a tragic love triangle?"

Connor tipped his head back and really laughed. "God, no! Ally kind of hinted around that she thought we'd be good together but we both knew it was just talk, especially since James was the one she got moony over."

"And that didn't hurt your feelings?"

"Not a bit. I was sort of confused about why anyone would want to date a nerd like my brother but, hey, we were just kids." Connor forked up some more macaroni. "This really is good, you know."

"Agreed. You should know by now that I'd never steer you wrong."

"You're right, I should. I won't doubt you again."

"'Atta boy. So how come you're *not* the Devlin that Ally got moony over?" Judah asked with a smirk. "Is James somehow even better looking than you?"

"Oh." Connor smiled too, though his gaze quickly shifted to his plate. "He totally is, yeah. He's not as big and rough as me and he's in better shape. Definitely got all the good-looking genes in the family, plus he's a lot more together."

What the fuck? Was this guy for real? Judah knew Connor well enough by now to know he wasn't fishing for compliments which made this inability to see himself clearly sobering. Judah set a hand on his forearm.

"Hey, I was kidding. You're being way too hard on yourself."

Connor immediately shook his head. "You wouldn't say that if you met him. And I knew my brother was sweet on Ally by the time we all hit high school. It didn't take a genius to figure out he stuck around the house more when Ally was over than not, but he didn't do anything about it for a long time. Heck, James was already at the Fire Academy when he made up his mind to take her out and he must have asked me a dozen times if I'd mind. It was like he didn't believe me when I said no, but it was the truth.

"Don't get me wrong— there was no big, romantic story between us, but I do love Ally a lot. We all did, Gram included. She and I were friends and we got each other through a lot of stuff." A frown settled over his features as he looked up and caught Judah's eye. "I like to think I'd have told her that I feel this way. About men, I mean. And you."

Judah's stupid heart fluttered in his chest. "Could you tell her now?"

"I don't see how."

"Because of your brother?"

"James wouldn't understand." Connor's gaze shifted, going far away, almost as if he was looking inward. He was wholly unaware of the way his words made Judah ache.

"Maybe you're wrong about that."

"I don't think I am. I hardly understand it myself, Judah, and it's happening to me." Connor gave Judah a wry smile. "James and I have always been different and he's more like you in a lot of ways. Confident. Always knows what to say and what to do."

Judah couldn't hide his frown. "I do *not* always know what to say or do, Connor and while I've never met your brother, I don't think it's a stretch to say he doesn't either."

Connor huffed a laugh. "I think you're the one selling yourself short now. And James may only be three years older than me, but he's had my back forever. Gram always said he helped raise me from the minute I was born."

"You love him." The food in Judah's belly was like a lead weight when Connor nodded. "And I'm guessing you don't want to disappoint him."

"No, I really don't. And that's just another reason I can't tell Ally about ... the way my feelings have changed. It wouldn't be right putting her in that position, knowing something about me that I hadn't told James."

Judah hardly knew how to respond. This didn't bode well at all for ... well, anything he might hope to have with Connor that went beyond friendship. And if James was even close to the conservative fuckface Judah could all too easily imagine him to be, he'd view Judah as a negative in Connor's life, whether they were just friends or something more. No, this wasn't good at all.

"Are you really sure you can't tell him?" he finally asked.

"I wouldn't even know where to start." Connor heaved a big breath, one hand coming up to rub the back of his neck in a gesture Judah now easily recognized as a sign he was feeling stressed. "I didn't tell James I stopped taking my meds because I didn't want him to worry, so how the hell would I tell him I'm attracted to men and expect him to understand? My brother is not one of those guys you were talking about earlier, Judah. He does *not* look at dudes the way he does women."

"Straight guys rarely do."

Connor's mouth opened and closed and, for a second, he looked sick. "I guess you're right. But I've always thought I was straight, and I'm not even sure which way is up at the moment."

Well, shit. Judah had tried to be gentle but, really, there

wasn't any way to talk around the topic of Connor's sexuality and the sooner he understood that the better off he'd be.

Still, Judah felt bad.

Reaching over, he took hold of Connor's hand. "I'm sorry. I'm not trying to make you feel bad. I want to be honest with you, though, because I think you need that right now."

"I probably do. My head is all over the place." Connor swallowed. "It's like trying to fit the pieces of a puzzle together but every time I reach for a new tile, I notice that the whole picture has changed. Does that make any sense?"

"Yes." Running his thumb over Connor's knuckles, Judah waded in a little further. "And also no. I figured out I was gay when I was a teenager, and there was never any uncertainty there, so I honestly don't know what you're feeling."

Connor gave him a small, uneasy smile. "Never any question in your head, huh?"

"Nope." Judah shrugged. "The prettiest girl in the city could walk into my shop and all I'd think about was how much yarn I could sell her. But when someone like you walks in ..."

Connor laughed. "Hey, you sold me yarn too. And you gave me a bag of free stuff!"

"Of course, I did." Judah laughed along with him. "You told me you wanted to buy some, Connor, so I was just doing my job. Doesn't mean I didn't find you any less attractive."

"Yeah?"

"Duh." He patted Connor's hand, then pushed back his chair. "Didn't I cover that earlier when I said I'd been thinking about kissing you for weeks?" he asked as he stacked their empty plates. "You're everything physical I like in a man, Connor, and yes, I like looking at you."

"I really didn't know." Connor wasn't laughing when he joined Judah at the sink. "And I feel like I should have since we've been hanging out a lot."

"Why? It's not like I wanted you to pick up on the way I was feeling. It sucks when someone you're not interested in is all up in your grill and I wasn't going to be that guy. I won't lie and say it wasn't tortuous at times."

"Really?"

Judah rolled his eyes but smiled to show he was teasing. "You need to look at yourself in the mirror more, man. But as I got to know you, I realized how much I enjoyed spending time together and soon it didn't matter that I couldn't mack on you because I already had you as a friend."

He turned on the faucet. "All this is just my way of saying I've got your back, too. Yes, I like you as a guy and, hell yeah, I like kissing you, but I'm also okay with going back to being friends if that's what you want."

Lips set in a straight line, Connor silently helped Judah rinse plates and stack them in the dishwasher. They were nearly finished when he did speak, and his voice was very quiet.

"I appreciate it, Judah. I honestly do. I'm just not sure I *can* go back to the way things were."

Oh, no.

Judah's heart fell right through the floor. "Really? Are you sure?" He licked his lips. "I meant what I said about it being okay if you don't want to be with me. I won't be hurt. I get that I'm not everyone's cup of tea and—"

"That's not it," Connor cut in over Judah's rambling, "but of course, you'd say that. It probably pained you to do it, too." He shook his head. "The thing is, I think I *do* want to be with you, Judah. I just have no idea what that even means."

His lips were on Judah's then, sweet and hot, wet hands at Judah's waist. This kiss was different, urgent in a way Judah hadn't felt from Connor before, and it made his head spin even as he fought to rein in his own reactions. He framed Connor's face with his hands and held on gently when Connor pulled back again, hoping his touch was steadying. But his own heart pounded at the confusion flickering in Connor's eyes, as well as the longing he saw there.

Despite the cozy kitchen, goosebumps rose on Judah's arms. God, this big man was simply intoxicating. His sharp mind and his strength, all wrapped around the tender heart he tried to hide from most of the world but willingly shared with Judah. And damn but Judah wanted to lose himself in the big eyes watching him so closely, especially after so many weeks of wanting Connor.

Judah couldn't do it though. Wouldn't. Not when Connor was still struggling to understand what had happened and Judah doubted either of them could trust his frame of mind just then.

"It's okay to not know yet, Connor," he said. "Because you will figure it out, and I'll help you as much as you need."

Connor closed his eyes and sighed. "Thank you." He pushed into Judah's arms for a hug. "I mean that."

Judah rubbed his back, affection brimming inside him. "I know you do. I'm glad I could be here for you." He hugged a little harder when Connor let out a shaky laugh. "You okay?"

"Getting there." Connor tipped his head back enough to meet Judah's eyes. "I guess I'm wondering what comes next."

"My advice? Do what feels right. You don't have to decide anything until you're ready and this is about you and no one else."

"What about you?"

"I'm happy to follow your lead. I might sneak in some more hugs and kisses here and there, if you let me though," Judah added with a laugh. "At least until we can dig ourselves out of here and you finally make your escape."

Connor's cheeks turned dusky. "You don't have to sneak. It's not like I stopped wanting to touch you either."

"I'm glad to hear it." Judah slid his arms from around Connor's neck and rested his palms on either side of Connor's sternum. "I just didn't want to push in case you'd gotten it out of your system."

"Oh, Judah." Connor covered Judah's hands with his own. "I think it's going to be a while before I feel anything like you're out of my system."

That's what a guy likes to hear.

Delight swooped through Judah as Connor leaned down and kissed him again, the touch lighter this time, as if he were exploring. Moving carefully, Judah drew him in, heat building inside him as Connor seemed to melt into the embrace. He teased his tongue between Connor's lips, humming low when Connor didn't hesitate to open for him, and skated the fingers of one hand down Connor's torso, sliding them up under the hem of the flannel bathrobe so he could get at Connor's heated skin. Connor grunted as he kissed Judah deeper and Judah's pulse picked up at the sound, his half-hard cock stiffening further. He had to swallow back a growl as he forced himself to pull away.

"Is this okay?" he asked, then bit his lip at Connor's quick nod.

"So okay." Connor whispered, heat in his gaze. His voice was a mere thread, surprise clear in his tone. "Kissing you, touching you ... God, you feel amazing. I want more."

"Shit." Judah couldn't help his groan. "I want that, too. I could make you feel so good."

Connor's eyes shone. "You do, Judah. Every time you touch me."

NINE

Judah rose up on tiptoe when Connor kissed him again, so their heights were more evenly matched, and damn, Connor liked that so much. This man made him feel things he'd never known before. Like he could fly. Like he was really awake—no, *alive*—for the first time in his whole life, and if that didn't exactly make sense right now, Connor really didn't care.

Groaning deep in his chest, he pulled Judah in, dizzy with the need to get closer, his dick hard again and aching. He didn't really think about what he was doing when he grabbed Judah up, hauling him against his own body, Judah's sharp inhale ringing in his ears.

"*Jesus*, baby."

Connor's knees trembled at the breathless endearment. He quickly set Judah down on the sink's edge, biting his lip at Judah's chuckle. "Sorry," he muttered, but smiled as Judah simply wrapped his arms around Connor's neck and snuggled a little closer. "Got a bit carried away there."

"I didn't mind," Judah said. "Never had a guy literally sweep me off my feet before but that was pretty hot."

Connor smothered a laugh against Judah's shoulder. "Is that your way of saying you like being manhandled?"

"Maybe my way of saying I like being manhandled by *you*." Judah was smiling when Connor pulled back and he looked almost blissful as he slid his fingers into the short hair at the nape of Connor's neck. "And mmm, I like this. Touching you feels even better than I imagined."

Heat flushed through Connor's core. "You thought about this? Us, together?"

"Oh, yes. Probably more than was wise." Leaning forward, Judah pressed his lips into the hollow of Connor's throat, the touch like sweet fire against Connor's skin. "I dreamed about you a couple of times," he said, voice lower. "And I was so hard when I woke up, it'd take me a few minutes to understand you weren't really there in bed with me."

Connor's breath hitched. Never in his life had he felt so much arousal from words alone. He stepped back as Judah slid down from his perch on the sink. "What did you want when you woke up?"

"You."

Fingers around Connor's, Judah led him out of the kitchen, saying nothing as they walked through the apartment. But once they'd reached Judah's bedroom, Judah moved to the bed and sat, gently pulling Connor down beside him, his expression earnest despite the fire in his eyes.

"I wanted you, Connor," he said, "here, with me."

Connor let out a shaky breath. "Oh, God. I think I want that too. It's just ..." he pressed his lips together for a beat. He felt *so* out of his depth here, regardless of how many times Judah assured him that Connor was the one calling the shots. "I'm not sure how this works, Judah. I don't have the first clue about how to be with a man and make it right."

A beautiful smile crossed Judah's face. "Stop thinking

about right and wrong, and you're going to be fine." The light in his face dimmed then, and he appeared almost somber as he folded his hands around Connor's. "I'll take whatever you want to give me, Connor. Because it doesn't matter which way I fly as long as I get to do it with you."

Nervousness fading, Connor met Judah's kiss without hesitation, aware once again of how easily this man made him feel good.

His skin tingled as Judah reached for the belt on the bathrobe and Connor leaned into the touch, sighing when Judah pushed the flannel aside and ran his hands over Connor's bare chest. Connor didn't hold himself back from touching Judah too, though he didn't feel brave enough yet to do more than slide his hands under the hem of Judah's sweatshirt. Awareness grew inside him as his fingers met silky skin. He *wanted* this. To touch Judah and see more of his body than the snatches he'd glimpsed under Judah's shirt collars. And Connor knew then that he had been thinking about a moment like this for weeks and he'd never even realized it.

A light shiver raced over him, like the thrill of awareness he always felt in the seconds after an alarm echoed through the station house. Throat tight, he watched Judah lift his legs onto the bed, then scoot over to one side of the mattress before he held a hand out to Connor. Taking it, Connor swung his legs up onto the mattress, too, his heart pounding so hard he could hardly breathe.

God. This is happening.

Judah waited for Connor to settle, then gathered him in his arms, his hold loose enough that Connor could have pulled away without trying. Connor snuggled in closer, closing his eyes as he met Judah's kisses, and warmth lapped at his insides as Judah gently teased his tongue between Connor's lips. The quiet noise he made when Connor opened for him turned Connor's whole body liquid.

He sank deeper into the mattress, arms around Judah's neck and his breath stuttering as Judah trailed the fingers of one hand down Connor's torso, leaving wisps of fire over Connor's already heated skin. Judah deepened the kiss, the slide of his tongue stiffening Connor's dick even further. He couldn't hold back his needy noise when Judah palmed Connor through the borrowed thermals, the heat and pressure on his dick so, so good.

"Christ," Judah muttered.

Connor wound his arms around Judah even more snugly. "Mmm. Judah."

"I've got you," Judah said, his voice rough in Connor's ear. He tapped his fingers against Connor's waistband. "Okay if we take these off?"

"Yes." But no sooner was the word out of Connor's mouth than Judah was moving, and Connor's entire being went cold. Wrenching his eyes open, he almost sat up, a protest half stuck in his throat. "W-what— "

"Just grabbing some supplies," Judah replied, his voice soothing as he reached over and opened the nightstand drawer. Plucking something from its depths, he turned back, a smile on his face and a slim bottle half-filled with colorless liquid in his hand.

"I meant it when I said I could make you feel good and figured this was as fine a time as any to introduce you to the joys of lubrication." Judah cocked an eyebrow at Connor. "Unless you're one of those enlightened straight boys who already has a favorite brand?"

"Um, no. Can't say I do." Connor knew his eyes had gotten big. He'd never found reason to consider lubrication when he'd been with women, but he'd studied medical journals and the human anatomy for long enough that he understood the mechanics of sex between men. His face heated at Judah's soft chuckle, but there was nothing mean in his friend's tone or words.

"Then you have been missing out," Judah said. "And you're going to thank me when all is said and done."

Connor couldn't help laughing too. He found he wasn't frightened or put off by the idea of using the contents of the bottle Judah set on the nightstand. Hell, he even felt a spark of interest at what other supplies Judah might be able to offer. "Do I want to know what else you've got stashed in that drawer of yours?" he asked and grinned at Judah's peal of laughter.

"Maybe another time." Judah's his eyes glowed with promise. "You should get used to the idea of just being with me before we do anything that might break your brain."

Climbing out of bed entirely, Judah bent over Connor and turned his attention to the thermals. He paused often as he stripped Connor down, massaging circles into Connor's muscles so Connor felt almost boneless by the time he lay nude. Heat flooded his face when Judah stood straight at last, but Connor didn't look away and quickly found his shyness faded under the awe in Judah's gaze.

"Damn," Judah murmured, his tone reverent. Raising a hand to Connor's chest, he stroked the fine blond hairs on Connor's pecs before moving to Connor's belly and Connor shivered at the lust zigzagging under his skin.

More.

As if he'd heard the silent plea, Judah straightened again and reached for the hem of his own sweatshirt. His movements lost finesse from there, though, and Connor bit his lip as Judah practically tore it over his head, then shoved his pants down, his actions jerky and hurried. He climbed back onto the bed but stopped when Connor reached over and touched him, spreading his palms wide over Judah's thighs.

Free from clothing, Judah's toned body was everything Connor's big frame was not; lithe like a runner's with lean muscles that spoke of dedicated yoga practice. His fair skin was more golden than Connor had expected with a delicate spray of freckles over his shoulders and scant, dark hairs sprinkled over his sternum. The planes of Judah's belly were entirely smooth until his navel where a trail ran from underneath it to his groin, ending in a thatch that framed Judah's dick, which stood hard and red against his abdomen. Connor stared, mouth going cottony dry, utterly unable to tear his eyes from the sight until Judah let out a pained-sounding noise.

"Fuck." Judah's eyelids were so heavy his eyes were practically slits. "You keep looking at me like that, big guy, and it's going to be game over before we even start."

Connor huffed a laugh that made Judah smile, and both sighed as Judah stretched out on the mattress again. They kissed some more, deep and languid, until Connor felt literally drunk. He wanted to grumble when Judah broke away, then thought better of it as Judah trailed his lips over Connor's jaw and neck, licking and gently sucking. He felt sure he'd lose his mind when Judah scraped his teeth against the muscle that connected Connor's shoulder and neck.

"Oh, *God*. Judah, please."

"I'm here," Judah murmured against Connor's throat. "Hang on to me tight."

Circling Connor's wrists with his fingers, Judah guided them to his shoulders, nodding when Connor grabbed hold. He climbed on top of Connor and lined up their bodies, and Connor gasped at the depth of sensation that delicious weight gave him. Judah felt so different from the women Connor had been with. Strong and hard, and all straight lines where they'd been curvy and soft. And though Connor was the bigger man, Judah's touch claimed him in ways that spoke to a part of him he'd never known existed.

He writhed and barked out a laugh as Judah gently bit at his neck again, though the laughter quickly devolved into a moan as Judah started sucking and his whole body jerked as their dicks met.

"Jesus," Connor got out, voice a raspy wreck. "Can't believe how good you feel. I wish ... wanna make you feel good, too, Jude."

"You will. Just touch me the way you like to be touched, and I guarantee I'll like it."

Judah's skin was sheened with sweat as he pulled back and reached for the lube. "And you're going to like this," he promised, eyes wild and breaths coming fast. "It makes everything feel a hundred times better."

Connor swallowed as he watched Judah wet his fingers, but he didn't hesitate to spread his legs wider when Judah reached for him. His balls throbbed at Judah's low oath, though, and damn if he didn't feel like he was on the brink of losing it himself.

Shifting close, Judah lined up their bodies again, then wrapped their dicks up in his hand, expression hungry as he watched Connor melt into the exquisite sensations of slick over steel and velvet softness.

"*Oh.*"

"Feel good?" Judah sounded smug as Connor's jaw went slack.

"Uhhh." Connor pressed his head back into the pillow, eyes squinched closed while every nerve in his body thrummed. "So good. So good, Judah, oh, my God."

Need barreled through him like a freight train. Unable to keep quiet, he groaned and called out, unaware of what he was saying or even that he was thrusting his hips up until Judah's whisper cut through him.

"That's it, baby. Show me how you fuck."

Forcing his eyes open, Connor was unsurprised to find Judah's gaze still locked on him, his eyes blazing.

A guy could get lost in those eyes. Even a guy like me. The words hit Connor square in the chest, making his throat knot.

"Wish you could see yourself," Judah murmured. "So goddamned gorgeous, all warm and relaxed and just for me."

He rolled his hips, sliding their dicks together, and the pleasure in Connor skyrocketed so high he thought he might scream.

"Oh, *fuck*. Fuck, Judah. I ..."

Judah's eyes slid closed. "Damn," he whispered, a shudder racking his frame as he moved against Connor. "You're swearing. So fucking hot, Con, and ... Jeez."

Pride bloomed hot and heady inside Connor. He'd done that. Made Judah come so undone he could hardly string two words together, groans coming steadily around his nonsensical pleas. And the power in knowing that pitched Connor over the edge almost before he knew what was happening.

Chest thrust up, he came apart on a shaky groan, muscles strung tight as pleasure—God, *joy*—pulsed through him in long, devastating waves.

"That's it," Judah crooned. "So gorgeous when you come."

He lost it then too, his head thrown back in a long, low moan. The hot slick of cum against Connor's dick sent a powerful aftershock through him, stealing his breath before it left him limp, and Connor had to press his face against Judah's neck as the understanding jolted through him.

He *loved* this. And what the hell did he do next?

"God*damn*." Judah's laughter soothed the worry rising in Connor's gut. "And to think I was afraid I'd break your brain if we went too fast. That was so *intense!*" Taking a corner of the sheet, he wiped them both down, his demeanor growing gentle when Connor didn't answer. "You okay?"

Connor wasn't sure what he was just then besides sated, sleepy, and freaked out all at the same time. He'd just fooled around with a guy and goddamn if it hadn't been the hottest sex Connor had experienced in his entire life. How had he gone over thirty years without knowing he could be attracted to men?

"Connor?"

"Not sure what I am." Connor hauled in a breath but choked on it and he quickly pressed his lips together when Judah dropped the sheet in favor of grabbing one of Connor's hands. "I didn't know, Judah. It's never been like that for me before. Had no idea sex could be so ... That it would feel good being with—"

"A man?" Judah finished for him, his voice soft.

"With *you*," Connor said, heart clenching when Judah's smile vanished. "Watching you. The way you touch me. I've never felt anything like that with anyone. It was amazing."

"For me too." Judah leaned down and pressed a kiss against Connor's forehead. "I hope you don't mind me saying that the selfish side of me is totally celebrating I got to do that with you, too." He sighed at the question he must have read in Connor's face. "Like I said, I'd wanted to kiss you for ages, but I never let myself think something like this would be possible."

"Same." Connor smiled but quickly cast his gaze down onto the mattress, face burning. He held onto Judah's hand a little tighter. "This really hit me out of nowhere, too."

"I can only imagine." Threading his free arm under Connor's neck, Judah settled back down beside him. "I'm honored you trusted me to be good to you, you know."

Connor's eyes stung. What the heck did a guy say to that?

"Pretty sure I'm the one who should be grateful," he whispered. "I don't even know how to thank you for ..." His eyes burned as Judah shook his head.

"Hey. I love having you here with me, Connor. I wouldn't change a minute of today."

He's just being nice.

Except Connor didn't believe that. Judah wouldn't feed him a line simply because he could. Judah was so confident and strong, just being around him made Connor feel a hundred times lighter than he usually did, and he'd been straight with Connor from the day they'd met. The shine in his eyes was like the warmth of ten suns as he smiled at Connor now, and Connor couldn't help basking in it, captivated by the attention.

Closing his eyes, he pushed into Judah's arms again, his skin tingling as they kissed. Yes. This. He wanted *this*. To quiet the voices in his head that insisted he *think*. Connor didn't want to think. He wanted to touch and taste and feel instead and lose himself in Judah. He loved being here with this man, the mere touch of skin on skin sending ripples of pleasure through him and the sweet buzz inside him growing stronger, leaving Connor wanting more, even if he wasn't entirely sure what more really meant.

They made out for a long time, the kisses cycling from sweet and gentle to dirty and hot again and again, Connor's desire building in a slow tsunami that had him clutching at Judah, only to find that Judah was coming just as undone. They were panting when Judah finally pulled away, Connor's body humming with a need he couldn't ignore, the desire in Judah's eyes too.

"Need you so much," he whispered, softly enough Connor thought he hadn't been meant to hear the words, but he was already moving, the bottle of lube in hand once more as he scooted closer to the foot of the bed.

Expression intent, Judah wet his fingers, then bent forward, pressing his mouth into the crease between Connor's hip and belly. Soft lips were followed by the prickling rasp of beard stubble, and that delicious contrast made Connor moan, his eyes going wide as he watched Judah nuzzle at the tender skin. He reached for Judah without really meaning to, and only just managed to stop himself as his palms made contact with Judah's hair.

"Do it," Judah said, his voice low. Once again, he circled Connor's wrists with his fingers, guiding Connor's hands to where he wanted them, only letting go when Connor's fingers were deep in Judah's hair. "Gonna suck you, Connor," Judah murmured, "and you can fuck my face all you want."

Fire swept through Connor, his eyes actually rolling as his lids fluttered shut. God, he wanted that. Wanted Judah's mouth. Wanted Judah to touch him freaking everywhere he could reach.

Lost, he moaned again when Judah cupped his balls with his fingers, and a shout built inside him as Judah massaged the soft skin behind Connor's sac in slow, maddening circles.

Connor dropped his knees open wide, Judah's appreciative groan curling around him like an embrace. Something about that really got to Judah. Then again, opening himself to Judah —giving himself over—got to Connor, too, and made his dick so stiff he almost hurt.

Judah trailed his fingers from Connor's balls to the cleft of his ass, and the shudder racing through Connor made him whine. Never had he wanted a thing as much as he dreaded it.

"I've got you, Connor."

A lump rose in Connor's throat. He knew that. Judah would stop if Connor asked, or go further if Connor wanted. No matter what, this man would be good to him and treat Connor right.

Connor floated, buoyed by sensation as Judah rubbed and teased his rim with one finger, the touches gentle so Connor couldn't help but relax. He shuddered when Judah finally slid the fingertip in, pleasure expanding through him so hard in a rush that he gasped.

"*Judah.*"

"I know, baby."

His body burned in the best way as Judah worked him open, the pleasure coiling tighter when a second finger joined the first. The achy-sting faded under Judah's whispers and the kisses he pressed into Connor's inner thighs, and when Connor peeled his eyes open, the mix of lust and affection he glimpsed on Judah's face knocked him for a loop. A strangled cry escaped him as Judah slid his mouth over Connor's dick.

He took Connor deep, the wet heat and pressure of his mouth quickly snapping the very last of Connor's control, leaving him a cursing, babbling mess and absolutely unable to look away from the sight of Judah below him, the most erotic thing he'd ever seen, lips stretched wide and eyes wet with moisture as he sucked and fingered. Without really meaning to, Connor tugged hard at Judah's hair, his bones turning to water as Judah's eyelids fluttered closed and he moaned around Connor's dick, the sound wanton and needy.

God. He loves this. And damn but, I do too.

Time lost meaning for Connor. He writhed and whimpered, helpless to do anything but surrender. His chest constricted as he watched Judah rut against the sheets, hips moving with an urgency that drove the fire in Connor even higher. Despite his own body's shaking, Connor didn't care anymore how or when he came. He only knew he wanted everything this man could give him and give it all back so Judah felt just as amazing as Connor did right now. Distantly, he heard himself beg.

Electricity crashed through him out of nowhere as Judah twisted his fingers, making Connor's dick jump and his hips buck. He cried out, toes curling as it happened again and again, until the coil inside him snapped. A sob in his throat, Connor unraveled, coming harder than he ever had before, fingers twined tight in Judah's hair.

He felt dazed and fuzzy when Judah pulled off, their breaths harsh in the otherwise quiet room. Then Judah was on him, his kiss bitter with Connor's cum, his dick like iron against Connor's hip. Something inside Connor crumbled at Judah's desperate noise and he quickly pushed Judah onto his back.

Propping himself up on his elbow, Connor mirrored Judah's movements as they both reached for his dick. He'd barely got his fingers around Judah when Judah's body jerked, and he stared in disbelief as Judah arched up into the touch.

"*Fuck*. Like that, yeah," Judah mumbled, eyes squished closed and his hand shaking as he brought it to rest over Connor's. "Love that. Fuck, Connor. You're ... uhhh, love how you feel. Gonna get me off."

Connor's breath hitched at the urgency he read in Judah's features. "Show me, Jude," he murmured. "Show me I make you feel good."

Judah gasped. "You do, oh, *God*," he got out before he arched his back even more and came, shooting so hard, cum striped his chest and neck.

Heat slashed through Connor. He needed this. Craved it. The weight of Judah's body, his lean strength. The way he took command of Connor and marked him with his teeth and lips and cum. The way he fell apart, shuddering in Connor's arms, Connor's name a reverent whisper on his lips. Jesus, just watching him now was enough to make Connor want to see it again and he had to clench his eyes shut against the sudden chill that fell over him.

How had this happened?

He held Judah close as he floated back down, mumbling endearments between clumsy kisses for Connor, clearly uncaring of the mess between them.

"You killed me dead," Judah said at last, his eyes closed and his limbs heavy against Connor's. "Hope you're happy."

Connor tried to smile. "Why would I be?"

"'Cause I'm about to pass out." Already, Judah's words were soft and slurred, and while Connor knew he was struggling to stay awake, he could tell it wouldn't be long before the battle was lost. "Is why I make th' worst boyfriend. Your fault this time, though."

Boyfriend?

Connor lay staring at the ceiling after Judah's breathing had evened out. He'd known their friendship was different well before they'd come up to this apartment to wait out the storm though exactly how hadn't been clear. Connor's world view had changed in the last twenty-four hours, however, and now a lot of things made perfect sense.

He wanted to be with Judah. As more than a friend. That was why he'd kept coming back to the yarn store every day. Why he'd looked for reasons to be around Judah, whether they were browsing stalls at the market or working with wool, or simply talking as they walked the neighborhood's streets. Why he sometimes caught himself watching Judah, his insides doing funny things when Judah smiled at him or his eyes caught Connor's just so.

Connor had felt jealous of Judah's ex when they'd met, and damn if it wasn't still true. The idea of Seb having been where Connor was in this moment—hell, that Seb could be here again —ate at him. Because Seb knew what he was doing. Really understood how to treat Judah right. Make him feel good, instead of bumbling around without the faintest idea of how to have sex with a man.

Is that what Connor wanted? To have sex with Judah? Be Judah's boyfriend the way Seb had been? Did Judah want that, too?

Connor's stomach twisted as a familiar floaty feeling he dreaded stole over him, like his brain was disconnecting from his body. He didn't know to answer those questions. He didn't even know what these encounters with Judah really meant. Were they still friends? Or was 'boyfriends' the more appropriate word? Just the idea of saying it out loud made Connor feel cold. How was he going to explain all this at work? To the people he knew?

A quiet chime cut through the hush, rising from the dresser where Connor had left his phone that morning after he and Judah had stripped out of their wet, post-drone-attack clothes. Connor knew the noise came from his phone because it was his brother's ringtone.

Connor pressed his lips against Judah's hair. How the hell would he explain this to James? Explain Judah? How much Connor liked him and that being with him made Connor feel better than any girlfriend he'd ever had, in *and* out of bed?

Fear rose inside him like a silent, black wave, swamping his senses, and the only thing Connor could feel was lost. It could be his heart wanted to figure out the answers to those swirling questions, but his head was another story. It wanted out of here, right here, right now, the urge to run pounding like a drum in his chest. And though Connor tried like hell to push his anxiety down, it got harder and harder to keep himself from drowning with every second that passed.

TEN

Judah felt the change in the air the second he opened his eyes.

He'd only meant to nap after fooling around with Connor, because he knew the big guy would want—maybe even need— to talk. Yes, Connor had said more than once that he'd wanted Judah, but frotting and getting off together were baby steps compared to having a man's fingers in your ass and their mouth on your cock. Especially if you'd only recently discovered your same-sex attraction.

But the warmth of Connor's body had been impossible to resist after he'd wrapped Judah up and held him. Judah had needed to be held just then. Yeah, he'd been lucky to have had good, caring partners who treated him well in bed and always made him feel good. Being with Connor had been something else entirely, however, and had catapulted Judah so high, his orgasm had been like an out-of-body experience. He'd been shaken as he came back down, his chest screwed tight enough it had been hard to breathe and Judah had *needed* an anchor to keep him from losing it entirely. That he'd found it in Connor's touch humbled him even more.

Judah still needed that anchor. His world had changed too, starting and ending with Connor and the feelings swirling inside him, feelings bigger than affection and friendship for the gentle bear of a man who'd walked into his shop only a month ago. Which just made the embarrassment Judah felt at conking out after having sex with that man sharpen to the point of pain as he stared at the empty space beside him in the bed.

Shit. I shouldn't have pushed him so fast.

Dread pricked at Judah's insides. It was early morning, judging from the light in the windows, which meant he'd slept through the night while Connor might have been awake and thinking God knows what. Sitting up, Judah ran his hands through his hair, the sheets pooling around his waist as he looked around the room. His mood tanked further when he spotted the bathrobe, thermals, and socks Connor had borrowed sitting in a neat pile on the dresser and abruptly the silence of the apartment around him grew oppressive.

He really hoped Connor had at least left a note.

Heartsore, Judah swung his legs over the edge of the mattress and forced himself to get up. He went through the motions of pulling on his sweats and stripping the bed, his brain still racing as he tried to work out his next steps. He and Connor could salvage their friendship; Judah wanted that if Connor did too. Things might be awkward for a while, but they were grown men—they could go back to the way things had been between them before the storm.

Connor already said he wasn't sure he could *go back. And what about you? Do you really think the 'just friends' scenario is going to be enough?*

A sinking feeling dragged at Judah. He really didn't know. As much as he enjoyed having Connor as a pal, he also liked him as a lover, *far* more than he should. He really wanted to try, though. Sex aside, Judah valued their friendship. Valued the time they spent together, even when all it amounted to was a few hours spent in near silence while they worked with their yarn.

With Connor, Judah didn't have to be anything but himself. He wasn't a business owner or editor or guardian to Levi. He was just Judah. Simple moments like those were scarce in Judah's life and now that he knew he could have them with Connor, he wanted to keep them just as badly as he wanted to keep his friend.

Bundling the bedding up with the bathrobe and thermals, he carried it all from the bedroom to the kitchen, then nearly dropped everything when he caught sight of Connor parked at the kitchen table.

For a second, hope and happiness surged in Judah. Connor was here. He'd *stayed*. They could come out of this okay. Talk it over and figure out what each of them really wanted and how fast or slow they'd need to move so Connor felt comfortable exploring this new side of himself.

Then Connor met Judah's gaze and Judah knew without either of them speaking a word that things were definitely not going to be okay. The anxiety on Connor's face—his white-knuckled grip as he clasped his hands together and the panic so plain in his eyes—made it very, very clear. As did the boots on his feet and the coat and duffle bag hanging on the back of his chair. Connor was halfway out the door already, even if he didn't actually know it.

Judah wasn't sure Connor would be able to get out the door without hyperventilating, though, because the guy looked about five seconds away from losing his shit. And that was down to Judah having let his friend down when he'd needed Judah most.

"Hey." Judah set the bundle of clothes on the nearest counter. "I'm really glad you're still here," he said, keeping his tone light. "Thought maybe you'd decided to brave a hike back home through the storm."

Connor just blinked. "It's mostly stopped," he said, his voice sounding hollow. He waved a hand at the windows. "Been like this for a while now."

"Gotcha." Judah glanced outside. Snow was still falling, but lazily, a sign the high winds that had buffeted the city for over twenty-four hours had calmed. "I guess we can chalk up your first big snowstorm as over then. The first of many, I'm afraid."

He cleared his throat against an ache. The weather? Is that really how Judah was going to play this?

"I'm sorry, Connor," Judah made himself say. "I didn't mean to fall asleep, especially since you probably want to talk about what we—"

"No. I don't." Connor opened his mouth like he was going to say more but closed it again just as quickly. He scrubbed at his face with his hands then dropped them, his cheeks pale under his beard. "I don't want to talk about what happened. I don't know how to do this. How to be with a man or be this guy you think I am or—"

"I don't want you to be anyone but you, Connor," Judah said as gently as he could. "And while I heard what you just said, I think it would be good for us to talk about what we did together."

"Yeah, but I don't."

"I really liked being with you that way, Connor." Judah gulped when Connor pressed his lips into a grim line. "But if you've decided you don't want me like that, that's okay too."

Connor drew his eyebrows together. "It is?"

"Yes." The half-lie sat heavy in Judah's chest. Connor not wanting him would hurt. Getting past it would take time. But Judah *could* do it. Wanted to if it meant having Connor in his life. "Nothing between us has to be any different than it was before we—just before. Nothing at all.

"I'm your friend. You know that, right?" he asked. "Last night doesn't have to mean anything about who you are unless you want it to. Straight or bi or whatever, you're still *you*. Still Connor."

"Yeah, well. I don't think I know who I am at all anymore." Connor looked so miserable, Judah stepped forward and his heart cracked wide open at Connor's visible flinch.

Oh, this was bad. And how the fuck had they come to this?

Judah drew in a deep breath. "I don't believe that. You know who you are, Connor. You're the badass paramedic. The guy who put himself through school not once but twice and did it all on his own in a new state that second time. Who lets kids play with his hair if it calms them down. Who brings kale smoothies to his partner even though kale makes you gag. The guy who likes chill house music and loved his grandmother, and still loves his big brother."

Judah gulped as Connor stood up from the table, every line of his body tense. For the first time ever, he saw Connor's size as something other than a physical attribute he admired. Connor was *huge* and strong as hell—Christ, he'd picked Judah up as if he'd weighed nothing at all last night. If he decided he felt like pounding Judah into sand, there was almost nothing Judah would be able to do about it but hope the guy changed his mind.

In his core though, Judah was certain Connor would never hurt him, no matter how upset he got. The tension running through his powerful frame right now was directed inward, not at Judah, and Judah felt broken knowing how hard Connor had to be struggling.

"None of those things about you have changed," he said more softly, "and they're all still parts of who you are."

Parts of a man I like so much.

Judah couldn't say that, though. Not when the fear in Connor's face had started to fade. And Connor just looked so tired, eyes rimmed red and his broad shoulders slumped as if he'd been carrying the weight of the world. Which, Judah thought, he probably felt he was. All at once, Connor's gaze went soft, and, for just a second, he looked at Judah with real warmth.

"Thank you," he said, voice weary. "I appreciate you saying that, Judah. You're a good f-friend."

The split-second stumble over 'friend' drove the fracture in Judah's heart deeper. He managed a smile, though it felt weird and wrong on his face.

"You're a good friend to me, too," he said.

Judah wasn't sure words had ever been more true and empty all at the same time. Connor had come to mean a hell of a lot to him. Last night, he'd even let himself wonder if maybe they could have more together. But now, as they stared each other down over the length of the kitchen, he had no idea if the friendship they'd started with was going to survive at all.

Turning, Connor picked his coat up from the back of his chair and just like that the walls were back up. Judah watched him draw it on and sling the strap of his duffle bag onto his shoulder, the awful, helpless feeling swelling inside him almost too much to bear. The pain left him almost breathless as he turned back to the laundry he'd abandoned.

"We should walk up to the Common and go skating at the Frog Pond sometime." Unlike his hands, Judah's voice was surprisingly steady, but he kept his eyes fixed firmly on the sheets. "Maybe drag Levi with us. Once the sidewalks are shoveled, of course."

"Sounds fun." Connor cleared his throat. "My brother and

Ally decided they'd take the train up to visit later this week, so maybe after that."

"Sounds good." Judah faced the laundry room instead of facing Connor. "We could go after your next knitting class."

Which is so not going to happen.

Judah was sure of it. He doubted he'd ever see Connor in Hook Me again, in fact, but he wanted to leave the door open anyway, even if Connor was just going to disappear right through it.

"Sure. I'll see ya, Judah."

"Bye, Connor. Don't be a stranger."

Judah flashed what felt like a smile in Connor's direction, but he didn't make eye contact; Judah wasn't even sure Connor was looking his way. And that meant he felt Connor slip away more than he truly saw it, but that was all right. Because while Judah would never have blocked Connor's way, he was damned if he was going to watch the man leave.

———

CONNOR HAD BEEN GONE for hours by the time Judah found the unfinished baby blanket on the side table by the sectional sofa.

He'd spent his day shoveling. At over two feet deep, the storm's accumulation had been impressive. Luckily, it was a lighter, fluffy snow that didn't make the project quite so back-breaking. Which still didn't make it an easy task for one person, between the rooftop garden and the sidewalks in front of the shop and around Judah's building, as well as the parking spaces at the rear.

Shoveling out was a neighborhood affair in the North End too, residents and homeowners pitching in with one another when someone needed help clearing an alley or digging out their car. And Judah had welcomed the added work, grimly using the straightforward physicality of simply moving snow as a distraction from his clusterfucked life until he was so exhausted his arms and legs trembled and he'd sweat through the clothes he wore under his coat.

Returning to the apartment, he soaked in the shower for a much longer time than necessary, his muscles filled with an achy burn as he got out and re-bandaged the cut on his forehead. He'd just opened a bottle of beer when his phone chimed, and though Judah felt too wiped out for conversation, he liked seeing his mother's name on the screen.

"Hey, Mom."

"He-e-ey, Jude!" she sang in return, the Beatles' lyrics dissolving into laughter at Judah's scoff. "How are you sweetheart? Up to your eyeballs in the white stuff?"

"Pretty much." *And a hell of a lot more*, he thought. "Been shoveling all day, so I'm kind of a big bag of garbage, but we should be good to re-open tomorrow, provided we don't get hit with another storm."

Molly clucked like a worried hen on the other end of the line. "Sounds like you haven't been watching the forecast. I suppose that's hardly surprising given you've been digging out all day, but it looks like another storm is already on its way and we'll get another eight to ten inches."

Judah let out a grunt that sounded pained even to his own ears. "Guess I'll be super ripped and hot after all this working out, then, and the gays will like that," he said, his mother's laughter merry. "Are you all doing okay up there?"

"Oh, sure. Your pops and I haven't had much trouble, what with Levi being here, not to mention the snowblower. I'm sorry you're stuck down there with no one to help you, though." Molly sighed. "I'd send Harvey or Levi back down if I didn't worry they'd get caught driving in the next storm."

Judah opened the refrigerator, intent on finding food that didn't require any kind of prep. "You're right to worry," he said, "and all of you should stay put until the forecast is clear. Besides, I'm fine!" Grabbing a tub of spinach dip from the fridge, he headed to the pantry for a bag of tortilla chips. "I've got plenty of help here if I need it."

"True, true. You could always call your friend, Connor! I'm sure he'd be happy to help."

The cheer in Molly's voice made Judah's chest ache even worse than his muscles. She'd made no secret of delighting in Judah and Connor's friendship though she'd stopped her matchmaking overtures once Judah had told her that he believed Connor was straight.

Except Judah wasn't sure what to believe anymore.

Fuck, what a mess.

"I'm sure you're right," he said, trudging into the living room. It was then he caught sight of Connor's nearly finished project and everything inside him went tight. "Listen, I'm really tired, Mom, so I'm gonna go."

"All right. You'll eat something that isn't chips, right? I can hear the bag rustling, so don't even think about lying."

"Umm. No? I'm too tired to cook and this tub of spinach dip called my name."

"Of course, it did." Molly fell quiet for a beat before she spoke again. "Are you okay, Judah?"

"Sure." Judah set the snacks and beer bottle on the low table in front of the sofa and sat. "Why?"

"I'm not sure. Your voice doesn't sound quite right."

"Hmm." Out of nowhere, emotions inundated Judah, clogging his throat and itching at his eyes, and he had to fight to keep his tone even. "Just tired. Two feet is a ton of snow to move when there's sidewalks, a roof, and a bunch of parking spaces that need clearing. Talk to you tomorrow, okay?"

"All right, sweetie. We love you, you know. Don't work too hard and make sure you get some sleep!"

Judah laughed against the prick of sudden tears. "Not gonna be a problem, Mom. I love you guys, too."

He waited until after he'd started his second beer before he picked up Connor's project. Despite all his snarled-up feelings over what had happened between them, Judah had no trouble admiring what had shaped up to be a truly beautiful piece. Connor might still be a novice knitter, but he was *good* with his needles. The fabric Connor had constructed was soft and plush and inviting, his impeccable stitchwork and the wools' colors coming together in a gorgeous, shifting palette that called to mind purple irises against blue skies. Judah couldn't wait to see it finished.

Provided Connor comes back to get it, the pesky voice in his head murmured.

Judah frowned. Of course, Connor would come back for the blanket—he'd invested too much time in the project to simply abandon it, right? Especially with what looked like only a half-dozen rows or so to knit before it would be finished. Not to mention the blanket was a gift for Olivia, a person Judah knew Connor respected deeply as a coworker and valued as a friend.

You were ready to write him off after he left this afternoon, Judah reminded himself, then winced as the thought settled in deeper.

He'd seen the impulse to flee in Connor's eyes and heard it in his voice—he didn't plan to come back, not when things had gotten so messy and weird between them. Again, Judah blamed himself. Yes, Connor had kissed him and yes, he'd said he liked the way Judah made him feel. But Judah had gotten so caught up in his own pleasure and need to *feel* more with Connor, he'd pushed too far and too fast, and it was no wonder at all that he'd scared the guy off.

Some fucking friend you turned out to be.

Judah relaxed into his misery. A couple of orgasms weren't enough to undo a lifetime of binary programming Connor had only recently begun to question; Judah didn't even have to think hard to know that. He was also the first man Connor had ever shown real interest in, for fuck's sake, so even if the guy really was bi or pan and not simply curious, Judah should never have allowed things to go beyond kissing and cuddles, at least not for a while.

"I could finish the blanket," he murmured, unsure why he had to say the words out loud. It felt good putting his voice to them, though, and like maybe—just maybe—doing so would help make things right with Connor, even if their friendship was dead in the water. Judah thought it was the least he could do *if* Connor didn't turn up to reclaim the baby blanket project himself.

In the meantime, Judah had his own project to finish while he waited Connor out. Something he'd started earlier in the week which would probably spin off some side projects since he and the rest of the city were about to be snowed in for a while longer.

Setting the blanket aside, he picked up his own knitting and stroked a finger over the sky-colored stitches. He wasn't sure why he'd been evasive when Connor had asked what he was working on. Maybe because Judah had jumped into the project without a plan. Maybe because he'd been wary of Connor thinking it weird that Judah wanted to knit something for him at all. Judah had been sure he wanted the wool as soon as he'd seen it, however, and that the lovely cerulean blue would complement the warm brown of Connor's eyes perfectly.

ELEVEN

"Why are so many of the restaurants in this neighborhood Italian?"

Connor glanced over his shoulder at James, who stood outside the open bathroom door watching Connor finish his grooming routine. "Because it's an Italian neighborhood? Hence the nickname 'Little Italy'?"

James scoffed. "I can hear your silent 'duh'. So, what—I can't just go out and get a burger?"

"Of course, you can," Connor said. "There are also hundreds of restaurants all over the city, so we can eat whatever kind of food you want."

Ally appeared next, squeezing past her husband so she could lean against the doorframe. "Don't pay him any attention, hon," she said to Connor. "Your brother's just being cranky."

"I'm just being *hungry*," James replied without heat. "Trying to figure out the easiest way to get us around in ass deep snow without driving, too."

He crossed his arms and mock glared at his wife, his wide shoulders seeming to fill the doorframe behind her. Though slightly shorter than Connor, James was equally broad and the hours he spent in the firehouse gym between calls made his six-foot-two frame extra jacked. Ally just rolled her eyes at James, clearly unimpressed.

"We could take the train," she began, but had to hide a smile behind one hand at James's grunt.

"*No*," he said with feeling. "Thank God the hotel is within walking distance because the less I have to ride that underground death trap, the better."

Connor turned back to the mirror and worked pomade into his beard. "That underground death trap is how most of the people who live and work in this city get around, you big goof, including you if you really plan on visiting me at the station tomorrow. Trust me, bro, driving in snow is a giant pain and parking is a total nightmare."

"I saw lots of open spots while we were walking around today," James said, his tone so thoughtful Connor almost tripped over himself nipping that idea in its bud.

"If by 'open' you mean there was a lawn chair in the space instead of a car, you should put any thought of moving that chair out of your head ASAP and I mean that." Connor met James's gaze in the mirror's reflection. "A chair means the spot is claimed and I am *not* kidding when I say people will legit defend their spots with their fists."

"That's the dumbest thing I've ever heard," James grumbled. "Though I guess the gun laws in this state are good for one thing at least."

Connor sighed. "Dude, you're acting like you've never been in a city before." Moving his hands from his beard to his hair, he raked pieces that had fallen onto his forehead back, then turned and faced his family. "So, what do you want to eat, anyway? You got something against pasta?"

"No." James smirked. "Pasta is fine. I was just bitching."

"Thought so." Connor turned his focus on Ally. "Any places catch your eye when you two were walking around earlier?"

"We were more focused on the historic landmarks," Ally said, "or, what we could see of them over the snow piles anyway. If it's all the same to you two, I say we just hit a place nearby, so Mr. Grumpy over here doesn't totally pop his cork."

James laughed. "Girl, come on."

Connor would have laughed too if he'd just had the energy. Ally had a high tolerance for what she called Devlin Boy Moods, but she never let James get away with sulking for more than a few minutes. She'd be after Connor soon too if he didn't shake off this funk, but he'd been working long, tough shifts on very little sleep since he'd walked out on Judah over a week ago and he was really feeling it today.

"Where is your favorite place to eat, Con?" she asked.

Shrugging, Connor sat back against the sink. "Not sure I have one. I don't eat out much, at least not for dinner."

Ally's eyes went round. "Why not? I'd have eaten in every single restaurant by now if I lived here as long as you have."

"That would get expensive," Connor replied, "particularly with rent being what it is in this town. Besides, I'm usually beat by the time I get home and I just want to chill with a sandwich. Quiet shifts are rare at Station 1 and you know we ride along with one of the busiest firehouses in the city."

"True." James frowned, and Connor didn't miss the way he swept his gaze around the tiny studio apartment before returning it to Ally. "Hey, what about the place the waitress mentioned when we stopped for coffee and cannoli at that cafe?"

Ally's face brightened. "Oh, right! She said it was her favorite and that the ravioli changed her life."

Connor chuckled. He wasn't hungry, but his own love of

dumplings gave those words real meaning. "Sounds promising. Where was this mystical ravioli palace?"

"Near the Catholic Church over on the main street," Ally said. "I'm pretty sure she said the name was Magica?"

"Magia," Connor corrected gently.

He knew the place, as did most people in the city. Well-liked by both tourists and locals, long lines of people waited for tables at Magia anytime its door was open for business, a door that just happened to stand diagonally across the street from Hook Me. The restaurant was one of Judah's favorite places to eat and he'd told Connor about the restaurant's life-changing ravioli on several occasions.

"I've never eaten there," Connor said, "but some of my, um, friends do."

"And it's not far from here, right?" James asked. "The sidewalks were icing up when Ally and I walked over and I'm not in the mood to fall on my ass. Not to mention you look like crap, even with this fancy look you're rocking."

Ally knocked her knuckles against James's chest. "You shush. How are jeans and a pullover sweater fancy? And you know Connor worked all day—he doesn't need you giving him a hard time just because your blood sugar's low."

She shooed the brothers away from the bathroom then, claiming she wanted to freshen up before they headed out into the cold, then shut the door in their faces. Unfortunately, that just gave James an opportunity to eyeball Connor some more, a development Connor wanted to curse because the longer his brother stared, the more worried his expression became.

"Are you feeling okay, kid?" James asked. "All jokes aside, you really do look whipped."

"I'm good."

"Yeah? 'Cause Ally thinks you're too skinny. And if those circles under your eyes get any darker, people are going to mistake you for a panda, especially now that you can't hide behind the Barbie doll hair."

Connor shrugged off the gentle jabs. James had been teasing Connor about his long hair for years and he supposed there was no reason to expect it would stop just because the hair was gone. If his appetite had been absent the last few days ... well. He'd get back to eating again when his stomach decided to let him, and food tasted less like ash.

"My sleep cycle's been messed up for a couple of days, but I'll get it straight eventually."

"Is it the ...?"

"The anxiety?" Connor walked past James to the hooks by the door where they'd hung their coats. "Uh-huh. You can say the word, bro. It's not like it's a secret at this point." He could almost feel James's eyes against the side of his face.

"I know it's not a secret, Con. I may not understand it any better tonight than I did when we were kids, but I know it's a real problem for you, especially when you can't sleep. I didn't want to assume anything, either. Has something been bugging you?"

"Nothing more than usual." Connor met his brother's watchful eyes, the lie bitter on his tongue. "And I'm sorry if it felt like I was getting in your face about it."

"It didn't." James licked his lips before he spoke again. "I thought the medication was helping you manage."

Rather than answer, Connor nodded, his insides twisting even harder, just like they always did when he hid the truth about his meds from James. "You know there are still times when I get off track."

And get wound up so tight I'm lucky to sleep a couple of hours a night.

"Okay." James's face was soft with sympathy. "Con, do you think you might have it easier back home with Ally and me?

You said you needed more than you could get with Howard County Fire and Rescue, but I don't know about this." He looked around at the studio again, his features pulling down. "Maybe being on your own up here isn't good when you're living in this tiny freaking box."

Connor managed not to roll his eyes. "I lived in a little box in River Hill, J. It just happened to be inside the apartment I shared with you and Ally."

"Okay, but we live in a house now," James said. "And hell, the in-law apartment over the garage is three times the size of this place. It's yours if you want it, and I already cleared the idea with Ally."

"What?" Connor frowned too. "Why would you do that without talking to me, too? I can take care of myself, James, and I've been doing it for a long time."

"I know you have but I still think you'd have it easier back home." Sliding his hands in his pockets, James sighed. "You'd have Ally and me, and the guys at the firehouse. You'd save a ton of money on rent and have so much more space than you do here."

"I don't want more space. Sure, this apartment is small but it's more than enough for what I need," Connor said. "Besides, even if I could get my job back with Howard County, I like it here in Boston, and I really like my job and Olivia, and the rest of the people at the station and firehouse."

"You sure about that? Because from what it sounds like, you don't see much of Boston at all and hardly do anything outside of work. I mean, Valentine's Day is in a couple of days and, yet again, it sounds like you've been too busy to find yourself a girlfriend."

Oh, boy. This was dangerous territory to get into right now.

"I ... said I don't go out much after shift. Not that I don't go out at all." Connor's words came slowly. "I do stuff on my days off."

Knitting for one, though it'd been hard even thinking about that since he'd walked away from Hook Me and left the baby blanket (and so much more) behind.

"Like what? Besides the trips to wherever the hell you go and buy clothes that make you look like a damned hipster doofus." Something like scorn crossed James's face as he looked Connor up and down. "I swear, I hardly recognized you when you met us at the hotel that first night. It was like my brother got made over by some Instagram jackass."

Swallowing hard against the tight feeling growing inside him, Connor rubbed his hands over thighs, smoothing the weathered denim with his palms. "I don't even know what you mean. I've had these clothes forever."

"If you say so." James reached over and nudged Connor's wrist with his knuckles, deliberately tapping the thin leather bracelets. "Never seen these before. And what the hell is up with your hair? When I saw you at Christmas, you told me you were never going to cut it off, and now it's shorter than mine."

"It was *green*, dude, I had to cut it off. The department was cool with me keeping it long, but a bad, accidental dye job was not going to fly." Heat stirred inside Connor when James didn't answer, because there was doubt in his eyes and James wasn't doing anything to hide it. "You don't believe me?"

"I didn't say that."

"You didn't have to. I see the way you're looking at me, James, and I really don't appreciate you thinking I'd lie about having to chop off my hair when you know how long it took me to grow it out. I felt ... It was harder to make the decision than you'd probably think." Connor wiped his mouth with an unsteady hand and James's face fell when he noticed the tremor, too.

"Hey. I didn't mean to make you feel bad. I believe you. So maybe it's more that *I* can't believe it's gone." James's gaze didn't waver when the bathroom door swung open, and he set his hand on Connor's shoulder, patting him gently.

"You're going to think this is dumb, but I worry about you sometimes," he said to Connor, his voice low. "You're up here by yourself and maybe on your own too much. And I worry about your job all the time. Like, I'm so proud of what you've done with your career, Con, but it's not easy with you being over four hundred miles away. I *know* how dangerous your job can be. The kinds of situations you're walking into every day with nothing but your kit between you and God knows what. When we worked for the same house, I felt like I could keep an eye on you myself, but Boston, really?" James waved a hand in the air, the motion slightly wild. "The least you could do is move back to Baltimore so you're not driving through assloads of snow for months at a time!"

Connor couldn't help his smile. "It snows in Baltimore too, dude."

"Not like this."

"Not usually, that's true. But what's on the ground here *is* going to melt, J. This isn't the North Pole."

"Close enough," James grumbled, though he managed a smile, and it got broader when Ally sidled up to his side. The loving looks they exchanged eased the tension in Connor's chest, too.

"I really appreciate that you care," he said. "I worry about you all too, and especially *you* with your job, James. But River Hill wasn't working for me and I'm not sure Baltimore would be much better. I didn't feel like me there. Like I wasn't being my whole self."

"And you feel like you are here?" Ally asked.

"I'm getting there." Connor rubbed a hand over his head.

Or trying to, anyway. "I know it probably doesn't make sense to you and I can't explain why things were different back there. Maybe everything was too familiar, and I needed a shock to the system. But living in Boston is working for me, whether you two can see it or not, and I really do like it here. It's not a perfect place, but it's been good for me."

James seemed to deflate just slightly. "I know it has." He ran his teeth over his bottom lip for a second. "I'm going to sound like a selfish ass, but I guess I'm maybe scared I won't know you at all when you feel like your 'whole self.'"

A sick feeling skewered Connor at his brother's verbal air quote. He was more than a little scared James wouldn't know the real Connor either. Worse, that James might not only have a hard time recognizing Connor's authentic self—he might despise him. And Connor just felt worse when he remembered what Judah had said to him the last time they'd seen each other.

None of the things about you have changed. They're all still parts of who you are.

Fear had pushed Connor to stay quiet about the feelings and needs he could no longer ignore. Pushed him to run from Judah, then cut him off cold. And God, Connor felt lower than an anthill every time he thought back to that morning and Judah's pained smile, his posture all tight and wrong as he'd hunched in on himself slightly, like even speaking with Connor had caused him physical hurt. The few messages he'd left in Connor's voicemail had been so hard to hear, too, because despite his easy words, Judah had sounded off and sad, as if he already knew that Connor ignoring the messages was a forgone conclusion.

Which it had been, of course. Connor hadn't called back or been anywhere near Hook Me. He'd even started using a different route out of the neighborhood that took him well out of the way of the shop, and *damn it* he hated the way he was acting because he was not *that* guy. He didn't ghost people he cared about or treat them the way he'd been treating Judah.

Except ... Connor had. He'd been that guy. Made a hard choice that hurt him just as much as it hurt Judah because he'd been so goddamned scared of what he might lose, no matter what decision he made.

Cutting Judah out was the best thing for them both—had to be—at least for right now. And once Connor had his head back on straight, he'd figure out a way to fix things. Not lead Judah on while they got close again and redrew the lines between friendship and *whatever* it was he wanted from Connor.

Judah wants the same thing you do, pal; nothing's changed about that, no matter how hard you pretend you never wanted more.

Connor swallowed hard as he pulled on his coat. Redrawing lines wasn't going to change the fact that Connor missed Judah more than he could have thought possible and that nothing in his world seemed to fit anymore. However, he would keep doing what was best for them both, even when it hurt to do so.

"I FEEL bad we got called out in the middle of lunch with your family."

"You knew it was bound to happen." Connor eased the rig into its bay inside Station 1. "James didn't even look surprised."

"He looked like he sort of loved it," Olivia said with a laugh. "Granted, I barely know the guy, but I'm betting he's an adrenaline junkie just like so many of the smoke eaters I've known. I'm surprised he didn't ask to ride along."

"He totally would have if Ally wasn't here with him. I'm

sure he died a little inside when we ran out of there and he had to stay behind."

Olivia was still snickering as she and Connor made their way into the station's kitchen, where they found James and Ally chatting over the remains of their food.

James lifted his right hand up for Connor to slap. "Hey, y'all. How'd it go?"

"How come you never use 'y'all' anymore, Con?" Olivia asked. Sitting, she pulled away the napkin she'd used to cover her salad when their ambulance had been called out. "It's like the Southern gentleman has been Yankee'd right out of you."

"The Baltimore accent isn't Southern." Connor played up his pronunciation of 'Bawlamore' so much that James and Ally laughed as hard as Olivia. "But I guess living here has helped kill it."

"It comes back a bit when you've spent time with your peeps," Olivia said around a bite of food.

"You're my peeps," Connor said with a scoff as he pulled off his insulated vest and took the seat beside her. As he'd suspected, the green stains on his uniform jacket hadn't come out, which meant he'd be rocking a standard issue wool sweater and vest combo in dark brown until he could get a new jacket set up with regulation patches.

"The call was fine," he said to James, then shook his head when Ally gestured to the yogurt he hadn't really been eating before he'd had to run off. "Kid pile up at the skating rink over on Boston Common, mostly bumps and bruises. One little guy managed to slash his hand up pretty good though, so he and his mom are having a heart-to-heart with some of the nice ED docs at Mass General."

"Poor thing." Olivia forked up more salad. "I deal with injured kids and their parents all the time on this job, but it's started to dawn on me that I could be one of those parents one day soon."

"Hopefully not," Ally said, sympathy all over her face. "And speaking of you and your soon to be mommyhood, someone dropped off a baby gift while you were out on the call."

"Really? Oh, my." Olivia's eyes went wide as Ally set a pair of white paper bags on the table in front of her. A chain of crocheted flowers decorated the handles of the larger bag, and the familiar purple, blue, and green shades on the petals sent Connor's heart sinking right past his feet even before he saw the Hook Me logo on the bag's side.

Oh, Judah. What did you do?

Numb, he watched Olivia run her fingertips over the crocheted flowers.

"This is so lovely," she said, her voice soft and pleased. "But how did you know it was a baby gift?"

"The guy who dropped it off told us so," James replied. "Said it was from Connor, as a matter of fact, and he was sorry the delivery took longer than it should have. The smaller one is for you, Con, and the guy said it was another order that you placed with him."

Olivia went still. The question in her face when she looked Connor's way sent misery creeping over him, even as he prayed she'd hold her tongue. Olivia knew all about Hook Me and how much Connor enjoyed his knitting lessons there. She knew Judah's and Molly's names too, along with the names of the other students Connor had become friendly with in the shop's basement workspace.

"Are you going to open it?" Ally asked Olivia, eyes bright. "I've been dying to know what's in there since the guy left and I almost called Connor to tell him to hurry his butt back." She was practically vibrating with excitement and if Connor hadn't felt so close to throwing up, he'd have gotten a kick out of that fact alone.

The uncertainty in Olivia's face disappeared. "Yes, of course!"

Pulling a bundle out of the bag, she peeled back the white tissue paper wrapping and promptly burst into tears.

"Oh, Con. It's *beautiful*." She stroked the finished blanket lovingly, almost like one would a cat's fur, before she abruptly set it down and grabbed him in a hug. "Thank you so much!"

This was really happening, right?

Connor patted Olivia's back, taking care to be gentle as that strange, disquieting question bubbled in his brain. He felt this way sometimes when the floaty, disconnected feelings took hold of him, like he wasn't truly there or real, and he gave himself a swift, internal shake.

More than once, he'd considered the idea that Judah had simply thrown out the abandoned baby blanket after he'd found it. Which just sounded ridiculous now because Judah would never have done such a thing. He'd *known* how hard Connor had worked to make that blanket. That he'd enjoyed every minute he'd spent on his craft and how much he'd looked forward to a moment like this, with Olivia so happy. And heck, Judah had probably thought Connor would come back for the project himself.

Because Judah always gave Connor more credit than he deserved and damn, but Connor's eyes burned that he hadn't done the same.

"You're welcome," he made himself mumble. "Really glad you like it."

"I *love* it." She pulled back and smiled at him, the questions still in her eyes as she glanced at the small card that accompanied the wrapped package. "Handmade for you with love," she read, choking on a hiccupping sob that brought fresh tears trickling down her face. "Ugh, fucking A."

Connor pressed his lips in a hard line, his usual impulse to laugh at her swearing utterly absent. He really needed to get out of here. "You okay?"

"Yeah, sorry." Olivia heaved a big sigh and wiped her cheeks with her hands. "My hormones are way out of control," she said to James and Ally. "I overcooked my oatmeal in the microwave the other day and got so weepy over having to clean up the mess, I ended up late for my shift."

"No need to apologize, ma'am," Connor heard James reply, but whatever followed got lost on the way from his ear to his brain.

Judah had finished the blanket. Without giving Connor a hard time about leaving it behind or ghosting him, or generally treating Judah like crap. And the naked gratitude Connor felt almost stole his breath, even as gravel clogged his throat. He didn't deserve someone like Judah at all.

"Your turn, big guy," Olivia said, then slid the smaller bag across over the tabletop to him. "Do you even remember what you, ah, ordered?"

"No." Lying made every muscle in Connor's face tight and Olivia's knowing look just made him feel worse. He didn't dare reach for the bag for fear that whatever was in it would crack him wide open. "I hardly remember being in the store."

"That's because you're a man." A smug look crossed Ally's face. "The guy who dropped off the bag was *so* handsome," she said, mostly to Olivia. "He looked like a television actor and I swear I nearly died just talking to him."

"Too bad he was about as interested in you as he was in watching paint dry," James put in, his voice dry, and yipped when Ally poked him in the side. "Hey, I'm just speaking the

truth, hon. The guy was hella gay and you know he was probably more into me than you."

Olivia laughed at Ally's pout. "How did you know he was
gay?" she asked James.

"From the button on his coat that said 'Hella Gay.'" James
laughed too. "He had a rainbow scarf and all, but anyone could
wear those, of course. The pin was the thing. I mean, even a
guy like me can put the pieces together when they're laid out in
plain view like that." He leaned over the table and nudged
Connor's elbow. "Right, dude?"

Connor thought his chest might burst. "Matching hat and
gloves?"

"Uh, no." James sobered then. He raised a hand and patted
the crown of his head. "He was wearing a skull cap. The kind
that Jewish boys wear?"

"A kippah?" Olivia suggested and James nodded without
hesitation.

"That, yes. Said he was on his way to teach a class at his
synagogue."

Connor stared. How the hell long had Judah been in the
station? "The delivery guy told you all that?"

James shrugged. "I asked where he was off to next.
Running deliveries around a city full of snow can't be easy.
And I guess my curiosity got the better of me when I saw the
cap. Religion and the gays—they don't always mix, you know?"

"Hmm. That's not true of every religion." Olivia wrinkled
her nose a bit. "Judaism isn't really like that. My husband is
Jewish, and I can tell you from experience that there's plenty of
room for LGBTQ in Judaism."

A thoughtful air fell over James. "I didn't realize that."

"She's right." The halting breath Connor drew next set off a
tremor in his body that quickly had him standing and James's
face changed in a flash.

"Con, are you—"

"I'm fine, I'm fine," Connor said, the top of his head tingling as he started to sidle off. "I'll just be—"

The station's alert system sounded, its siren instantly rerouting the anxiety building in Connor's head. Closing his mouth, he stood poised to move if needed, aware that Olivia was re-wrapping her lunch for the second time.

"Ambulance P1, medical emergency at 322 Washington Street," the dispatcher called. "Man down, suspected overdose 23-C-5."

Olivia stood, her expression stony. "Let's hit it. I'm glad you restocked the NARCAN this morning," she said, "because we may be in for a long day."

Connor tipped his chin at her, then quickly met James's eyes, unsurprised at the question he saw there.

Are you all right?

"I'm good," Connor said aloud as he grabbed his vest from the back of the chair. They both knew he was leaving regardless of his brother's opinion or the words between them that would go unspoken for now. Timing was everything with opioid poisonings and the sooner Connor and Olivia got to the victim, the better their chances were for saving his life.

"Go," James said anyway. "We'll meet you at your place after your shift."

"Copy," Connor replied, then ran after his partner without another word.

Saved by the bell, he thought grimly, *but for how long?*

TWELVE

Hours passed before Judah felt truly able to let go of the tension that had crawled through him upon meeting Connor's family. Even inside the synagogue, a place he sought out when he wanted to feel centered, his insides had been knotted, and it had taken a long time to shake off his nervous energy.

Though worn out, he felt somewhat better now as he rode the subway back home. If Judah was honest with himself, he'd acknowledge that his nerves had started even before he'd laid eyes on James and Ally Devlin. Like when he'd had the wild idea that morning to hand deliver a bag of knitted goods to Boston EMS Station 1 and maybe get Connor to talk to him for a couple of minutes.

You want more than talk. You want him back in your life.

Judah stared out at the tunnel beyond the train window. Yeah, he wanted Connor back. Attraction aside, Judah was at a point where he'd do almost anything to fill the void Connor had left in Judah's life after he'd walked away. If Judah hadn't missed the guy so horribly, he'd have hated him for it, too. He hadn't been this down since things had gone bad with Seb and fuck if losing Connor didn't somehow hurt even more.

It was still easier for Judah to blame himself for things falling apart. He'd let his guard down and gotten in too deep with someone who needed more time to find himself. And though Judah had known better than to gamble on more with Connor, he'd done it anyway.

Back at Hook Me, he found Levi talking with a customer, so he made his way to the office where he left his things. Levi was alone by the time Judah came back out onto the shop floor and the expression in his eyes when he turned to Judah was searching.

"Are you okay?"

Judah raised his eyebrows. "Me? Sure, why?"

"You went to synagogue and it's only Friday." Levi cocked his head. "You don't usually attend service until Saturday."

"I felt like going today."

"Okay. Any specific reason why?"

"I needed it." Judah leaned into the counter and set his elbows on its top. "Just like I need to figure out why I keep making the same mistakes."

Levi was quiet a moment. Then, to Judah's surprise, he moved out from behind the counter and walked to the shop door. He flipped the cardboard sign from 'Open' to 'Closed' and turned the locks, his face somber when he faced Judah again.

"Is this about Connor and how he's stopped coming around?"

Jeez.

"You've been down since I got back from Vermont," Levi continued. "And by 'down' I mean sub-basement level grumbly. At first, I thought you were just annoyed because that stupid drone hit you in the head and dented your handsome." He smiled at Judah's snort of laughter and crossed the room to the counter again.

"I'm not actually that vain, you know." Judah made sure his voice sounded chiding. No, he hadn't loved wearing a bandage on his head, but the small cut was healing nicely, and he was down to a small adhesive strip that was almost easy to ignore.

"When the dark clouds stuck around day after day, I figured it was something else," Levi said, "and that's when I noticed Connor wasn't parking himself in the big chair almost every night."

Judah sighed as his brother nodded toward the overstuffed chair Connor had favored during his visits to Hook Me. Of course, Levi was right. Judah had fallen into a funk after Connor had disappeared, and the mood had only grown darker the longer the silence continued.

Judah hadn't tried very hard to hide his dejection, primarily because he hadn't wanted to. The last ten days had seriously drained him. He'd been alone in the apartment and shop for longer than he'd expected after another big snowfall had delayed Levi's return from Stowe, a development he really hadn't needed in the wake of the drama with Connor. Without his family or Connor to remind him to take breaks, Judah had worked *a ton* of overtime hours and though he craved company more than usual, he had no energy to seek it out, even now with Levi back home.

"The bad mood has been about Connor, yes," Judah said. "And I'm sorry if I've been a sulky ass because that's not fair to you."

"Jude, no."

"The dark clouds are also about Seb, though, and maybe even Jeremie, the guy I dated before Seb."

Levi frowned. "The writer?"

"Yes. The guy who wanted me to quit working with Mom and go back to editing full time because owning a shop wasn't artful enough for his tastes."

"I remember him." Levi wrinkled his nose. "He was kind of a doucheface."

Judah chuckled. "You're right, he was. And not necessarily because he was a writer."

"If you say so." Levi shook his head when Judah laughed outright. "But what does Connor have to do with Seb and Jeremie?"

"Nothing and everything." Judah rapped his knuckles softly against the countertop and furrowed his brow. "I've come to realize Connor is part of a pattern of guys who don't want the same things I do and probably never will."

"Not to be a jerk, but I could have told you that." Levi grimaced at Judah's glower. His voice was gentle when he spoke again, however. "Connor is straight, dude. It was never going to happen."

"Turns out Connor is not exactly straight." Judah watched his brother's eyes get big. "The trouble for me is that Connor may not believe that to be the case, which is where things get complicated."

"Oh, damn. Are you sure he's really queer?"

"He likes dick, Lee, or seemed to like mine, anyway, and that's a thing your typical straight dude really does not."

"Wow, okay."

"You asked."

"I did. I just wasn't prepared for that level of candor." Levi cleared his throat. "So-o-o, do you want to talk about it?"

"If I say no, will you let it go?"

"No. Especially since you just brought up Connor's sexual

orientations and kind of waved them in my face. I bought cookies for tonight's stich-and-bitch while you were out you know, and I'm sure no one will notice if we sample a few while you talk."

They relocated to the basement workshop and though Judah didn't have any appetite for cookies, watching Levi enjoy them made him feel lighter. At least until he copped to having walked over to Connor's place of work today and Levi started asking questions.

"So, you didn't even talk to him?"

"Ah, no." Judah raised his mug to his lips. "I didn't exactly walk into the station after I got there."

Wiping crumbs from his fingers with a napkin, Levi simply stared until Judah wanted to squirm under that too-sharp gaze.

"I chickened out," he said at last. "I got all the way to the station doors and it was like my insides froze. I ended up in the park across the street while I tried to figure out what to do."

Levi chuckled. "You're such a creeper, dude."

"It's not like I could see anyone. The station doors were closed the whole time! Well, until Ambulance P1 pulled out." Judah's face heated at Levi's continued laughter. "That's Connor's rig and I knew he'd be in it if he was on duty."

"Did you memorize his schedule, too?"

"I didn't have to. He works four eight-hour shifts a week and he's usually on days, so all I had to do was math from the last time I saw him. Besides, I planned on leaving the bag with the blanket whether he was there or not. Which I did, in the end."

"With Connor's brother and sister-in-law, you said," Levi mused. "Talk about a stroke of luck!"

"Yeah, I guess."

Judah sipped some more tea. He wasn't sure what to call

what had happened today when he'd walked into Station 1. He'd honestly thought he was hallucinating when the receptionist who greeted him had called James and Ally to the front desk. Discovering that Connor's family were nothing like the grumpy conservative characters Judah had painted in his head had been almost as shocking.

Like Connor, James was a *big* man, the muscles on his broad frame easily visible under his navy-blue Henley. Though closer to Judah's height, he'd still seemed very, very tall as he'd fixed stormy gray eyes on the paper bags in Judah's hand. Judah wasn't too proud to admit he'd almost quailed under the intensity in that stare when it shifted onto him and James had looked Judah up and down, lingering for an extra beat on the Pride button affixed to Judah's coat.

But then the burly guy with the stern demeanor had turned out to be pretty goddamned friendly. He'd appeared much younger than Judah had imagined, especially when he'd smiled, and deep dimples appeared on his clean-shaven cheeks. He'd made polite chit-chat about his and his wife's stay in Boston and even mentioned that Connor was a medic in case Judah hadn't known, his brotherly pride both obvious and adorable. James had clearly been smitten with his wife Ally too, a spritely young woman with sparkling brown eyes who was even more outgoing than her husband. Ally stood maybe five-foot-two, but exuded enough energy to power a city, and she wanted to know all about what it was like to run a craft shop in a region that was so focused on business and the sciences.

Judah had trouble picturing bashful Connor with his extroverted family, but James and Ally had seemed genuinely nice. Kind, too. Their affection was obvious, both for each other and the absent Connor, and Judah could only imagine how protective they'd be of him. James had even asked how many more deliveries Judah had left to make in the snow and simply nodded when Judah had blurted out some kind of nonsense about being done with deliveries and on his way to teach class at his synagogue.

So why had Connor been so sure that his being not straight would torpedo his standing with those nice, kind people? Better yet, why did it matter to Judah? And why, now that he'd met Connor's family, did he feel even more sad about Connor turning away not only from the spark that existed between Judah and himself, but from their friendship entirely?

You're upset because you fucked up. Somewhere along the way, you fell for the big lug, even though you knew it was the worst idea in the world.

Judah rubbed a hand across his face and let out a muttered, "Fuck." He saw sympathy in his brother's face when he lowered his hand, though Levi gave him a small smile, too.

"It's like that, huh?"

"Yeah. I got attached, Lee." Several seconds passed before Judah could continue. "More than attached if I'm truthful. And Connor's not going to feel the same way. Or, not in the way I really need him to."

Levi's eyes were sad. "You don't think he'll come around to getting right with his own feelings?"

"Jesus, I really hope that he does. Even more for himself more than me," Judah said. Imagining Connor struggling against his own feelings—continuing to hide—was too terrible to contemplate. The guy deserved far better than that kind of life. "But even if Connor gets okay with being queer, he may not want me. And while I get that he's still trying to figure out his world, this is exactly what I was talking about with Seb and Jeremie." He clasped his hands together on the tabletop. "I *promised* myself I would stop going after guys who weren't right for me and then I turned around and did it again with the guy who is the *most* wrong for me in so many ways."

"To be fair, you did think Connor was straight." Levi clapped Judah on the shoulder and squeezed the muscle. "From what it sounds like, you never actually pursued him, either."

"True, but I didn't do a lot to avoid him."

"And why should you have? You guys were friends, Jude, and you had no way of knowing he was questioning his identity."

"You're right. I think that's why the ghosting hurts so much. After Seb, I kind of shut down emotionally and I was ... I don't know if lonely is the right word, but it's close. I started coming out of it after becoming friends with Connor and, honestly, I liked that. I'm sure I sound ridiculous."

"You don't. You *were* really closed off after Seb. I'm not sure I realized how much until you started hanging out with Connor every freaking day," Levi said, and shrugged when Judah looked at him askance. "You can't think I wouldn't notice, man, not with a big Viking dude in that chair upstairs. And all those lunch breaks you took when you usually eat standing at the counter? Why do you think I noticed when he *stopped* coming around?"

"Fair." Judah grumbled. That was exactly why Connor cutting him out made Judah feel like shit. He absolutely understood why Connor would be afraid of his shifting sexuality and he'd have supported him in any way he could on that journey. Connor hadn't even wanted to talk to Judah about being that friend, though and that loss—the drop from sixty to zero overnight—stung. And try as he might, Judah was having a hell of a time getting over it, especially in this shop and city, where it felt like a Connor-shaped space dogged him every time he turned around.

I could leave, Judah thought. *Maybe not come back until I feel more ready.*

Licking his lips, Judah met Levi's gaze. "Do you think Mom would be upset if I switched places with her and Harvey for a while?"

A troubled expression crossed Levi's face. "No. Why would you think that? And what do you mean? Like, you'd move to Vermont and Mom and Pops would move here?"

"Yes," Judah said, "but just for a little while. I know I'd be uprooting their life and maybe yours too. Mom and Pops have their own space here just like you and I do in Stowe, but we both know they prefer it up there just like we prefer staying here." He chewed the inside of his cheek for a beat. "It's kind of a big ask, right?"

"Yes, but I think Mom would do anything for you if you really needed it, Judah. Pops too. Fuck, they'll drive home tonight if you call and tell them what you want." Levi sighed. "But are you *sure* it's a good idea to cloister yourself up there? You said it yourself—your home is here and if you're up in Stowe everyone you might choose to hang out will be three hours away."

"Stowe's never been my first choice, true," Judah replied. "Business is a lot slower up there and sometimes it's so quiet out at the house I swear I can hear my hair grow." He paused at Levi's bark of laughter. "Quiet sounds okay, though. I'll end up working fewer hours in the shop and do more editing. It'd be a good opportunity to recharge my batteries and practice more yoga, too. Things I just can't do here right now."

"Like maybe pick up a guy at the nearest gay bar and screw his brains out, right?"

It was Judah's turn to laugh until he almost choked. "I hate you. And hookups are not what I'm looking for right now."

"That's where your opinion and mine will differ because I

think some screwing around would do you a lot of good," Levi said. "If you don't want to, then fine, you don't get laid. But if sex isn't the thing you need, what is?"

To get over falling for a guy who I really liked calling my friend, Judah's brain supplied.

"A break." He swallowed when his voice cracked and damn, he hated the worry he saw in Levi's eyes. "From lots of things."

Levi patted Judah's hand where it lay on the table. "Including me? I know it can't be easy acting as a glorified babysitter to your college-aged brother but you're actually really good at it."

"Because I'm not your babysitter, Levi. I haven't been for … shit, a really long time." Judah frowned. "Honestly, I feel like you take care of *me* half the time, even though you're still an undergraduate. When I say I want a break, I don't mean from you as much as I mean everything." He snorted on a soft laugh. "Fuck, maybe myself most of all. Because I don't want to keep going like this."

"Okay. So, are you going to call Mom tonight?"

"Yeah, I will. But she might freak and insist on making the drive before we even hang up. We should be ready for that. I'll try to put her off though, so we can do dinner on Sunday just like always and not have yet another overload of drama. I'm kind of over it if you know what I mean."

"I do."

"Why not wait until Sunday and talk about it over dinner?"

"Because Mom and Pops would have to go back to Stowe to pack up a bunch of stuff and that's hardly fair."

"Good point. Why don't we call her together tonight then?" Levi sat up straight in his chair. "We'll Facetime and get Pops in on it too. That way, we can talk it through as a family and nip any drama in the bud."

"Good idea," Judah said and smiled.

With some help, he could get through this—Judah was sure of it. And, for the first time in over a week, he felt like maybe he could see past the clouds that had hung over him and refused to clear.

THIRTEEN

"Are you ever going to open it?"

Blinking, Connor lifted his gaze from the little white bag that sat on the rig's dash in front of him and shifted his focus to Olivia.

"I'm not sure I want to," he replied, then winced as pain rolled through his gut. As predicted, they'd been called out repeatedly over the course of their shift and while staying busy had kept Connor's anxiety mostly at bay, his brain hadn't shared the memo with his stomach, and it ached like he'd been punched.

Olivia watched him swig from the travel mug of peppermint tea she'd forced on him just before their last call and both pretended Connor's phone hadn't buzzed in his pocket for the fifth time that hour.

Finally, she sighed. "You're not going to be able to eat the dinner your sister-in-law is planning if you keep going like this."

"I know." Connor didn't even want to think about food, let alone sitting down with his family tonight. "They'll be all up in my grill about it, too."

"Because they care about you and want to know you're okay," Olivia said gently. "Put yourself in their shoes. You moved hundreds of miles away, so they see you once, maybe twice a quarter, and you have a high-stress job in a department that dispatches over a hundred thousand incidents annually."

"One hundred and fifty-six thousand last year," Connor muttered.

Olivia snorted. "No wonder I'm tired. And no wonder *you're* tired and look like you could sleep for a week." She paused, her voice quieter when she spoke again. "But I think we both know it's not the job that's been messing with your sleep."

"You're right. Damned sure James and Ally have figured it out, too."

"Then, talk to them, Connor. Or, hell, talk to me if you want. Consider it practice if you like."

"Practice?"

"For unloading whatever has been weighing you down and making you jumpy as fuck this past week. You could start with explaining why you pretended you weren't the one who knit that beautiful baby blanket. Because I know you did."

Connor set the mug in the cup holder by his hip. "I didn't know how to tell you. James and Ally don't know I've been looking for alternative ways to manage my stress."

"And that's entirely your prerogative, no question. I'm not sure why you'd basically lie about a hobby, though."

"Yeah, well." Connor scrubbed a hand over his head. He was full of stupid ideas these days. "I was just so *surprised* to see the bag from Hook Me. I never asked for the blanket to be delivered."

"Huh." Olivia frowned. "So how—"

"I didn't even get a chance to finish it. The blanket, I mean," Connor said. "I left it behind one night at ... at a friend's place and I guess he finished it for me." Another ache skewered through his gut and, for a second, Connor thought for sure he'd be sick. "God-fucking-*damnit*."

Olivia whistled low. "Damn. I know it's serious when you start cursing. You okay?"

"No, I'm not." Propping his elbows on the steering wheel, Connor put his face in his hands. "I just lied to you, too. I feel like that's all I do these days, lie to the people in my life and myself and I *don't* want to be that guy, Liv."

"I know you don't." Olivia set her hand between Connor's shoulders. "It makes me sad you'd feel like you have to lie to me about anything but I'm sure you have your reasons."

"Maybe, but I'm starting to see those reasons are shitty."

Olivia laughed. "Understood." She rubbed a slow circle into Connor's back. "You know I'm here for you, right? As much as I like to hear my own voice, I'm a good listener and if you ever want to unload about anything at all, you can."

"Thank you."

Sitting back in his seat, Connor eyed the paper bag on the dash for a moment before he pulled it toward him. He withdrew another soft, tissue-wrapped bundle from its depths and unwrapped it carefully, his heart clenching as he looked over a beautifully knitted scarf, hat, and gloves nestled against the white paper.

"Oh, man," he whispered, Olivia's soft sound of approval in his ears. He fingered the stitches fashioned in blue yarn, unsurprised when Olivia reached over and did the same.

"I don't know, Con," she said. "I'd think you'd uncovered a true hidden talent for needlework except your face tells me you didn't knit these."

"No, I didn't. Judah made them."

"The knitting instructor, right?"

"Yeah. This is a basket cable pattern and he told me it was

one of his favorites. He didn't tell me he was making these when I asked him about the yarn, though."

Connor hated the way his voice shook. He hated the spectacular mess he'd made of his life even more, and that he'd let his fear control him and hurt someone he really cared about. The idea Judah must despise him for it made Connor ache and, weighed down by dread, he picked up the small white card tucked among the folds of the scarf.

Stay warm, Connor, and be well he read, his eyes stinging at the graceful 'J' inscribed below the note.

Judah didn't hate Connor at all. He was too good a person to get bogged down with bad feelings and he'd finished the baby blanket in Connor's place because he'd known how much making that gift for Olivia had meant to him. Hell, Judah had brought the blanket to Station 1 and that couldn't have been easy for him after the way Connor had acted.

Judah may not be a First Responder, but he's a hundred times braver than you've ever been.

Connor met Olivia's eyes. "Judah delivered the blanket today. I could tell from the way Ally and James described him. He ..." Connor licked his lips. "He covered for me. Pretended I was just a customer so James wouldn't know about the knitting or that Judah and I are ... friends."

"I see." Olivia furrowed her brow. "Well, honestly, I don't. Why would you not want James to know Judah was your friend?"

"Because it turns out Judah is more than a friend. Or at least I hope so. Last week we—"

What? Hooked up? Messed around? How the hell did Connor describe the intensity of feeling he had for Judah Bissell and how much it had changed his world?

"We connected," Connor said, his voice steadier. A sense of power rushed through him then because holy hell, did he like saying those words out loud. "I stayed at Judah's place during the big storm last week and finally figured out I am very attracted to him, Liv. As in, more so than to anyone else in my life, ever. I like him so much I'm not even sure what to do with myself."

The soft smile on Olivia's face made him feel light. "Connor, thank you for trusting me with that." Holding her hands out slightly, she turned them palms up. "Would it be okay if I gave you a hug?"

"Heck yeah." Head spinning, Connor leaned over the console and met her halfway, his breath whooshing out of him all at once. "Oh, my God, I just ... I came out to you."

Olivia laughed gently. "You sure did, honey. And did it feel good?"

"It really, really did." Connor blinked against sudden tears, the swell of emotion inside him so powerful he found himself fighting not to sob.

"I'm so glad!" Pulling back, Olivia reached up and wiped Connor's cheeks with her fingers, her eyes shiny with tears of her own. "I meant what I said earlier, okay? I'm here for you, no matter what, whether you want to talk about it or not."

"I know. Thank you, Liv, really. I needed this. So much more than I even realized." Sniffing, Connor frowned at the knitted goods that still lay in his lap. "I just have to figure out how to tell James and Ally. Fix things with Judah, too."

"What happened there? Why would you say you hoped Judah was still your friend?"

The fracture in Connor's heart reappeared. "I was an ass and I hurt him. And if I'd been in the station when Judah showed up today, I'd have done it again, probably even worse."

Olivia shook her head. "That doesn't sound like the guy I know. What's going on with you?"

"Too many things," Connor said. The idea his partner

might hate him as much as he hated himself for the way he'd acted toward Judah just made Connor feel sick all over again. He rolled his eyes as the radio squawked, then turned his attention to his seat belt.

"Of course," he muttered. "Of *course*, they'd call us now."

"Ambulance P1, water rescue in progress at Aquarium Plaza," the dispatcher said. "Male, late forties reported overboard by vessel's captain. 14-C-1, alert with abnormal breathing and cold exposure."

"Ugh, I hate the wet ones, especially at this time of year." Olivia reached for the radio. "And don't think you're off the hook, guy. We're not done talking."

"No, we're not." Connor was surprised to find he meant it. He wasn't done talking about Judah by a long shot, even if it meant his relationships with the people in his life changed forever.

Oddly enough, that certainty strengthened Connor on his journey home that evening, new scarf wrapped around his neck and the hat snug on his head. Of course, his relationship with his family would change—it had been changing for a long time, most recently with his move to New England. And while it was clear James still wasn't fully on board with Connor's decision to leave Maryland, his love for Connor hadn't lessened, a sign Connor wanted to take as a sign the bond between brothers could survive even bigger challenges that might lie ahead.

Right?

"Right," Connor muttered to himself.

He *had* to be honest about himself and not only about his evolving sexuality. He wanted James and Ally to know he'd discontinued his meds too, and about the alternative therapies he'd been exploring. The secret-keeping had to end if Connor wanted the people in his life to know him, regardless of how daunting the prospect seemed.

Steeling himself, Connor walked into his studio only to find James alone in the tiny kitchen with a pile of salad ingredients and Ally nowhere in sight. The place smelled amazing though, like baked cheese and bacon and sweet, fresh bread, and for the first time in days, Connor felt hungry.

He inhaled deeply as he peeled off his bag and coat, then ran a hand over the blue infinity scarf Judah had given him, using its soft warmth to self soothe. He decided he'd leave it on.

"Hey," he called out to James. "Where's your better half?"

"Went out to buy some dessert." James didn't quite smile at Connor across the room. "She's been gone a while, though, so I think it might have been wife code for 'I'll leave you boys alone to talk.'"

Connor toed off his boots. "She always was a lot smarter than you."

"No need to rub it in." A beat passed before James spoke again. "There's some beer in the fridge if you want. We thought it'd go good with the mac 'n' cheese bake."

A bittersweet ache curled through Connor at the obvious gestures James and Ally were making to reach out. However hard it was going to be for Connor to talk real talk tonight, he hated the idea that he might hurt them, especially James who'd thrown himself into protecting Connor from the world for such a long time.

Crossing to the refrigerator, Connor pulled two bottles of beer from the pack on the bottom shelf. "I'm sorry if I've been worrying you and Ally."

James stilled, his gaze on the carrot he'd been shredding. "You have. A lot, Con," he said at last and went back to grating. "You seem way more stressed out than you have in a really long while."

"I know. It hasn't been too bad until recently, believe it or not, and even when it is, I have ways to get my chill back while I'm on duty."

"Uh-huh, but what about when you're off duty? I don't like the idea of you popping Ativan when you're here alone."

Connor twisted the tops off the beer bottles, then went to the cabinet where he stored his glassware. "Outside of emergencies, I try not to take Ativan at all. Or any meds. I stopped taking them a while ago and I lied the other night when you asked me about them."

"What?" Salad prep forgotten, James stared. "Why?"

"I started having trouble concentrating in class and on my coursework." Connor set two pilsner glasses on the counter. "The insomnia came back too, worse than ever."

James's face fell. "Damn. They worked so well for you when—"

"When I was younger, sure. It's possible something in my body chemistry changed and made the drugs work differently, but all I know is they made me feel scattered when I needed to be sharp." Connor shook his head. "So, I weaned off and started using non-drug therapies."

"Such as?"

"I went back to counseling and started in more with exercise, and deep breathing. I'm working on learning meditation but so far I'm not very good at it."

"And you didn't think you should share that with Ally and me?" James huffed loudly. "What the hell?"

"I wanted to tell you, I really did. But I put it off and I put it off." Sighing, Connor turned his attention to pouring their beers. "Next thing I knew, it'd been months and I stopped wanting to tell you at all. Mostly because I didn't want to admit to you or myself that I didn't trust you'd let me live my own life."

Naked hurt was on James's face when Connor looked up again. "You didn't trust me?"

"Not to let me make my own decisions, no. You've always had trouble with that, and you know it." Connor picked up his glass. "I understand. You're my brother. You want what's best for me."

"Meaning what I want and what's best aren't always the same thing?" James asked, his speech slow, as if speaking the words pained him. "I am seriously at a loss, dude. What the hell do you expect me to say?"

"I'd like it if you'd listen," Connor said quietly. James jammed his lips into a hard line, and it was all Connor could do not to reach out and hug him. "Whatever else you're feeling about me hiding things from you, I need my brother right now, maybe more than I have since we were just kids waiting for Gram to come get us because we'd been left on our own."

James paled. He'd been ten years old and Connor seven when their parents had disappeared on a binge and simply chosen not to come back. For the better part of a week, James got Connor and himself to school and back every day, but they'd run low on food and neither had any money. The day James had finally called their grandmother marked the very last time either boy spent a night under the same roof as their parents. And from then on, though the Devlin family had splintered, the bond between James and Connor had grown immeasurably stronger.

"What's wrong?" James asked. "Are you sick? And what do mean by 'things'? What else haven't you been telling me?" He looked even more stricken than before. "More importantly, *why* are you hiding? I know we don't see eye to eye a hundred percent of the time, Con, but I'm your brother and I want you to feel safe telling me anything."

God, I hope he means it, Connor thought. Setting his glass on the counter, he reached over and squeezed James's shoulder.

"Slow down, okay?" He gestured toward a pair of bar stools on the other side of the island. "Leave the salad for a sec and come sit with me. I'm okay," he said as they carried their glasses to the stools. "I'm not sick and, like I said, I'm managing the GAD without drugs."

James looked at him askance. "I watched you start spiraling over a baby blanket today, dude, so excuse me if I have some questions about just how much managing you're doing."

"God*damnit*, J." Connor scraped a hand over his face as James's eyes went wide. "This is what I meant about listening. Yes, the spikes still happen, and yes, I still worry. My stomach has stayed weird and my sleep too, and all that was true even when I was taking meds because my anxiety problem is probably a lifetime deal."

"You're right," James replied, his voice quieter. "So, you stopped taking meds. How long? You said something about coursework so that means—"

"I weaned off after the move to Connecticut," Connor said, then winced at the shock on his brother's face.

"Jesus, Connor. That was *years* ago. I can't believe you've been sitting on this the whole time!"

"I know. I didn't want to worry you or Ally, but I had to figure out ways to manage so I could study and work and do a respectable job, which is exactly my point. I did it, and I kept going."

James set his glass down and simply stared at it for a while. "The counseling and other stuff are working for you?" he asked at last.

"Yes, and it's a process, just like with the meds. I struggle sometimes, more so since being promoted to medic. But I'm hanging in there." Connor gave his brother what he hoped was an encouraging smile. "It helps that Olivia gives me great suggestions too, like yoga and knitting."

"Knitting?" James frowned at his beer. "Like old ladies do with the pointy sticks and yarn?"

"It's not just old ladies." Connor chuckled. "Some people find Zen when they run ten miles, some when they knit a scarf. I'm lucky that I can do both. I made the baby blanket that was delivered to the station for Olivia today," he said, his humor fading. "And the guy who delivered it was my instructor, Judah."

"The gay kid?" James asked. Under different circumstances, the bewilderment on his face might have been funny, but Connor had never felt less like laughing. "He acted like he hardly knew you. But you're telling me he's your teacher?"

"The way you and Ally described him—the button on his coat, the rainbow scarf ..." Connor shrugged. "I'd have guessed it was Judah even before you mentioned he was wearing the kippah."

"Then what's with all the cloak and dagger stuff?" James threw his hands up. "The receptionist at your station told the kid—"

"Judah," Connor cut in though James plowed on without pausing.

"—that Ally and I were your family, so why the hell didn't he say something then?"

"I'd have to ask him to be sure, but I think Judah was covering for me."

"Covering *what*? That you learned how to knit? Or that you hang with a kid who wears buttons like 'Hella Gay' for the entire world to see?"

"Yes." Connor said, his tone so flat that James instantly fell silent. Nerves skittered along Connor's spine and he found himself pushing hard to get words out past his lips. "I wasn't sure you'd understand the knitting. And I definitely didn't know how you'd feel about Judah."

Disdain crossed James's face. "Man, I'm not sure why I'd feel anything at all about your knitting teacher. The guy seems ... a little out there, I guess, but nothing like some of the genuine weirdos I'd come across back in Howard County. But hell, I don't care. It's not like I need to know this Judah, right? And if the knitting helps you feel better, then more power to you." Sitting back in his chair, James squinted at Connor, his gaze piercing. "So, how about you tell me what's really going on here, Connor, and what you're still not saying because I know just from looking at you that there's more."

"You're right, there is." Lifting a hand, Connor held on to the scarf around his neck, seeking out its softness with his fingertips as he spoke. "Judah is more than my knitting teacher. More than a friend. Having him in my life is important, and yes, I'd want you to know him. Judah means a *lot* to me. More than anyone I've ever been interested in."

Whatever James might have replied next, he froze at those words, his eyes wide and his face blank, and it took everything Connor had to keep going.

"I know you didn't see this coming," he said, his voice not quite steady. "But you have to believe me when I say I didn't either. It was like ... damn, I don't know, like one day something inside of me clicked and from there everything that never fit before finally slid into place."

James blinked once and again, slowly, like he was rousing himself. "What are you saying, Connor? That you and the knitting guy are dating? That you're with a-a-a guy?"

Connor's heart broke at his brother's spluttering, but he refused to flinch when anger suddenly flashed in James's eyes. "Yeah, I'm with a guy. Or I'd like to be. Judah and I haven't exactly been dating but—"

"So, you're gay now? After over thirty years of being a straight guy?" James's voice grew louder with each word. "When the hell did this start? When you moved up here and got cozy with the libtards, right?"

The rattle of the doorknob on Connor's front door couldn't have come at a more opportune time, but Ally's expression was alarmed as she hurried inside, a white cake box in her hands.

"James Devlin, what on earth is going on in here?" she exclaimed. "I could hear you shouting from the top of the stairs!"

James sucked in a huge breath and closed his eyes, visibly reining himself in. "I'm sorry, hon. Con and I were just talking. He took me off guard with six kinds of *bullshit* and I guess I lost my cool there for a second."

Opening his eyes, James cast a glare in Connor's direction and the ice that Connor saw there cut him to his core.

Oh, God.

"It's not bullshit," Connor said around the wool choking his throat. The top of his head felt like it was about to fly off and no, no, *no*, he had to hold it together right now. "It's who I am. This has all been confusing for me, too, J. I'm ... I'm still figuring it out, but I wanted you to know the truth. To know *me*. The man I'm trying to be and—"

A terrible sound came out of James, at once scornful and sad. "This isn't you, Connor. I have no idea who I'm looking at right now, but I know it's not my brother."

Sweat broke out over Connor's whole body.

"Okay," he whispered. Everything inside him went tight, like he was being squeezed on all sides. "I'll understand if you don't want to—"

See me anymore? Be my brother? Talk to me ever again?

Those poisonous thoughts stole Connor's voice completely. He didn't look up as he got to his feet and though it sounded like maybe James and Ally were still speaking, Connor pushed through the haze clogging his brain until he was inside his tiny bathroom where he could lock the door and fall apart in private.

Eyes closed, he pulled the scarf from his neck and crouched down with his back against the door, folding himself up as small as he could manage. The sharp voices in the room beyond were like jagged shards of glass in his brain, and though Connor couldn't focus enough to understand what words were being thrown around, each drilled deeper and sharper inside of him until he couldn't take it anymore and heaved up what little he'd ingested that afternoon into the toilet. He stayed down on the floor for a long, long time.

The apartment was silent by the time the storm inside Connor quieted some and every inch of him ached. However, while James had disappeared, Ally sat waiting for Connor on the futon and she waved him over immediately, her expression careworn, then smiled gently when he didn't move right away.

"Can we sit a minute, Connor? Because I'd really like to talk with you."

"So tired, Al," Connor mumbled, then made his feet move. "I hurt."

Ally's smile wavered and Connor saw her eyes were red-rimmed. "I know you do, hon, and I'm sorry. What can I do? Do you need to take anything? James said you keep meds for emergencies if that would help."

"No. Not yet. If I can't ... get my head back together on my own I will." Connor sank onto the futon beside her and stared at the scarf in his hands. "Is he coming back?"

"Of course, he is. I told him to walk around until he'd cooled off." Ally patted Connor's hand. "I know James lost his head and said some hurtful things, but in his defense, you *really* blew his mind."

A laugh pushed its way out of Connor, but it caught in his chest and came out all wrong. "I don't know what to do." He closed his eyes as she shifted closer.

"We'll figure it out," she said, her voice very soft. "We'll talk some more in the morning and get this whole mess straight."

"How? You heard him. He said ... He said I wasn't his brother."

"He didn't *mean* it." The fierceness in Ally's tone made Connor's eyes water but he still couldn't look at her. "Your brother can be an asshat on occasion, but we both know he loves you, and it'll just take some time for him to figure out how he feels about learning his brother is bi or however you see yourself."

"What if he can't figure it out?" Connor's voice broke. "What if he doesn't want to? You guys are my family, Ally, the only ones I've got left. I love you both so much and I can't ..." He bit his lip as his tears spilled over. "I can't lose you over this. Not over me wanting someone in my life, even if that someone is a man."

"You're not going to lose us," James said from the door.

His face was ashen as he stepped inside, eyes bright with pain. His earlier anger had gone, however, and he didn't hesitate to cross the room and sit on Connor's other side. He promised over and over that everything would work itself out and, through his tears, Connor clung to the words as fiercely as he did the people who folded him up in their arms and held him close.

FOURTEEN

A bag over each shoulder, Judah stepped inside Hook Me, his stepdad Harvey following close behind with the backpack Judah used to carry his laptop and another tote full of stuff. Molly came around the counter immediately and met them in the middle of the space, her expression uneasy as she looked Judah up and down.

"Honey, are you sure you want to do this? Today, I mean, instead of driving up on Monday morning?"

"Oh, I'm sure. I'm still not sure what time I'd have to leave on Monday to even get to the shop in time to open."

"Just after ass o'clock in the morning," Harvey said with a wink. "Which is why your mother and I let the assistant manager open on Mondays. I'm still not a morning person after all these years and the traffic in this state is a total nightmare, no matter what time we get on the road. You're welcome to continue that schedule, Jude, because I'm certainly not going to push you to open on Mondays either."

Smiling too, Judah shrugged at his mom, then stooped so he could set his bags by his feet. "I'll keep that in mind. And I'll stop by the store once I reach Stowe and check in, then head for the house."

"As long as you get to Stowe before the snow starts," Molly said, though she immediately pursed her lips. "You should pick up some groceries on the way. Obviously, your pops and I keep the refrigerator pretty well stocked, but I know for a fact there are no corn chips or dip because Levi ate all that snacky stuff when he was with us during his break and I only ever buy food like that when you boys are going to be around."

"Yes, I know," Judah said, "but thanks for the heads-up. I'll buy extra of both in case I get snowed in."

"Yes, because chips are so much better for you than fixing a full meal." Molly rolled her eyes at Judah. "Is there really nothing I can say to convince you to stay here tonight? I was hoping we could talk some more and, honestly, I hate that you won't be here for Sunday dinner. Your pops and I look forward to sitting down for a meal with you boys all week."

Judah sighed. "I know you do and I'm sorry I'm going to miss it, especially since it's Levi's turn to cook. But we talked last night, Mom, not to mention again over breakfast, so I kind of feel like whatever you had in mind that needs to be covered has already been talked out and I could use a break from the topic of How Judah Can't Keep A Man."

"No one said any such thing!"

The sheer force of his mother's instant outrage made Judah laugh, especially with Harvey hiding a smile behind one hand. "I know, Mom, I was just kidding. But, like you said, I should get on the road and settled at your house before this next storm rolls in, especially knowing I might have to wait for the plows to dig out your road in the morning. I promise I'll come down for dinner next week if the weather cooperates, okay?"

"You'd better," Harvey said, his blue eyes twinkling despite his dry tone. "You know she'll drag Levi and me up there kicking and screaming if you don't and then we'll all be snowed in together talking about how you can't keep a man and then where will we be?"

Molly cocked an eyebrow in his direction. "What is wrong with you? And, really, is it so bad that I'd like to have dinner with my sons? It's not like I get to see them every day."

Oh, boy.

As Judah had expected, last night's family meeting hadn't gone smoothly. Molly's alarm at Judah's request to swap out their households had been abundantly evident, and it had taken a while to talk her down enough to carry on a substantive discussion. Having Levi and their Pops standing by had helped Judah diffuse the tension though, as had using video so his mom could literally see his body language and understand that, aside from the unusual ask to get out of town, he really was in good health. Molly was still worried for him and Judah suspected there was nothing he could do to help ease that.

She and Harvey had started packing *immediately* after the family conference had concluded, departing Stowe at such an early hour this morning they'd arrived in the North End to find Levi still asleep and Judah barely caffeinated and not even showered. Molly had insisted on making a huge breakfast spread so they could talk it all through one more time too, and though Judah had worked at being patient as he answered her questions, he hadn't missed the way her face had fallen when she'd understood just how eager he was to get the heck out of Dodge.

Judah did feel bad about taking off like his ass was on fire, especially knowing his parents were bummed that he'd miss the family dinner. But the idea of rehashing Judah's reasons for wanting to be in Stowe for yet a third time just made him tired and he knew he'd never make it through that discussion without getting drunk or emotional or both and that wasn't going to help anyone.

Reaching over, he wrapped Molly up in a hug, chest pinching when she squeezed him back tight. "Come on, Mom —it's not like I'm moving cross-country. I'm staying in your house! And if the road isn't buried next Sunday, you'll see me whether you want to or not."

"Of course, I'll want to see you," Molly said with a grumble. She shot him a quick smile as she let Judah go, but the furrow in her brow remained. Her voice was soft when she spoke again, and tighter than Judah liked to hear. "I can't help being worried about you. If this ... estrangement with Connor bothers you so much, why not reach out and see if he's ready to talk?"

"I tried, Mom. I called him a few times and when he didn't call back, I decided to give it a rest." Judah tried to smile, though it felt weird and wrong on his face. "I don't want to be that guy, pushing Connor to do something he's not ready for and might never want. That wouldn't be fair to either of us."

She blew a noisy breath through her nose. "Yes, I see your point even if I hate that you're being so goddamned pragmatic about everything."

"Would you rather I throw a tantrum?"

"If it made you feel better, then sure. I'll bet it would too because venting really can be a liberating experience."

"Venting has always been more your thing than mine," Judah pointed out and smiled as his mother turned her eyes skyward.

"Oh, I know. My point, however, is that it's not like you to hide away from the world, Jude, even when you need some space. And that's exactly what you'll be doing while you're holed up in Stowe instead of trying to fix the thing that's broken."

Damn, but his mom saw a lot.

Judah swallowed hard. "I'm not hiding, Mom—I'm trying to get my shit back in order. And I definitely need this break. Yes, it's my own fault for burning the candle at both ends but being away from Boston will give me quality time to chill that I won't get otherwise."

"Quality time in the woods. On your own. Which you normally hate," Molly said, her expression and voice going so deadpan Judah had to laugh. She looked slightly less serious as his snickers trailed off, but the earnestness in her eyes tugged at his chest. "I still think it's a shame you'll be missing out on chances to at least talk to Connor, because that's something I don't think either of you want."

Pressing his mouth in a tight line, Judah scooped his belongings up from the floor, the sadness he carried inside him far heavier than the bags. He cast a lingering glance at the big chair by the counter before meeting his mother's gaze.

"Maybe you're right," he said quietly, "but I'm not sure what Connor wants, Mom. He doesn't want me, at any rate, at least not right now. That's something I have to respect, but it's insanely hard to do when he's so close but farther away than ever at exactly the same time."

Molly and Harvey exchanged a look, communicating in silence the way so many long-time couples seemed to do, and the sympathy in their faces when they turned back was like a smack to Judah's gut.

"Do what you need to, son," Harvey said, hand coming up to gently clasp Judah's elbow. "If your mom or Levi or I can help in any way, you be sure to tell us."

THICK CLOUDS HAD ALREADY GATHERED OVERHEAD when Judah arrived in Stowe that afternoon. As promised, he made a quick stop at the shop in town to say hello to the Hook Me staff and gather up the schedules that had been prepared for the coming week. He forced himself to leave before the urge to tidy shelves and fill inventory overcame him, then raided a nearby market for more snacks than a person had any business eating before he headed for his parents' place, pulling his old Jeep into the driveway just as the first flakes fell.

Though Judah hadn't been in the A-frame house for a couple of months, he was immediately struck by how different the place felt the moment he let himself in the door. It was familiar, of course, big open room bathed in what remained of the daylight through the giant windows that covered the house's front wall, the décor easy and comfortable and the smell of his mother's stovetop orange-cinnamon potpourri still lingering in the air. But Judah's last stay had fallen in December when he and Levi had joined their parents to celebrate the eighth night of Hannukah as a family, and the place had been bright with talk and laughter over that weekend. Their banter had carried easily over music or TV shows playing in the background, and the teasing had even grown a bit raucous during what had turned into several *epic* sessions of Mario Kart.

A thick silence permeated the place now, inside and out, the woods beyond the huge windows in the main room turning white under the falling snow. For a second, Judah simply stood, bags still in hand, and soaked it all in, new awareness stealing over him. He really did want to be here. He *wanted* the quiet and stillness, and to slow things down for a change. Yeah, he'd be working at the shop in town and he had some documents to edit, but if Judah paced himself and was diligent about not taking on more, his schedule would be mellow in comparison to the North End store.

He had only himself to manage while he stayed in this

house and being here on his own could feel like he'd gotten away from the buzz of the city.

Boston isn't the thing you're trying to get away from.

Carrying his bags to the spiral staircase located toward the back of the main room, Judah climbed them to the loft where he slept anytime he was in town. His brain had a point, of course, as had his mom. Judah hadn't left his home for a vacation-esque stay in the woods. He'd wanted to lick his wounds in private and get his head on straight but, most of all, force himself to *stop* waiting around for Connor to walk in to Hook Me and explain why he'd been acting like a big jerk.

"Not like that's going to happen," Judah murmured to himself.

Knowing that sucked. Worse was the suspicion that Connor probably wasn't having an easy time of it either. Maybe Judah was overinflating his own importance in Connor's life, but he'd gotten to know the guy pretty well during the weeks they'd spent together. A tremendously sweet and kindhearted soul lurked beneath Connor's burly frame and though Judah had seen it many times in flashes as their friendship had blossomed, Connor had laid it out in plain view during the hours they'd sheltered from the storm together and quietly invited Judah to get closer.

He'd made no secret of the value he placed on his relationships, especially with people he held close to his heart like his family and Olivia. And though it stung even thinking that maybe Judah had managed to carve out a small niche for himself in that big heart before things had gone all to hell, he felt it was very likely true which meant that having to sever the connection between them had probably hurt Connor just as much as it had Judah.

Judah could only hope he was wrong.

Slowly, he pulled his phone from his pocket and opened

the messaging app, staring at the thread he and Connor had shared. Full of quick notes and stupid memes, he'd come close to deleting it at least a dozen times, especially after the few calls he'd made to Connor had gone unanswered. Judah hadn't wanted to be a pest and, honestly, being ghosted sucked, but a part of him *still* wanted to check in and make sure Connor was okay. There was no way he'd simply blown off what had happened between them and gone about his business as if nothing had changed. Connor wasn't wired like that any more than Judah was, and even now, he wondered how things were going for that shy guy and whether he'd found another place to buy his yarn and maybe start another knitting project.

I hope he's all right.

He blinked as a gust of wind rattled the glass in the small windows behind him, Mother Nature's way of announcing that the stormy part of that evening's program was about to begin. Judah gave himself a quick shake before he slipped the phone away again, then headed downstairs for his second load of stuff from the car while also making a mental note to check the snowblower once everything was safely inside.

If he were a betting man, he'd say his odds of being plowed out before Monday weren't very good. Judah felt okay about that, though. He had a new manuscript to work on and an online yoga program he looked forward to trying, not to mention a refrigerator packed with food; being ass-deep in new snow didn't worry him at all. It almost felt symbolic in fact, like the universe was helping him wipe a slate clean. And if that was the case, he was overdue to turn the page and move on, too.

FIFTEEN

"You feeling okay, kid?"

Connor stifled a groan. This had to be the fourth time he'd heard that question since meeting James and Ally at their hotel. And Connor *was* okay. He still felt drained and low on energy, but he was in one-hundred percent better shape than he'd been only twenty-four hours ago.

He appreciated his brother's concern more than he could say, though. Those awful, fraught moments from the night before still loomed large, when he'd been so certain he'd done irrevocable damage to his family; every time Connor thought about them, his insides curled with dread. If James and Ally had been different people, Connor could have lost them. Been utterly helpless to do anything but watch them turn their backs on him and walk away, exactly as he'd feared.

Kind of like the way you turned your back on Judah, huh?

A lot like that. Bringing his hand up, Connor curled his first two fingers around the blue infinity scarf and gave his brother a small smile. "I'm good."

He meant it. Talking to James and Ally last night and

hearing their assurances that they weren't going anywhere had helped immeasurably, even if there were a million things they still needed to hash out. Connor had been exhausted but much calmer by the time he could persuade them to go back to the hotel for the night and, wonder of wonders, he'd crashed and slept a solid seven hours, his body and brain finally giving in to the fatigue that had been building all week and crested in the wake of his panic.

His shift on the rig today had been a unique kind of torture, but thanks to Olivia's patience and repeated mugs of herbal tea, he'd made it through and still felt up to meeting James and Ally at the Public Market for some quick errands before they found a place to eat what would be their last dinner in town for a while.

James sipped a cup of hot cider, voice easy when he spoke though his gaze was intense. "You sure?"

Damn. Maybe he still didn't trust Connor to tell him the truth. Or it could be James sensed that Connor's emotions were as tangled and messy right now as his early attempts at knitting had been. Because while James was trying to get past Connor's secret-keeping and lies by omission, Connor *wasn't* entirely okay and wouldn't be until he talked to Judah.

Connor glanced around at the crowd in the Public Market, chest hollow with melancholy. He'd suggested coming here without a second thought, knowing how much Ally enjoyed the cheery buzz of the place and wanting to give her that treat once more before she and James climbed aboard the train back to Baltimore tomorrow afternoon. Unfortunately, the sights and smells and sounds of the place reminded Connor forcefully of Judah and any appetite he might have worked up had gone right out the window as soon as he'd stepped through the door.

Forcing himself to swallow a little more of his own cider, Connor shrugged. "I'm good, I promise."

"Okay. 'Cause you're acting like your cup is full of poison."

"Dude, come on."

"I'm just saying." James smiled at Connor's soft laughter. "You want to talk about it? We've got time to burn while Ally buys all the French pastry she can lay her hands on and you know I don't mind listening."

Connor smirked. "I'll bet you five bucks you eat most of that box before your train even hits Providence tomorrow."

"That is a bet you will totally win." James snorted on a laugh. "I called dibs on the cookies 'cause we all know I'm not eating those vegan cupcakes she picked up at the other counter. Not even sure why she wanted to stop there, to tell you the truth."

Connor glanced down at the purple bakery box on the table between them, his voice and smile growing softer. "I told her how much Judah and his family like the stuff from that bakery," he said. "And hey, maybe you should try them anyway. Judah's mom says their stuff is some of the best she's ever had."

James sipped his cider in silence for a beat, a wariness coming over him that hadn't been there when he and Connor had seated themselves at this long, communal table in the market's main seating area. "What about you?" he asked at last and damn, he sounded oddly careful. ""How do you like their stuff?"

"I haven't tried any of it." Connor squirmed a little under his brother's stare. "You know I'm not big on sweets."

"I know you've got it in your head that you shouldn't eat them because you think they'll slow you down on the job. Doesn't mean you can't every once in a while, Con. It's not like I eat cookies or cupcakes on the regular, you know."

"Umm, except you do. That bakery you like over on Daybreak Circle would go out of business if you stopped going in three times a week."

James huffed a laugh. "Okay, fair. You didn't answer my question, though. When I asked you if you wanted to talk about whatever's got you looking like you got knocked over sideways. But I guess I already know the answer. Your friend, right? Judah?"

Heat crept up Connor's cheeks as he cast his gaze out onto the market floor. "This place reminds me of him. We used to have lunch here and hang out sometimes, grab hot drinks on our way downtown. I haven't been here without him in a while and it feels strange. Wrong, maybe." Connor swallowed before meeting his brother's gaze once more. "I miss him, you know?"

James's expression was uneasy. "I guess I do," he said, words coming slowly. "If it's anything like the way I feel when I'm away from Ally for a while because I'm on a long tour or when one of us has to go out of town." James furrowed his brow. "It's like that, right? Even though he's a guy?"

"Yeah." Connor spoke without hesitation. "Exactly like that. I've missed girlfriends after breakups in the past. Not that Judah and I even got a chance to be together officially, but it still hurts. And I never felt like this about any of the girls. Like something is missing." He rubbed his knuckles against his chest. "Something important. And I really want it back."

Silence fell over them, James fussing with his cup while Connor died a little each second watching the tight set of his brother's mouth. But James simply looked confused when he finally met Connor's gaze again, and more than a little regretful. "I wish I understood this better. But I want to, for you, Con, I really do, and I promise I'm trying my best."

Connor pulled in a deep breath, head going light as relief crashed through him. "I know, J. And it's good. Exactly what I need from you right now, too."

James gave a tight nod, like he was deciding something right then and there. "Okay. So, what happened with Judah?"

"I messed up. Walked away and cut him out." The back of Connor's neck went hot. "He didn't deserve that. Judah was nothing but really good to me the whole time we were friends and I treated him like crap."

"Because of me?" A crease worked its way between James's brows. "I know I was an ass to you when you told me who he is to you but—"

"It wasn't because of you," Connor cut in gently. "Or at least not in the way you might be thinking. I hurt Judah because I was scared. I was afraid I'd disappoint you and Ally when you realized who I really was and worried that I could lose you. But I was afraid of what I was feeling, too, maybe more than anything. I never ... I had no idea I could feel this way about a man, and I didn't know how to handle it. How to explain to *myself* who Judah is in my life and how much he means to me, so how the heck was I going to tell my coworkers or you and Ally?"

"You told Olivia." The sorrow shimmering in James's eyes had Connor reaching over the table so he could set his hand on his brother's arm.

"I told her a few *hours* before I told you, J. And, God, I was so freaked out the whole time, even knowing she wouldn't judge me for being ... me. It was the first time I said the words out loud, even to myself, admitting that Judah is way more than a friend and I'm not the straight guy I always thought I was. And I needed to say those words out loud because it was killing me to hold it in. I just couldn't take it anymore."

"I'm glad you told her. As much as I hate that you were afraid to tell me." James covered Connor's hand with his own and drew an unsteady breath. He looked haunted and so unsure of himself, it was like talking to a whole other person. "But I get it now. I just hope you know that I'm sorry I wasn't ready to hear you last night."

"I do." Connor had to force the words out past the boulder lodged in his throat, but James's face fell further.

"I should have handled it better."

"Hey, I should have, too." Connor managed a creaky chuckle. "I'm not going to apologize for not telling you about Judah before I figured it out myself, but I should have been honest with you and Ally about the meds. And damn, I should have been better to Judah. Fought harder not to let my fear get the best of me and trusted him to keep being my friend while we figured out if we could be more. The hell of it is that I wanted to. I just didn't trust myself enough to let him all the way in."

He paused as Ally slid onto the bench beside him and immediately wound a slim arm around Connor's waist, her expression open and serene.

"So, what comes next?" she asked, her smile so kind. "Do you trust Judah enough to let him in now? Because from what I heard when I walked over here, the ball is in your court, hon. If you really want something with your man, it's on you to let him know."

Connor's chest warmed. *His man.* Damn, he liked the sound of that even if James's cheeks had gone a little bit pale.

"That's gonna take some getting used to," James muttered, though he visibly rallied before Connor could even begin to fret. "Pretty sure the lady is right, bro, so I'd take her advice if I were you."

He's trying, Connor thought, an understanding that made him feel even better than he would have thought.

Ally wrinkled her nose at her husband. "You're such a Leo. I'm not giving advice, silly, I'm *listening*, something you said you were going to work at doing more when it's Connor's turn to speak."

"I have!"

"He really has," Connor agreed over Ally's snickers and gave his brother's arm one last squeeze. "But you've totally got a point, too, Al. It's on me to fix things with Judah or at least try to, which is why I'm going to go back to knitting class tomorrow and try to convince him to talk to me."

"There is no try, only do," Ally said solemnly, then grinned at James's groan. "Sorry, but you know I love me some Yoda."

"Yeah, we do." James shook his head at her. "I think the real question here is whether Connor's 'only do' will be enough."

Connor ran a hand over his mouth. "I hope it will be. I know I hurt him pretty bad, though." Of all the hopeless feelings he'd had in the last week and a half, knowing Judah had felt pain because of him had been the worst. "But I can't let it go without telling him I'm sorry, not even if he hates me for it."

THOSE WORDS RANG in Connor's ears as he stood on the sidewalk across the street from Hook Me on Sunday afternoon, heart hammering beneath his ribs like it was going to beat its way out. He'd seen James and Ally off at South Station before turning for home, and though he'd had to coach himself the whole way to the North End, he made it without once stopping. Actually stepping inside the yarn store was another story though, because finally being this close to Judah had Connor scared out of his mind.

What if this thing between them couldn't be fixed? And what the hell was Connor going to do if it turned out that Judah really did hate him?

Connor wasn't sure he could take that. Not when his heart yearned for Judah so badly.

Just as he had before his first knitting class all those weeks before, Connor focused on breathing until he felt ready to cross the street and reach for the handle on the shop's door, but his insides still trembled, a sensation that only worsened when he saw Levi at the counter instead of Judah, wearing an expression more somber than Connor had ever seen.

Connor pulled the door closed behind him and softly cleared his throat. "Hi."

"Hi, Connor."

Levi's greeting was even and almost friendly, but his gaze shuttered as he watched Connor cross the room. Connor wouldn't have expected anything less; he'd been certain Judah would have told his family about their friendship having soured and knew he'd need to prove his worth more than once before this got any easier.

"You're early if you're interested in sitting in on a class," Levi said, "but you're welcome to go down to the work room if you'd like. It'll be about thirty minutes before anyone else shows up."

"Thanks, but I'm not here for class." Connor used his scarf to self-soothe but even that wasn't enough to steady his voice entirely and he knew Levi had heard the tremor by the way his gaze instantly softened. "I'd really like to talk to Judah, though, if he thinks he has time before he starts?"

The long pause that passed while Levi simply watched him scraped at Connor's nerves.

"Judah's not here, Connor," Levi said at last. "He and Mom decided to switch shops for a while, so he's up in Stowe. I'm ... shit." He blew out a breath, cheeks puffing, then ran a hand over his head. "Judah hasn't said when he'll be back."

Connor blinked as Levi came around the counter, unsure if he could trust his own hearing. "Judah ... moved? Why? What happened?" he asked, before understanding hit him like a slap of cold water.

You happened, pal.

Connor's stomach sank right through the floor. "Is this because of me?"

"Sort of, yes. But there was more going on with Judah, too." Levi slid his hands in his pockets, eyebrows drawn together and eyes going distant as he seemed to think something through. Then he blinked and gave Connor a crooked little smile. "Can you stick around for a little while? I think we should talk about the stuff Judah told me, so you have the whole story."

Near numb, Connor made himself nod. "Of course. I'll do whatever it takes to—"

"Connor!"

—fix this.

Connor's words caught in his throat as Molly Abrams's voice rang through the air. Oh, man, he was in for it now. The *last* person this very nice woman was going to want to see was the big oaf who'd hurt her son, badly enough the guy had freaking left town, apparently. Connor wouldn't blame her for tearing him a new one or even for banning him from the store. Bracing himself, he turned, ready to make his case, and his heart stuttered when instead of sharp words, he was met with Molly's smile.

"I am glad to see you," she said, "because this family really needs your help convincing that son of mine to get his ass home where he belongs."

SIXTEEN

Pretty much any time Judah drove along the winding road to his parents' house, his heart ended up in his throat. Particularly if he was driving in the dark or through snow, both of which were true as he drove on this Friday evening. He squinted at the road ahead, sure this would be the trip where he'd encounter a deer or moose or axe-wielding maniac in the twin beams of his headlights and he gritted his teeth against the curses piling up in his head that were trying to slip free.

He didn't bother stifling himself as he turned into the driveway and spotted a man-shaped figure on the front steps, though, and only luck kept him from driving into the bushes that sat beside the drive. Still, the strange, squeaky shout that wormed its way out of him hurt his throat.

"What the *fuck* is this?"

No one answered of course, unsurprising when one remembered the nearest neighbors were a quarter mile in either direction. At least the floodlights attached to the house switched on as Judah pulled in, bathing the driveway in yellow light as well as a second SUV he didn't recognize.

Pulse speeding, he jerked the parking brake into place and killed the ignition. He snatched glances through the windshield as he gathered his things, trying to suss out if that figure was friend or foe, and felt sure the ground had opened beneath him when he got a good look at the guy's face because that sure looked like Connor Devlin standing on the front steps, bigger than life and just as gorgeous, with a familiar blue scarf wrapped around his neck.

If he'd been able, Judah would have sworn again, then followed up with every other oath he knew. His throat seemed to have closed up though, leaving him distinctly breathless by the time he opened the car door. Setting his feet on the ground, he stood, glad his suddenly wobbly knees supported him, but he stayed silent as Connor walked down the steps. Unwanted thoughts crashed into Judah's head then, none of them comforting, and helped him find his voice at last.

"What's wrong?" he asked, voice rough. "Is it Mom or Pops? Is Levi okay? Are you ... Did something happen?"

Connor strode toward him through the white flakes, hands up in a quelling kind of motion. "Everyone's fine, Judah," he said, gaze intense. "Your mom and pops and Levi are all good."

"Okay." The air in Judah's lungs left him in a rush that made his head light. "Jeez. You took a fucking year off my life."

Connor stopped by the Jeep's front fender. "I'm sorry. I didn't mean to scare you. Didn't really think about how it'd look for me to show up unannounced."

"It looks weird as hell. And of course, you scared the shit out of me, man, what did you expect?"

Judah rolled his eyes, more at his own babbling than anything else, then pursed his lips at the wince on Connor's face. Playing nice with the guy who'd stomped on his feelings hadn't been on tonight's agenda and Judah was mightily tempted not to give a damn. But Connor moved closer and

Judah noticed the snow crusting the shoulders and hood of his coat. How long had this guy been waiting? And why was just looking at him enough to make Judah's resolve to be a hard ass waver?

Damnit.

"What are you doing here?" he asked as gently as he could. "I don't mean to be rude, but you're the last person I'd have expected to see anywhere and especially here at my parents' house."

"I came to apologize," Connor said without preamble. "To tell you I'm sorry for taking off that morning. For not returning your messages or coming back to class. That I'm sorry I hurt you."

Judah pressed his lips together hard, chest pinching at Connor's sigh.

His face flooding with color, Connor slid his hands into his pockets, but kept his gaze locked on Judah's as he continued. "I also wanted to thank you for finishing the blanket for me, Judah. And for the scarf and hat and gloves." He hooked the fingers of his right hand over the slash of sky blue at his throat. "I've caught Olivia trying to steal this at least three times this past week."

A rusty chuckle pushed its way out of Judah. "You should probably knit one for her." His traitorous heart wobbled at Connor's grin. "And we both know I didn't finish that blanket so much as bind it off, wrap it up, and drop it off. You did all the work." He ran his teeth over his bottom lip a moment. "I thought for sure you'd come back for it."

"I wanted to. I really did. I just ... couldn't." Connor walked several steps closer. "At first, I thought maybe you'd thrown it out."

Judah made a pained noise. "Never," he muttered. "Not after you worked your ass off to make it. And I knew how much you wanted Olivia to have that blanket. Did she love it?"

"Oh, yeah, she did." Connor smiled. "And she knew without me telling her that I'd made it, too." His expression sobered. "Just seeing the blanket—knowing you'd come to the station—

made me face some things I'd been trying to ignore, namely you and me and the way I've been acting.

"I wish I could turn back time and do things differently with you Judah, but we both know I can't. So, I'm hoping—and I mean *really* hoping—you'll let me make it up to you and give me a second chance."

"Second chance to do what?" Judah asked. His voice sounded small, even to his own ears, and no wonder considering he felt like he would literally fly into pieces if this man so much as touched him. "I'd like to think we could be friends again, but I don't know if I'm up for it, Connor. Not when—" He pressed his lips tight against the stupid trio of words he still ached to say.

"Respectfully, I disagree." Connor gave him a sweet smile. "I totally think we can be friends again. More if you're ready for that."

"If *I'm* ready?" Judah blinked at the sky, trying to get a read on just what the hell was going on. "A couple of weeks ago you couldn't even say the word 'friend' to me without hesitating and now I'm the one playing catch up?"

Fuck that noise.

Real anger bloomed in Judah. Setting his jaw, he stared at the man who'd upended his life and tried hard to screw up the courage to order him to leave. But Connor's next words knocked the wind right out of Judah and nearly put him on his ass, too.

"I came out to James and Ally," Connor said, his tone even.

"Olivia, too. I told them about you and me and how important you are in my life."

Judah gulped. "Holy shitballs. I ... You know, I hoped someday you'd do a little groveling, but I truly did not expect you to lead with that." He tried to smile at Connor's laughter but couldn't quite manage it. Judah knew how much James and Ally meant to Connor. The idea he'd told them he wasn't the straight guy they'd known their whole lives was awesome and humbling. "Connor, wow. Are you okay?"

Connor nodded, his expression both shy and pleased, if just a touch downcast. "Yeah. James was floored. Betrayed really, since I told him about quitting my meds, too. We still have some work to do." He shrugged. "He and Ally want to be there for me, though, and that's what I need from them."

Now Judah really could smile. "I'm so glad to hear that, man. Good for you."

"Thank you." Connor smiled back. "It is good for me. Really good, if I'm being honest with myself, which is something I'm working at being better at every day."

"Me too. That's one of the reasons I came up here," Judah said when Connor raised his eyebrows. "To get some clarity. Recharge. Just *be*, you know?"

"I do." Connor glanced around at the snowy woods. "How's that been going?"

"Meh. I'm out of practice with the concept of relaxing, but it's going okay. It's snowed every goddamned day since I got here, though, and the snowblower is on the fritz, so I mostly feel like I picked up a new hobby that no one sane calls extreme shoveling."

Connor's laugh echoed through the night. "Yikes, Judah. I'm glad I cleaned up the driveway and walk before you got here, then."

"You didn't have to do that, but thanks." Judah waved a

hand at the flakes falling around them, more heavily than they had been a half hour before. "My guess is this isn't going to let up until tomorrow morning at least and if the road doesn't get plowed in time to open the shop, I'll have extra time to shovel. Certainly wouldn't be the first time," he muttered and started for the house. He wasn't surprised that Connor fell into step beside him. They had talking to do and, however angry Judah might still be, he wasn't going to turn Connor away after he'd been so candid.

"When did you get here?" he asked.

"Maybe an hour ago," Connor said. "I wanted to catch you at the shop in town but traffic from Boston was murder. By the time I got off the interstate, I figured you'd be closing up soon and decided to come straight here."

"Okay but how exactly did you know where *here* is? You could look up the shop, obviously, but this house sure isn't listed on Hook Me's website."

"I didn't need to look it up because your mom gave me the address."

Just short of the front steps, Judah stopped dead in his tracks. "My mom?" Turning, he stared at Connor, sure the words would make more sense once he'd had a chance to process them but nope, they really didn't. "When did you talk to my mom about this house?"

"Last Sunday, before and after knitting class." Walking halfway up the steps, Connor picked up a cloth bag that sat at the top. The bag's shape told Judah it held something both wide and flat, and Connor held it carefully at his side as he faced Judah again. "I was there to find *you* of course, but Molly told me you'd decided to move up here and go full hermit."

Judah groaned. "I said I wanted a *break*," he grumbled as he climbed the steps too, "never that I was moving here permanently. She knows this!"

"Levi and your Pops said the same on Sunday and today, but I don't think she's been much in the mood to listen."

"You saw my family today, too?"

"Uh-huh." Connor waggled the bag in his hand slightly. "Molly asked me to bring you some stuff, namely a lasagna from Levi and homemade bread from your pops, plus a box of cookies she threw in. She made me promise to eat a couple, by the way, and I hope that's okay."

Despite the amusement in his voice, Connor looked serious when they faced off at the top of the stairs. "My guess is they're worried you might change your mind and decide not to come back at all. You blew them off for Sunday dinner last week, Judah, and she seemed to think this Sunday wasn't going to go any better."

"It's not my fault this place has been buried nearly every day. And no, I haven't even considered relocating." Judah unlocked the door. "The fact I have to drive everywhere, including synagogue, is reason enough to go back—I straight up hate this goddamned road they live on. Besides, Mom's lived out of the city long enough to get grumpy about the lack of privacy, especially in the North End where everyone is packed in on top of each other. She'll come and kick me out herself when she gets fed up enough."

"I can picture that. James bitched all the time about the city being crowded during his visit and the guy lives in a town with over a hundred thousand people."

Connor followed Judah to the kitchen area in the corner, then set the bag he'd been carrying on the counter, gaze appreciative as he ran it over the space.

"This place is nice."

Judah chuckled. "It's all right, especially if you're into woods. Which my parents are, of course." He scrunched his nose up at Connor. "I'm sure they're itching to get back here."

"They want you to be okay first, Judah. Levi too." Connor gave him an earnest look. "I hope I don't have to tell you how lucky you are to have them."

Judah nodded. Though guilty of taking his family's love for granted in the past, knowing Connor had given him perspective he'd needed and welcomed, even as it had bruised his heart. He was phenomenally lucky to have his mom, Pops, and Levi, and wouldn't trade them for the world, even when they drove him crazy, like right now.

"I don't mind if you tell me. I can't believe they sent you up here with an apology and a food bribe, though."

"Ah, no." Connor held up a finger. "The food bribe was their idea, but the apology is all me."

Judah rolled his eyes. "Then I'm surprised Mom didn't give you crap for not driving up here as soon as she fed you that line about me not coming back to Boston last Sunday."

"Oh, she did," Connor said. "I had to arrange for a couple of days off, though, in case you wouldn't speak to me and I had to wear you down. Once I explained that to her, she cut me some slack." Color flooded his cheeks. "Said she's been rooting for us since my first Knitting 101 class."

Good Lord.

His own face hot, Judah peeled off his coat. He wasn't sure how to feel about his parents and brother banding together to help Connor execute this little stunt, but at least he had time and geography on his side to figure it all out.

"That definitely sounds like Mom," he said.

"They miss you," Connor replied, and Judah had to laugh.

"Yeah, I miss them, too." Shifting, he leaned his ass against the counter and crossed his arms, pleasure curling inside him when Connor did the same. "And the city. Yoga class. Christ, the store. I even miss riding the goddamned Green Line, which just goes to show you where my head is at."

Connor hummed. "What about people?"

"I already said I did, right?" Judah murmured. "Some of it started before I made the trip up here though, so I guess you could say I've been living with it for a while." He closed his eyes and sagged a little when a big hand clasped his shoulder. "I thought it would get easier, but so far no luck."

"Same here."

Neither spoke as Connor slowly pulled Judah into his arms. Once there, though, enveloped in a bear hug, Judah's eyes stung. Burying his face against Connor's broad chest, he drew what felt like the first deep breath in weeks and reveled in it, inhaling Connor's scent: woodsy soap and a mild, earthy beard pomade, underscored by faint traces of the peppermint tea he liked to drink in the afternoons. Judah slipped his arms around Connor's waist, sighing at Connor's soft noise, and Connor pressed his lips against the side of Judah's head, voice was rough when he spoke in Judah's ear.

"I missed you so much, Jude."

"I missed you too." Judah burrowed closer. "Do me a favor and don't disappear on me like that again, okay?"

"I won't. But you have to promise not to move out of town without at least telling me first."

Judah smiled against Connor's shirt. "I already told you I'm not moving but yeah, I can do my best."

———

CONNOR STUCK CLOSE as he helped Judah throw a quick meal together, brushing his fingers along Judah's as they worked and resting his hand on Judah's arm or the small of his back. Those touches were intoxicating for Judah, who'd been so hungry to see Connor over the weeks they hadn't spoken.

They talked and caught each other up, and though Judah's

heart broke to hear of James's struggles with Connor's coming out, he felt pure relief knowing both brothers were committed to making it work.

He felt certain that Connor was feeling that same relief, probably in massive portions because he'd changed remarkably in just a couple of weeks. This Connor was more at ease with himself and the world around him and if he still did daily battle with his anxiety, it seemed he won more than he lost right now.

"I decided I'd finally get serious about yoga," Connor said around a mouthful of salad, "so, I went to that studio at the top of Hanover Street that you mentioned. I hurt in places I didn't know existed after my first class, but I also slept like a rock afterward. Took me forever to get out of bed the next morning."

"Because you didn't want to wake up?"

"No. Because I ached so much, I almost cried."

"Baw." Judah laughed. "It really does get better the more often you practice. Are you still doing the relaxation breathing, too?"

"Oh, definitely. I've been doing it in the back of the rig." Connor's tone was so easy, it took Judah a second to catch on.

"Do you mean in the back of the ambulance?" He could literally feel his eyes get big. "That's not against regulations?"

"Nope. As long as I'm not sleeping and we're in between calls, it's cool. I switch the lights off and set my watch and practice deep breathing for five minutes a couple of times a day." Connor shrugged. "Liv asked me once if I didn't feel closed in but, honestly, there's probably more space back there than in my bathroom at home." He smiled. "We should take a turn hanging at my place when you come back to Boston, I think. Your apartment is definitely nicer than mine, but it's not fair for you to host every time."

Warmth settled in Judah. Yeah, he'd like to see Connor's studio apartment. He liked the idea of going out together when their schedules lined up too or staying home and knitting if the mood struck them. He didn't feel quite ready to say so, though, especially since something kept niggling at the back of his brain, and that funny, uncomfortable energy made it impossible for him to fully relax.

It wasn't until Connor had set a plate of butter cookies on the table that Judah understood a not so small part of him was waiting for the other shoe to drop.

"It's really coming down out there," he said as they munched. "Did you plan on driving back to Boston tonight or ...?"

"I'd say my answer is up to you but that wouldn't be fair." Connor looked so earnest. "I'd like to stay if that's all right with you, Judah. We still have a lot to talk about and, honestly, I'm really enjoying just seeing you again."

"Same." Judah breathed in deeply. "But I wasn't kidding about the road not always being plowed in a timely manner. You could be stuck here a day or two, depending on the weather patterns."

"Then I guess I'll be snowbound for the second time this year," Connor said. "And that's fine. I'm not on shift again until after the weekend and I've got nowhere to be until then."

Judah hummed in response. He liked the idea of talking. And being with Connor even more. He'd missed him way too much to send him on his way just yet.

Still ... he wasn't sure how to feel about having Connor *here* in this house. Judah had come up here to get his head on straight, *away* from the guy sitting across the table who'd wrung Judah's heart out like a pile of wet wool. And now Connor was here, hope and nervousness mixing in those brown eyes as he waited for Judah to speak and damn that got right under Judah's skin. There were three bedrooms plus the giant couch, after all—no reason they couldn't inhabit the same space without getting under each other's feet.

"You're welcome to stay," he murmured, voice softer than he'd wanted it to be. "If you'd really like to."

Damn, he felt raw and vulnerable just then and maybe like he was taking a bigger chance than he wanted. Something of those feelings must have shown in his face because Connor rubbed the back of his neck, that now familiar gesture reminding Judah he wasn't the only one putting himself out there. Connor had taken a big chance driving up from Boston just so they could talk face to face. Hell, Connor had plucked up the courage to walk into Hook Me and talk to Levi and Judah's *mom*; everything he'd done to get here had probably been a great deal more stressful for him than it would have been for Judah.

"I'm really glad you're here, you know." Judah smiled to show he meant it. "Not sure I've said that yet, but it's true."

A shy smile blossomed on Connor's face. "I'm really glad I'm here too."

He dashed out to his rental after they'd cleaned up the remains of their dinner and Judah put a playlist on to stream, more to distract himself than anything else. He was still standing there in front of the TV when Connor re-entered and dropped a bag by the door, but Judah didn't have time to fret too much about where that bag was going to end up before Connor was in front of him, laughing as he gestured at the big, sectional couch.

"This can't be a coincidence," he said. "I think it's even the same color as the one in your apartment!"

"Not quite, but close. It was my housewarming gift to Mom and Pops." Judah felt very smug as he watched Connor practically dive on to the cushions. "For me, it's the one spot in this place that really does feel like a home away from home."

"I can see why." Arranging his long limbs with a heartfelt sigh, Connor rolled onto his side and propped his head on his hand. Despite his smile, Judah thought he saw something rueful in his face.

"What is it?" he asked, then took the hand Connor held out to him.

"I was just thinking it would be nice to do some knitting." Gently, Connor tugged Judah's hand, then scooted back on the cushions to make room for him to sit. "I bought some new needles and wool from your mom last week, but almost left them at home, in case you told me to stick my apology in my ass."

"I thought about it." With his free hand, Judah smoothed Connor's hair back from his forehead, watching a line form between his eyebrows.

"You did?"

"Yes." Judah hauled in a deep breath and blew it out through his nose. "It was touch and go for a bit while we were standing in the driveway. You wrecked me and I'm only human —I had an impulse to wreck you back."

Misery flashed over Connor's face and he closed his eyes for several seconds. "I'd have deserved it."

"I'm not so sure. You learned a huge thing about yourself, Connor, and it changed everything you thought you knew. Even though I was hurting, I didn't blame you for needing time to understand what it meant to your life, especially after I pushed you to get physical."

"You didn't push, not really. I *wanted* it, Judah. Wanted to be with you like that." Connor tightened his grip on Judah's hand. "I just ... I got caught up in my own head about how I was going to make it all work with my life. How to talk about it at the station and with friends. With James most of all. Every-thing kind of hit me at once. Even though I knew what was happening, I couldn't step back enough to talk myself down. Maybe if I'd figured myself out when I was younger. Been able to talk about it and understand what I needed, I'd have been ready for you when we finally met."

Judah squeezed Connor's hand in return. "Don't do that. There's no such thing as a sexual identity playbook, Connor. Not everyone has a lightbulb moment when they're kids. For some people, it takes a lifetime to understand how they're wired, and I will never give you a tough time for wanting space to understand how you want to come out as bi or gay or whatever fits you best.

"I really wish you had let me in, though." He tried not to mourn the days they'd wasted not being there for each other. "You should have had support while you were working on figuring yourself out. That feeling you described about it everything hitting you at once? That can be a scary, lonely time and I know coming to terms isn't always easy on your own."

"I wish I'd stayed. Not just for me, but for you." Connor levered himself upright. "Walking away that morning, cutting you out—those were the worst things I could have done to either of us. If I could go back and do it all over, I would. I'm sure I'd still get something wrong but at least we—"

"—could have been there for each other," Judah finished. Melancholy filled him at the understanding he saw in Connor's face. "That's why I hated the idea of telling you to fuck off. There are a lot of things I still have to learn about you, Connor, but I knew from the day we met that you have a good heart. There was no way you weren't hurting too during these last weeks, especially on top of having to relearn how you fit into the world."

Connor cupped Judah's face in his palms. "That is such a *you* thing to say. Caring, decent, and kind, even after the way things went down between us. I don't know how you do it."

"Well, I'm actually kind of selfish," Judah whispered. "Not so sure I could do it for anyone else." He wasn't surprised when Connor shook his head.

"You should give yourself more credit, Judah. I do."

Judah had no answer to that. Not with the man he loved smiling at him, his pretty eyes shining.

"Judah," Connor whispered, his breath warm against Judah's chin a second before he brushed their lips together.

Oh.

Just as the first time they'd kissed, even that feather-light touch jolted Judah's system. He forced himself to hold still, determined to follow Connor's lead, but it was so fucking hard as Connor kissed him again and Judah sighed into it, unable to resist the way this man made him feel.

A need to touch and be touched unfurled in Judah. He sank down with Connor onto the sofa cushions, their kisses slow and potent, neither in a hurry to do anything more than connect. Judah's bones turned liquid.

Buoyed by sensation, he swept Connor up, heat pooling in his core when Connor melted into him. He slipped his knee between Connor's and kissed the tiny moan off his lips, desire unfolding inside him as Connor squeezed Judah's thigh with his own. Sliding his hand under Connor's shirt collar, he stroked his warm skin, luxuriating in the simple contact. He groaned when Connor ran his fingers through Judah's hair, reveling in the shivers that raced down his spine, and kissed Connor deeper, his heart pounding at the slide of their tongues.

He shivered when Connor broke away only to press his forehead to Judah's.

"I need you, Judah."

Connor's quiet voice cut through the hormones hazing Judah's brain. There was reverence and passion in those words, and they stripped Judah bare. This was more than lust for them both. This attachment went deeper than sex, and Judah knew it in his bones.

He was in love. And he felt in his heart that Connor wasn't far behind.

The last remnants of Judah's doubt started to crumble as he cradled Connor's face in his hands. "I'm here," he said, and they shared a smile before they got lost in one another again.

SEVENTEEN

A feeling of being settled—steadied really, after navigating shaky ground for too many days—expanded inside Connor as the evening unfolded. God, he'd missed this so much. Talking and laughing with Judah. Judah's kisses. The way he held Connor so close. His smile that always made Connor feel like his heart was too big to fit in his chest.

Missing Judah had infiltrated every part of Connor's life, but he hadn't realized just how deeply this man had gotten under his skin until tonight, when he'd been given a second chance to grab hold of everything he'd turned his back on just weeks ago. And Connor was going to do his utmost to make sure he wouldn't need a third chance because he wasn't going anywhere without this man by his side.

He just needed to convince Judah that he was serious about making their relationship work. That's what Connor wanted with Judah: to pick up where they'd left off and continue transforming their friendship into the something more he'd glimpsed during that first snowstorm. Something strong. Maybe ... Jeez, maybe something that looked a lot like the big, romantic story Connor knew Judah wanted. Having a forever person wasn't something Connor had ever considered for himself, but he thought it sounded damned amazing now, and not even a little bit terrifying.

Try not to get ahead of yourself, pal—you've still got a lot of work to do.

Connor sighed. He could always count on his brain to deliver a dose of reality. But Judah still harbored doubts. Connor could see them in his eyes sometimes when he met Connor's gaze, flashes of surprise and wariness, as if he couldn't believe Connor was there, mixed with something raw that dented Connor's heart. It didn't matter that Judah would blink and find a smile in the next second, seeming to shake off any dark clouds. Connor knew he was still hurting. The shadows under his eyes spoke silent volumes. Hell, the guy had packed up and moved himself two hundred miles to the *woods* in an effort to put Connor behind him. No way Connor was forgetting that anytime soon, or the stark fear that had bolted through him as he'd talked with Levi and Molly the week before and realized Judah really was just gone.

More than anything, he wanted to erase the pain that lingered in Judah's gaze. To gain Judah's trust back and know he'd never doubt that Connor was in this with him, deeper than he knew how to say.

Not that Connor knew quite yet how he'd go about doing that. He was ready to try anything necessary to fix things between Judah and him, however, and he'd keep at it no matter how long it took.

They'd made out for a long time on the couch, passion waxing full and fiery before it gentled again, over and over, and the pure pleasure of just feeling Judah against him had made

Connor's body buzz. He'd reveled in Judah's soft, needy noises, though neither made a move to go any further than tangling their limbs together as they petted and groaned.

And while Connor had loved that—loved Judah's gasps and shivers and the way his own body had throbbed with want—he'd craved reconnecting even more and he'd basked in being with Judah while the rest of the world had faded into the background. He'd felt how badly Judah had needed that too, in the way he'd clung to Connor, eyes so, so serious as he'd moved his gaze over Connor's face, as if trying to memorize every detail in between kisses that had been so deep and drugging Connor's head had spun.

They'd even drowsed together, so drunk on touch and comfort that it had been easy for Connor to coast into the twilight space between wakefulness and true sleep, only to surface again and start over, nuzzling at a dozy Judah until he woke and kissed Connor back.

"Much as I know how much you love this couch, there are actual beds on the premises," Judah murmured now, his lips moving against Connor's temple. "You're gonna have to move first though, because you've got me pinned pretty good."

Connor snuggled in closer and gave Judah another squeeze, tightening his thighs around Judah's hips because he knew how much Judah liked that. Sure enough, Judah loosed a low groan, his groin hard and hot against Connor's high.

"Killing me slowly here, Con."

"That's the plan."

"Wait, you have a plan?"

The smile in Judah's voice sent a happy pulse through Connor and he smirked as he levered himself up into a sitting position. "Mmm-hmm. A plan that includes keeping you here in this house by hiding all the snow shovels, so we take tomorrow off," he said, teasing Judah with his own words. "Maybe do something outrageous like make pancakes and bacon for brunch *after* we sleep in until noon."

Judah squished his eyes shut and really laughed, the peals ringing through the big room around them. "You're such a smartass," he said, still chuckling as Connor hauled him up, though that merry sound trailed off into an appreciative sigh when Connor took Judah's mouth in a heated kiss. "I think I might like this plan," he murmured, still sipping at Connor's lips. "Especially since I bought some pancake mix just the other day on my lunch break."

"That's my guy." Connor sat back enough to get a look at Judah, but his heart sank a little when the sparkle in those gray-green eyes clouded over. "What is it?"

"You called me your guy," Judah said, all traces of laughter gone. "Kind of took me by surprise."

Ignoring the heat rising in his face, Connor took one of Judah's hands in his and weaved their fingers together. "As in a good surprise or bad?"

"Good, I think." Judah drew a deep breath and slowly blew it out. "What do you see happening between us from here, Connor? Earlier, you said you're ready to be more than friends and I really like the sound of that. You already know I care about you and the physical stuff well ... I'm so down." He smiled at Connor, but faintly, and his eyes stayed terribly serious as he continued.

"I can't help wondering if you're ready to even *have* a guy." He gave Connor's hand a quick squeeze. "I'm not going to try to tell you your own mind or pretend I know what you need better than you do yourself. That said, coming to terms with being queer isn't an overnight thing for most people and, excuse me for saying so, but I suspect you're still working to get there."

Connor cleared his throat. "You're right about me working on coming to terms with being queer. I'm not even sure how I identify though I guess it'd be as bi or pan. And I know it's going to take time to be truly sure. I'm done fighting it though. I have things to learn about myself and trying to close off pieces and pretend they don't exist ... it's not good for me at all and I need to face that, even when it scares me a little."

"God, you're strong." Ducking his head, Judah raised Connor's hand to his lips and pressed a kiss against his knuckles. "I'm so proud of you, Con, and I hope you are too."

"I'm not ..." Connor huffed a sigh. No, he wasn't ready to pat himself on the back just yet. "I just want to be me, Jude. And stop being *afraid* to be me, as much as I can."

"Okay. But I need you to understand that dating a man is going to change how the world sees you, not just once but over and over. You'll lose track of how many times you'll have to decide whether or not to come out, just in the course of living your regular life."

"Is that why you wear the Pride pins? To send a signal to the world?"

"No. I wear the pins for me." Judah gave Connor a gentle smile. "They definitely send a signal, sure, but how a person chooses to interpret it is on them."

Certainty, as warm and comforting as the softest blanket, wrapped itself around Connor. "I'm ready to send signals of my own," he said, "and, honestly, I think that's down to you more than anything else."

"What does that mean? That you want to try out dating a man and start with me? Because I'm not ready to be anyone's test drive, Connor, and definitely not yours. Not when I—" Judah stuttered to a stop, ears turning red as his throat worked. A sudden, haunted expression settled over his face, his eyes turning glassy as he continued. "You mean too much to me to put either of us through that."

Pulse speeding, Connor pressed a quick kiss against the corner of Judah's mouth. What the heck had he been about to say to Connor before he'd stopped himself?

"No, I don't want to *try*," Connor said, "I want to do, and *only* with you." Ally's teasing about Yoda came back to him but Connor had never felt less like laughing. "I don't need a test drive with you, Judah, because you're the one I want. Have I put a lot of thought into what it would be like to date other men? No. I have thought a lot about dating *you*, however, because you're the right person for me." He shrugged. "And maybe I know that because we were already halfway there without really realizing it and that makes it easy to *know* I want that and you every day."

"I'm not sure I understand."

"Okay, well, what would you call the stuff we usually do together? The knitting, the shopping, the hanging out over coffee or a meal?"

"I guess I'd call them low-key dates." Judah's words came slowly. "Huh. I mean, I'd do the same with any friend, but I knew from the start I liked you as more than a friend, even if I never said so."

"Exactly." Connor smiled. "I felt the same but just didn't know it, and we had all of that *before* I ever even thought about kissing you."

Judah shook his head. "Jeez, you're right. Not sure I'd ever engaged in unconscious dating before I met you, but I liked it all the same."

Connor barked out a laugh. "We'll have to come up with another name for it though, because 'unconscious dating' sounds super weird." He kissed Judah again, softer this time, and lingered a little as he worked up the courage to ask a question that had been circling in his brain for the last several minutes.

"What do *you* see happening between us from here, Judah?" he asked, insides going tight even as he forced out the words. "Do you think we can pick up where we left off? Because I want that with you so much. I know you probably don't trust me after everything that happened, but—" he made himself stop when Judah shook his head and hardly dared to breathe.

"I'm not sure it's as easy as picking up where we left off. I'm not even sure it would be smart to go about it that way," Judah said, each quiet word like a stone against Connor's heart.

"Okay," he got out, his throat gone so narrow he practically croaked. Dropping his gaze, Connor shifted his weight carefully, trying not to jostle Judah as he stood, but Judah was ready for him, moving just as swiftly to stop Connor's flight.

"Damn, I'm sorry." He caught hold of Connor's chin with his fingers, touch gentle but firm, regret rolling off him in big waves. "I didn't mean that the way it sounded, Connor. Like I didn't want to try at all. Because I do."

Slowly lifting his gaze, Connor stared at Judah, breath catching at the affection he saw there in his face. "You do?"

"Yes, baby, so much."

Connor had to shut his eyes at the endearment, the hope in his heart leaping so high it was like a kick in the chest. He let out a shaky breath as Judah gathered him into a hug, voice low and soothing as he spoke.

"What I was trying to say was that I think we should start *over* and not just again, so we can do things right. I need to set things straight with you too, and that way we both go into this with our eyes wide open. It's not right for me to hold back things you need to know because I'm second guessing whether you're ready to hear them."

"What do you want to tell me?" Connor sat back, frowning at the way Judah was chewing the inside of his cheek. "I can't promise I'll always know what to say, but you can tell me anything, Jude, and I'll always want to listen."

"You need to be careful with a promise like that, Con, because I'm going to hold you to it." Judah gave an unsteady laugh. "The thing is, my heart was ready for a lot more before you ever kissed me, but I wasn't ready to admit it even to myself. But I know now that I was never going to be able to stay just friends, even if you hadn't walked out on me."

Connor pushed in closer, spreading his hands wide over Judah's ribs. "God, I wish I hadn't. And I'm so damned sorry I hurt you."

"I know." Judah's voice was thin, like fraying threads. "You did though, and if I hadn't felt like my heart was in pieces, I'd have hated you almost as much as I hated myself for letting it happen."

"Hey, no." Vision blurring, Connor blinked hard. "What happened wasn't your fault. I'm the one who messed up. And once the fear got the best of me, I couldn't get hold of it long enough to stop what I was doing. I was afraid to choose you—*us*—and be honest about who I am, most of all to myself."

Judah nodded. "I understand that. I've felt the same kind of fear, going back to when I was a kid and just figuring out I was gay. But if we're really going to do this and start over so we can do things right, then you need to know where I stand. I don't want another day to go by where I don't tell you I love you because I'm afraid of scaring you off."

Oh, holy shit.

Connor's breath caught, the world around him grinding to a halt. Hope shone in Judah's eyes, but there was something darker there, too, echoed in the way he lifted his chin, meeting Connor's gaze head on. Resignation, maybe. Like he was steeling himself for the worst. Probably because he was waiting for Connor to freak out and run out the door, just like he had the last time Judah had put himself out there.

EIGHTEEN

What is wrong with you?

Judah heaved a quiet sigh. He really hated how much that voice in his head sounded like Levi right now. But seriously, why was he like this? He and Connor were in the middle of patching up their friendship. Still figuring out who they were to each other and where the lines between them lay. And fuck, Judah had *just* said all kinds of things about starting over not even five minutes before he'd gone and blurted out an "I love you" like it was no big deal.

Except it was a big deal. And how Judah had been feeling for this man for what seemed a very long time. He was tired of keeping it quiet and tired of drawing lines. He thought Connor had a right to know how Judah felt, too, and that Judah wanting to be around him wasn't just about making himself feel good, in or out of bed. Judah wanted to give Connor more. Everything, if Connor would let him. Provided Judah hadn't just scared him off for a second time.

"Damn." Working hard not to freak out at Connor's very wide eyes, Judah ran his hands over Connor's shoulders and gave him a small smile. "I really meant to work up to saying that and not just lob it at you without any warning like a snowball. I think being up here with no one to talk to but Siri every night really messes with my filters."

A smile ghosted over Connor's lips, and oh, that quieted Judah's spinning thoughts so much. "I'll bet. Did you mean it?" he asked, voice whisper-soft, eyes liquid and so shy, like even looking at Judah was hard. "No one outside of family's ever said something like that to me before and—"

"I meant it. And I've felt this way for a while now." Judah raised a hand to Connor's cheek, brushing his knuckles over the bristly beard. "I know it seems fast, especially since we're still figuring things out and not even living in the same city at the moment. But somewhere between your first knitting class and that first kiss ..." He ducked his head, face absolutely on fire as he laughed softly. "I was just gone." His insides trembled as Connor pulled him close. "I really didn't mean to tell you *now*, though, but it's like my brain and mouth aren't connected. I'm sorry if I'm freaking you out."

Connor spoke over Judah's rambling. "You're not. Whatever you're thinking right now about me being scared or put off or whatever, I'm not feeling any of that." He rubbed Judah's back with one hand, big circles that loosened some of the tension in Judah's body. "Jeez, Jude. You okay? You're strung so tight, it's like you're about to snap."

God, this guy. He really was too much. Judah couldn't help but smile even as he buried his face in Connor's neck, forcing himself to exhale past the emotions crashing through him. Joy and relief that Connor wasn't running, mixed with real fear that he absolutely would once he'd had a chance to think it all through. Because for all his caring looks and words and gestures, Connor was still so new to this and had been nowhere near ready to hear the three words Judah already wanted to say again, let alone say them back.

"I don't mean to be," Judah said. "I'm ... nervous."

"About what?"

"Saying the wrong words, like maybe I just did, or not saying enough. And of making the same mistake as last time and pushing you for too much, too soon."

"You're not pushing me for anything." Connor's lips moved against Judah's ear. "You didn't before, either. I *want* to be here, Jude. Why else would I have dragged my sorry self to Vermont?"

"To get snowbound somewhere new?"

"No." Connor chuckled, voice gruff when he spoke next. "To be with you. Start over, like you said, and learn how to do this together. I want that for us, and I wouldn't say so if it weren't true."

"I know you wouldn't." Judah pressed a kiss against Connor's neck before he sat back. He did, too. Connor had always been honest with Judah, even when lying would have been easier for them both. "And I'd love to start over with you, too. Kind of a spoiler alert, though, since you already know I'm stupid for you."

Connor smiled brighter than Judah could ever remember seeing. "I'm not complaining about that." He wrapped Judah up in a rib creaking hug. "Not gonna complain if you want to kiss me some more, either."

"Oh, I want," Judah got out past a groan filled with equal parts promise and pain. "Though you need to ease off on the bear hugs, big guy, or our first try at starting over is going to happen in a hospital because you broke more than my brain."

He covered Connor's laughter with kisses, sweet and deep, gladly losing himself in those touches for a little while. His and

Connor's breaths were coming fast by the time Judah pulled back again, and he smiled at Connor's soft noise of complaint.

"Like I said, there are beds we can use." Judah stood, one hand out to Connor who immediately grabbed hold so Judah could pull him up. "Plus, mornings are hella bright in this room thanks to the windows, and your eyeballs will thank you for moving come dawn."

Hands linked, he led Connor to the spiral staircase which they climbed in near silence, and Judah couldn't resist pulling Connor in the second they stepped into the loft. They got across the room somehow in between kisses, the air between them crackling with an urgency that made Judah's skin pebble with goosebumps. He tugged his t-shirt up and over his head, then helped Connor do the same, drinking in the expanse of peaches and cream skin with his gaze.

Running his palms over Connor's chest, Judah's groin throbbed as he stroked the light blond fur, while Connor simply watched him, hands on Judah's waist, his expression almost dreamy.

"Is this okay?" Judah asked, his voice quiet despite the lust rolling through him. He needed Connor's 'yes' right now as much as he needed Connor's touch.

"Very okay," Connor's deep rumble went right to Judah's balls. "I missed this, Jude." He leaned in for another kiss. "Missed you, so damned much."

Judah's throat went tight. "Me too."

Gathering Connor close, he delighted in the heat rising off his skin, and he feasted on Connor's mouth, their lips meeting again and again. Connor met him kiss for kiss, stroking Judah's shoulders and back with his hands, his touch unhesitating as they slowly stripped each other down. Judah bit his lip as Connor's cock sprang free of his boxers, rigid length bouncing gently against his abdomen as Judah laid him out on the mattress, then stepped back so he could simply look his fill.

"Gorgeous," he whispered, almost without meaning to, his heart expanding under the force of Connor's beautiful smile. Connor set a hand on Judah's hip, seeming to need that contact, and a small sigh came out of him as he stroked the meat of Judah's thigh. Judah's cock twitched in time with his groan.

Quickly pulling lube from the nightstand, he climbed into bed beside Connor, who moved the hand from Judah's thigh to his lower back, guiding him so Judah could settle on top of Connor, both moaning as their dicks came in contact. Connor gasped as Judah ground down into him, hands coming up to grab Judah's ass now, and he gasped again when Judah moaned louder.

"Fuck, Connor."

"Yeah."

Connor's eyelids fluttered closed under another scorching kiss. He was so *hard* against Judah, little noises of pleasure stoking Judah's need. There was fire in his gaze when he opened his eyes again, but the look he leveled at Judah—the raw trust there, woven all through with tenderness and desire—made Judah's heart squeeze.

"Never expected this," Connor said, "or you. The things I feel for you ... They're so much bigger than you can know, Jude. Bigger than I can say even because I just don't have the right words." Bringing a hand up, he cupped Judah's cheek, his expression changing, filling with wonder, and knowing and a fierce happiness Judah could only imagine matched his own.

He feels it too.

The something between them that was deep and strong, despite the time they'd spent apart. Connection. A bond. Love.

Connor dragged his thumb over Judah's lips and fuck, Judah had to fight to keep his eyes open.

"Never wanted to be around someone the way I do you," Connor murmured. "And maybe that's because I never needed someone like this. I was good mostly being on my own. But not being with you feels like something important is missing."

"I feel the same. But you have got me, Connor. I'm here."

"I know. You've got me, too."

Parting his lips slightly, Judah pressed a kiss against Connor's thumb then took it in his mouth, lust searing inside him as the intensity in Connor's face changed again, his features going slack and dazed. Movements slow and deliberate, Judah sucked and toyed with his tongue, making a show of it, until Connor gently pulled his thumb from Judah's mouth and captured his lips in a deep kiss that made Judah's breath catch.

He melted into Connor, rutting slow and easy, the movements too small and gentle to get either of them off as the heat between them mounted. Connor wound his arms around Judah, squeezing him tight, but at the same time spread his legs wide so Judah could leverage his weight and pin Connor down, eyes rolling behind his closed lids. God*damn*, he liked that this big, strong man turned to putty in his hands. The way Connor just *yielded* to Judah in moments like these, really let him in and take control.

Their ragged breaths echoed around the loft as they made out, and Connor shuddered hard when Judah palmed his cock.

"Oh, Jesus." He canted his hips into Judah's touch, a whine in his throat. "Need. Mmm, Jude. Need to touch you, too. Please."

"Yeah. Want that too." Judah backed off enough for Connor to get a hand between them, gut clenching hard as a big, hot hand wrapped around him. "Oh, *fuck*. Love your hands on me," he whispered, then moaned into Connor's kiss, the urgency he felt in it slowly dismantling what remained of Judah's control.

God, he was going to lose it from kissing and Connor's hands on him alone.

"I love it too." Connor's cheeks and neck were flushed red when he drew back, skin sheened with sweat, and the eager light in his eyes made Judah grin. "Want more, Jude. To get closer. Feel you all over. Make you fly, the way you do me."

"You do, baby. But I want to fly together." Reaching for the lube, Judah waggled the little bottle between his fingers and raised an eyebrow at Connor. "Trust me?"

"Always," Connor said, that one word and everything it carried hurtling through Judah like a shot.

This man was here to stay. Wherever 'here' was of course, be it Boston or Stowe, or wherever their paths might take them. Judah could feel it, deep in his core. The bond between them, so fucking strong, wrapped in emotions so thick Judah could almost touch them.

He took Connor's mouth again without warning, going deep with his tongue and fucking until Connor's moans were steady. He lay wrecked and breathless when Judah sat back, and he looked shell-shocked as Judah straddled Connor's waist with his knees.

"I'm gonna blow you," Judah said as he wet his fingers with lube, and he chuckled at the way lust instantly transformed Connor's face, eyes going heavy-lidded and dark. "Uh-huh, I thought you'd like that."

Connor's cheeks turned pink, but he laughed too, his smile big as he slung his arms around Judah's neck. "You know I do. But what about you? I want to make you feel good, too."

"I love that you asked." He pressed a kiss into the hollow of Connor's throat before he handed him the lube. "I also love being jacked while I suck dick, and you liked that when we did it together, right? Driving me nuts with those big hands of yours?" He gasped when Connor palmed him, his insides going all melty. "Fuck. Keep doing stuff like that and you'll get me off in no time, plus you'll have a chance to explore."

Connor's eyes gleamed. "I can do that. Wanna find out what you like best." He kept his hands on Judah as they got him turned around so he faced Connor's feet, dragging his fingers over Judah's shoulders and spine and ass, his touches trailing fire. "Mmm. Love the way you feel."

More of that murmured praise in his ears, Judah crouched over Connor, grasping his hips with his hands and easing them both onto their sides

Heat blasted through Judah as he eyed Connor's tight abdomen, his dick red and rigid and mere inches from Judah's face. Though dying to taste Connor again, Judah pressed his face into the juncture between Connor's hip and groin first, kissing the soft skin and breathing in soap and musk and Connor, groaning softly when Connor brought his knees up and cradled Judah between them, his powerful thighs pressing into Judah's ribs and squeezing just so, turning Judah's crank even tighter.

Judah bucked his hips when Connor took him in hand, a low growl in his throat as slick fingers grasped him, and quickly took Connor's cock in his mouth. Pleasure rattled up his spine at Connor's gasp and he wasn't surprised when Connor's grip loosened only to recover a heartbeat later, a soft whine reaching his ears. But then Connor's mouth was on Judah's belly, pressing lingering kisses there as Connor slowly jacked him, breath hot and fast against Judah's skin.

Judah gorged himself on Connor, wrapping his hands around the small of Connor's back, urging him through touch to thrust deeper and harder into Judah's mouth. Pleasure circled in his core, coiling tighter each time Connor thrust into

Judah's mouth until Judah was so aroused, he felt like he was floating.

He loved sucking cock enough that he could sometimes get off untouched, especially when he felt close to his partner, the way he did with Connor. Judah had never felt this level of connection to another man before, however, and he felt seconds away from blowing, especially since Connor *wasn't* letting him go untouched. His first few strokes had been somewhat tentative, but he was working Judah without hesitation now, grip not too tight, thumbing the cockhead with each pass while massaging Judah's balls with his other hand, doing his part to spin the feedback loop of sensation between them even higher.

Eyes still screwed shut, Judah slid the first two fingers of one hand in alongside Connor's shaft, triumph bolting through him at Connor's loud curse, the oath quickly devolving into a drawn-out moan. Judah pumped the fingers slowly, teasing Connor's shaft with his fingertips before he pulled them from his mouth and slid them along the cleft of Connor's ass, lust radiating through him as Connor's body tensed. Judah circled Connor's rim, groaning when Connor's released a strangled cry, his thrusts coming faster.

Heat licked up Judah's spine. He teased Connor, intent on fingering him until he lost his mind, but his eyes flew open as wet heat suddenly bathed the tip of his own dick.

Oh, my God.

Judah shuddered hard, his groan so wild it didn't sound like him at all. A mouth on his dick always felt amazing, but this was *Connor* gently sucking and licking, and that heightened everything Judah was feeling to almost unbearable levels. Pulling off, he swore weakly, the desire inside him electric and unpredictable, like a live wire. He wasn't going to last long like this.

"Fuck," he got out, voice a raspy disaster. He struggled for moment, almost more desperate to see Connor than he was to come. "Connor, you don't have to—"

"Want to." Connor pressed another kiss against Judah's shaft. "Been thinking about this for a while now. Hoping I'd get a chance to try it with you."

His growly tone made Judah burn white hot. He'd only heard Connor sound like that once before, when they'd been tangled around each other in Judah's bed back in Boston, and he'd made Judah come so hard he'd seen stars. Connor uttered a low, pleased sound now as he took Judah slightly deeper, hands wrapped around Judah's ass, and all Judah could do was take Connor back in his mouth and make him come before he lost it himself.

Sinking one finger deep inside Connor, he curled it and sought out Connor's prostate, the change in Connor's body immediate. He trembled in Judah's arms, needy noises forlorn and nonstop, his body jolting every time Judah tapped the gland. He pulled off Judah without warning, Judah's name on his lips as he came in big shudders, face pressed to Judah's thighs as his cock pulsed, the bitter salt of his cum everything Judah wanted.

Only after Connor was a boneless heap on the mattress did Judah let the spent cock fall from his lips, and he was breathing hard like he'd been sprinting, his body practically vibrating with his need to get off. His movements were unsteady as he scooted backward slightly, but he felt a surge of pride as he met Connor's gaze along the length of their bodies and Connor held out a hand, his eyes aglow.

"C'mere," Connor murmured, his voice thick. "Was that okay when I—?"

"*So* good. Perfect. God. Almost lost my mind." Crawling up beside Connor, Judah settled into his embrace and he hissed loudly when Connor once more spread his palm over Judah's cock, pulling words from him in a torrent. "Oh, *fuck.* You ... Didn't wanna come in your face your first time. Not unless I could see it, anyway. An' I do want that, some time. Because God, I need that."

"Me too." Connor's laughter buoyed Judah up, but it was the promise in his eyes that made his heart squeeze tight and start to fall apart in earnest.

"Mmm, Con. I'm gonna come, baby."

"Good. Want that. Want you to come on me."

"That's ... totally gonna happen, right fucking now."

Holding Judah close, Connor rolled half on top of him, smiling at Judah's breathless hum. He dropped kisses all over Judah's face as they worked his cock together and Judah lost it within seconds, orgasm rolling through him in giant waves that cracked him wide open. Soaring high, he hung suspended for an endless time, too far gone to return Connor's kisses as his cock pulsed between them, but he knew he told Connor he loved him because he wanted to, and he meant every word.

His thoughts went distant and fuzzy for a bit, but he was aware of Connor holding him the whole time he floated back down. Funny, how only yesterday Judah would have been nervous—frightened even—of a moment like this, and so sure Connor's nerves would get the best of him and that he'd run.

That fear *had* faded to almost nothing in the last several hours, though. They still had some work left to do to get their relationship back on track, not least being that Judah needed to get back to Boston where he belonged. But he didn't doubt that Connor *wanted* to do the work every bit as much as Judah did, or that every second would be worth it.

Once his brain had come back online, Judah used a corner of the sheet to wipe them down, and though he tried like hell not to, heaved a mighty yawn that made Connor smile.

"Sorry." Judah chuckled. "Orgasms tend to zap my batteries, but I promise I'm not going to pass out this time."

Connor settled back onto the mattress with a quiet sigh, his cheek on Judah's shoulder. "I wouldn't mind if you did. I like being with you like this."

"You like me passed out and snoring?"

"I like that you'll hold me even then, yes," Connor shot back with a laugh. "But I like pretty much everything we do together. The way you make me laugh and your cooking. Our talks." He tilted his head enough to meet Judah's gaze. "Just being us."

"Me, too." Judah ran a finger over the color blooming in Connor's cheeks. "What's that about?"

"I love the way you look at me. Like—"

"Like I love you," Judah said with a soft smile.

"Yeah, like that." The roses in Connor's cheeks grew brighter, but his gaze was soft and adoring. "I meant it when I said I haven't had that with anyone before, Judah. Never had anything serious with anyone I've dated, like you have."

Oh, hell. Connor feeling even a little insecure over Judah's past relationships was the last thing Judah wanted. Especially since every one of those past relationships—even with Seb—felt almost insubstantial compared to the feelings he had for the guy in his arms.

"I've had more practice with relationships, true, but they weren't like what we have." Judah licked his lips when Connor raised an eyebrow. "You told me that figuring out you were attracted to men was like understanding your whole world had shifted and everything looked and felt different from that point on. That's what loving you is like for me. I've had feelings for other men before, yes. But none of those men were you, Connor. This ..."

This could be forever.

Judah drew a deep breath, his heart leaping at the thought, sweet-scary words that he knew needed to go unspoken for now as he and Connor found their way back together.

"This thing you and I have is different," he said instead, and smiled at the soft expression that fell over Connor's face. "Special. That may sound like a line, but I promise you it's not."

"I know." Connor's smile warmed Judah like sunlight after a rainstorm. "I feel that way too. And like nothing would make me happier than giving you everything." He laid his palm over Judah's heart and smiled. "I'm glad I got to have this with you."

NINETEEN

One year later - Thursday, January 9

CONNOR SMILED at the sleepy baby sprawled on his chest. "I know how you feel," he said. He'd been lounging with little Titus in the overstuffed chair by Hook Me's counter for twenty minutes now and both were losing the battle against sleep. Not that Connor minded. Unwinding with Titus after a shift was one of his favorite ways to close out a day, even if the little guy tended to conk out after Connor fed him his six o'clock bottle.

"You guys all right?" Olivia asked, voice quiet as she sorted through wooly hanks of yarn. She smiled when Connor slid his gaze in her direction without moving.

"I'm good," he said just as quietly. "Titus isn't going to make it upstairs awake, though."

"I'm not sure you are either, my friend—you look entirely too comfortable." She glanced toward the door that led to the basement workroom, then set the yarn down. "You want me to take him?" she asked. "I can shop another time if you want to head up now."

Connor gave a small shake of his head. "No worries," he said. "Judah shouldn't be long."

At Olivia's nod, he fell quiet again, his blinks steadily growing longer as he soaked in his surroundings. The muted music and soft chair. Voices rising and falling from the workroom below. The warm, easy weight of the baby asleep on top of him.

This is nice.

He stirred at a light touch along his hairline and blinked, his head muzzy. Judah leaned over him, hip pressed against the arm of the chair. He smoothed back some stray hairs that had escaped from the knot Connor wore at the crown of his head, an indulgent grin on his face.

"Hey, gorgeous." He glanced from Connor to the baby's still form, then caught Connor's eye again. "You boys ready to take this sleepy party upstairs?"

"Uh-huh." Connor leaned into Judah's touch. "Didn't mean to doze off. Is the circle all set?"

"Yup. Levi's got them until eight," Judah said, his tone smug. "It's not often he volunteers to take over the stitch-and-bitch, so I figured I'd take him up on it while I had the chance." Pausing, he dropped a soft kiss against Connor's temple. "You didn't need to wait for me, you know—you could have gone on up."

Connor nodded. "I know. But I like coming in here even if I'm not working with needles or a hook and yarn, and Liv needed to pick up some stuff. Is she all set?"

"Yes, she is," Olivia said and held up two big bags. "Judah got me sorted out when he came upstairs, right after he took about a million shots with his phone of the two of you napping."

Her evil grin became laughter when Connor made duck lips with his mouth. Ears reddening, Judah ducked his head, but he was smiling, because he knew Connor really didn't mind having his photo taken. Connor thought it was cute that Judah loved seeing him with Titus and he couldn't have cared less if his man told everyone in the city.

Straightening up, Judah held out a hand. "Much as I hate to bug you when you're so comfortable, we really should get out of here while we can. If anyone in the circle wanders up here and gets an eyeful of you with that baby, we'll be stuck here forever."

Connor knew his eyes got big. He shot a furtive look at the door leading to the basement and muttered, "I'm gonna need a little help to get vertical," then held his breath as Olivia set down her bags and reached for her son.

Somehow, they got Titus wrapped and out of the shop without waking him and carrying the baby stroller around the corner to the resident's entrance did Connor good too. The chilly air chased the cobwebs from his brain and just holding Judah's hand gave him a much-needed charge of energy.

Connor smiled. Touching Judah always made him feel better.

Lovely, cozy feelings filled him as Judah opened the door to their home over the shop. Connor sometimes wondered when the thrill he felt in these moments would fade, but, then again, his world had changed radically in the last year and maybe it was no wonder he was still growing accustomed to it. He certainly wasn't taking anything for granted, especially the man in front of him.

"I'll open some wine if you want to give Liv a hand with Titus," Judah said. "Ally gave me her recipe for chicken and dumplings," he added for Olivia's benefit as he helped her out of her coat, "and I rebooted it with some kickass matzo balls. I am not kidding when I say that Levi lost his mind a little after tasting it."

Olivia hummed, swaying the baby in her arms gently. "That sounds fantastic. Dimitri is going to be so bummed that he missed out." She laid her cheek against Titus's head. "Okay if I put him down on your bed?"

"Absolutely," Connor replied. "We set up the pillows and the blanket before we left for work this morning, so you should be all set. Go on and I'll be there in a sec."

He waited for Judah to hang the coats in the closet before pulling him into a hug. "Hi," he said, contentment running all through him at Judah's smile.

"Hi." Linking his arms around Connor's neck, Judah reached up with one hand and carefully tugged at the band that kept Connor's hair in a knot. He ran his fingers through the long tresses as they tumbled free, long enough now that they lay on Connor's shoulders. Judah pressed a quick peck on Connor's lips. "How was your day?"

"The usual—bananas." Connor grinned back. "Better now, though." He kissed Judah not once but twice, and only let go when a little sigh came out of him.

"You don't play fair," Judah murmured, his eyes glowing hot. "You're lucky that's one of my favorite things about you."

Stretching up on his toes, he bussed Connor loudly on the cheek then peeled himself away, twisting out of reach when Connor made a playful swipe in his direction. "Go on," Judah said with a wave toward the bedrooms. "Make sure Olivia's got what she needs before she thinks we forgot about her."

Olivia had already settled Titus on the bed when Connor walked in, and she was fluffing the ring of pillows they placed around the baby to keep him from rolling too far while he slept.

"You are so gone for that man," she said. "And he's just as

bad. I'll never forgive you if I don't get an invite to your wedding."

Connor laughed softly through the heat that rose in his cheeks and reached for the blanket that lay across the foot of the bed. "Who says Judah and I are getting married? Do you know something I don't?"

"Would you be mad if I did?" Olivia snorted at Connor's wide-eyed look. "I'm *kidding*, Con," she said. "I know you think about forever with this guy though, so I'm stating for the record that I want an invite to the wedding, whenever and wherever it happens. You wouldn't have even met Judah if it weren't for me!"

Connor shook his head and smiled some more but knew his friend had a point. Without Olivia's urging, he might never have walked into Hook Me, a simple act that had changed him in ways he'd never have imagined.

Life without Judah was unimaginable. Connor couldn't comprehend not coming home to this snug little flat. Not knowing Levi and Molly and Harvey and their seemingly endless love and support. Or sharing everything he had here in Boston with James and Ally who loved him just as fiercely.

Olivia ran a hand over the weighted blanket that covered Titus's sleeping form. Judah had fashioned it for Connor from a pearl gray, super chunky wool and used his arms in place of needles. The blanket's thick, massively oversized stitches gave it a delicious weight that made being wrapped in it feel like settling into a full body hug. That sensation of almost being swaddled helped tame Connor's thoughts when they raced too fast to allow him to unplug, and the effect was more than double if Judah was there to hang on to Connor too.

"This is my next project," Olivia said with a nod toward the blanket. "Titus always naps so hard when he's here, I'm hoping

I can replicate the magic at home. Is it really a one-night project?"

"Judah can knock one out in under an hour, so sure," Connor replied, "and Titus isn't the only one who naps hard with that blanket. I brought it with me the last time Judah and I visited River Hill and my brother was *all* over it. Kept stealing the damn thing when my back was turned." He smiled. "Judah ended up knitting another one for James before we left just so we could hang on to this one. I'd have made it myself, but I was still working on figuring out how to crochet so I figured I'd let the guy who does it best take the lead."

Though James's name wasn't mentioned again, Connor's smile lingered as he and Olivia made their way to the kitchen, meeting Levi on the way. Connor's happy feelings always doubled when he considered how far he and his brother had come in the last year.

Accepting Connor's changing sexuality hadn't always been easy for James. But while none of the Devlins would forget that awful night when James had denied his brother's feelings for Judah, Connor had forgiven him without hesitation. Connor had tried to deny those feelings himself in the beginning, after all and, hell, he'd practically run away screaming. Holding a moment of weakness against anyone else just seemed wrong, particularly if that someone worked as hard as James had to repair the parts of their relationship that had cracked.

Ally had helped bridge the gaps, of course. She'd been there for both brothers when they needed her and taken it upon herself to reach out to Judah after she and James had gone home to Maryland. A bond had formed between them with almost no effort at all, fueled by their mutual desire to make the men in their lives happy. They swapped recipes and crochet tips, talked ad nauseum about baseball and *True Detective*, and they were practically old friends by the time Connor had visited River Hill late that summer for James's birthday.

Judah chose to stay home for that trip. He'd soothed Connor's fretting with simple words about wanting to give James more time, though Connor had felt sure that Judah had been the one who'd needed more time; his obvious concern that his presence would make the trip awkward for everyone had wrenched Connor's heart. His absence had been felt all weekend, however, with even James asking about him and after repeated Zoom calls with all three Devlins, Connor felt sure Judah had gotten the message that he was welcome in James and Ally's home any time.

He'd joined them virtually for birthday cake and beamed when James had opened the joint gift from Connor and himself. James's eyes were big and awed as he stared at the gorgeous Aran sweater and Connor had gotten rather choked up too. He knew how much effort had gone into crafting the complex patterns in that cream-colored wool and seeing the satisfaction in Judah's face when he met Connor's eyes through the tablet's screen made Connor fall for him a little more.

That trip to see his family had been the last one Connor had made alone. He'd moved into Judah's apartment as soon as the lease on his apartment had expired and hadn't looked back once. Yes, it had been almost a shock at first, going from the quiet solitude of his little studio to living with someone again, especially since Judah and Levi were currently a package deal with busy, vibrant lives and bigger than life personalities.

Connor loved every minute, though. Loved sharing ups and downs with Judah and learning new things about each other every day. He caught Judah's eye across the table now, as Olivia laughed at Levi's joking, and the two exchanged a smile. Connor would never grow tired of watching those gray-green eyes light up.

"SORRY." Connor groaned as Judah pinned him against the mattress, then bit his lip to quiet another needy noise. "Didn't mean to be loud."

"You're fine," Judah said, his voice amused.

After dinner, they'd ordered a Lyft for Olivia and Titus and walked them downstairs, then Connor had retreated to the bathroom for a hot shower. Judah had been in their room after Connor had emerged and he'd wasted no time peeling the bathrobe and boxer briefs from Connor's body before pushing him down onto the bed. He'd kissed Connor hard and deep and there'd been a mad scramble to strip Judah of his clothes because, *yeah*, Connor wanted more.

Even so, he liked to keep his lovemaking with Judah somewhere below a quiet roar whenever Levi was in the apartment. He was a great kid who totally respected Judah's and Connor's space, but his bedroom was just across the hall and not one of the doors in this place was soundproofed. But Judah responded with another dirty-hot kiss and Connor couldn't help moaning again as a hard dick met his own.

He grunted when they finally came up for air. "You're killing me here, Jude. Levi's—"

"Not even here." Judah's kiss was softer this time, and he wove his fingers into Connor's hair which lay loose and still damp against the pillow, an action that never failed to drive the heat in Connor higher. "Levi is at Billie's tonight," Judah said, "and they're doing a study group until late."

Connor grinned up at him. "You sure about that?"

"So sure." Smirking, Judah ground down into Connor again. "Told him not to come back until after eleven because I'm going to make you scream tonight and I don't want him scarred for life."

Connor's laughter quickly turned to sighs as he and Judah grappled with each other, but it was Judah's turn to gasp when Connor palmed his dick.

"Oh, fuck."

The desire in his voice sent fire coursing under Connor's skin along with an itchy impatience. He bit back a whine as Judah pushed up onto his knees, and he spread his palms over Judah's thighs, needing that connection. He watched Judah lean toward the nightstand and, a moment later, a bottle of lube landed on the mattress by Connor's hip.

"Love you." Connor's chest squeezed as Judah bent over him again.

"Love you, too," Judah said, voice just the least bit raw, a sound that made Connor ache in the sweetest way possible.

They made out for a while, rocking together and gorging on sensation as the heat between them built. Skimming his hands over the small of Judah's back, Connor stroked and petted Judah's ass, his own skin pebbling with goosebumps as Judah wound his arms around Connor's shoulders. He lifted his knees and caged Judah between them, then put just enough pressure on Judah's ribs to make him shudder.

"Fuck, I love it when you do that," Judah whispered, his eyes already glazed. His hands weren't quite steady as he grabbed hold of the lube. "Need you so much."

Quickly wetting his fingers, he took Connor's dick in hand. Connor hissed and arched up into the touch, desire rattling down his spine, and he slung his arms around Judah's neck, his kisses growing steadily more desperate as Judah slowly jacked him. Judah waited until Connor's moans were steady before he reached down and slid a finger inside him. Connor nearly sobbed.

"*Judah.*"

"I know, baby."

Judah kept up the stroking as he worked Connor open, though he made sure no one touch was enough to get Connor off. Connor held on for dear life, his breaths growing ragged as he fought the urge to beg and come and oh, my God, fuck. He really did whine when Judah finally pulled his fingers free.

"Judah! Shit, shit — I can't. I ... *please*."

A sly smile crossed Judah's face. "That's what a man likes to hear," he said.

Judah shifted back. He pushed Connor's knees toward his chest and, rising, aligned their bodies. He used the tip of his dick to trace circles over Connor's rim and Connor held his breath when Judah finally pressed forward. He split Connor open, the razor-edged pleasure so damned good. Heart in his throat, Connor framed Judah's face with his hands.

Judah pushed deeper, his gaze moving from where their bodies were joined to meet Connor's and the world around them stilled. He bottomed out and the burn in Connor bloomed into a delicious pressure he craved more than almost anything. Judah rocked in and out, bliss in his expression, and Connor slid his hands down over Judah's shoulders and arms, then dropped his head back into the pillow, unable to speak beyond a shaky exhale.

"That's it," Judah whispered.

He bent over Connor, grasping him hard around the shoulders, and the full body contact jolted Connor's pleasure higher. Connor brought his legs up around Judah's waist. He abandoned himself to sensation, already so far gone his kisses were clumsy when Judah took his mouth. The coil inside Connor tightened more with each thrust, and he'd barely gotten himself in hand before his balls drew up.

"Close," Connor got out. "More, Jude. Harder. *Need*."

"I'm here."

Fucking Connor hard, Judah reached between them and

when he set his hand over Connor's, that was all it took. Everything went out of focus as the orgasm swamped him. Cum striped Connor's chest and he shook and gasped, aware only as he came down that he was squeezing Judah so tight with his legs that Judah could hardly move.

"Fuck, I love this. Love *you*," Judah panted, a second before his body stiffened and his voice broke. "Oh, God!"

His back arched as he hit his peak and his cry made Connor's heart clench. Gathering him up, Connor held Judah close, sharing lazy kisses with him until they were both calm.

"Liv was teasing me tonight in the shop while you were asleep," Judah said, his voice drowsy and amused and fond all at once. He'd cleaned them both up and helped Connor under the sheets, then spread the weighted blanket over him like a big, cushy cocoon before dimming the lights. "Had a lot to say about you and me getting married."

"Hah, me too." Connor pressed his nose against Judah's skin and smiled through the heat rising in his face. "I was sort of terrified Levi would hear her and we'd end up with a full-fledged drama once your mom and Ally got wind because we didn't talk to them first."

"That would be unfortunate." Judah chuckled. "But they know you're the guy for me, and I think they'd be fine once we explained. We'd just remind them that the only timetable we need is the one we're making up as we go along."

Connor hummed. Judah was right. They'd already come so far, and they'd taken every step together, neither moving forward until the other was ready. Whatever came next, including the forever he wanted with this man, they'd handle it in their own time. Connor trusted Judah—and himself—to get them there.

Tilting his head back so he could catch Judah's eye in the half light, Connor bit his lip. "You're it for me, too, you know."

"Yeah?"

"Uh-huh. I think I knew it early on, too. I mean, you scared me so hard that first night I almost died, but I still signed up for your class."

Judah laughed into Connor's kiss. "And thank God you did," he said. "I was hooked on you from the minute we met, Connor Devlin, and I'll always be glad that you came back to me."

Fin

BONUS SCENE

I could squash this guy like a bug.

Forcing a smile, Connor set his hand over Judah's where it lay on the pub table, though he took care not to squeeze too hard. It wasn't Judah's fault that Connor's jaw was so tight it ached. No, that was on Seb, Judah's blue-haired ex-boyfriend and thorn in Connor's side, who sat across the table from them, talking up a storm. Seb, who brought out a side of Connor he hardly recognized, a sullen, *grumpy* side that wanted to growl anytime Seb so much as touched Judah. Which Seb did of course, being an affectionate guy who freely doled out hugs and kisses to his friends.

Seb had brought a date tonight at least, a fellow musician named Ellis who played the French horn and seemed perfectly nice. Connor was still fighting his grumbly feelings, however, even as a tiny line between Judah's eyebrows told him he might not be doing such a great job. Which sort of made Connor want to kick his own ass. He'd said yes when Judah had suggested they meet Seb for dinner, after all, and even suggested they meet at this pub, a low-key place he liked for its no-frills burgers and beer, as well as the fantastic view of Boston Harbor the pub offered from its back windows.

You suggested coming here because you didn't want Seb in Judah's apartment.

Okay, that was true; seeing Seb in the apartment over Hook Me was something Connor liked to avoid. He didn't like that Seb was so obviously at home there, moving through the rooms with an ease Connor wasn't sure he felt yet himself, even after six months with Judah. Then again, Seb had lived in that apartment with Judah for over two years, and they shared a history Connor couldn't change if he'd wanted to.

And he didn't, really. Connor didn't want to break up a friendship, not when he'd parted on good terms with every one of his own exes and still kept in touch with each through emails and texts. Seb was also fiercely loyal to Judah and a rock-solid support, things Connor honestly admired when he wasn't acting like a possessive jerk, and the guy could be a lot of fun to hang out with, too.

"This food is fantastic," Seb said now, his expressive face aglow as he worked his way through a platter of broiled scallops. "I'm kicking myself for never coming in here before tonight though, and that's something I blame on you, babe."

Judah aimed an arch look across the table at Seb. "Yeah, no. *You* are the one you should blame, girl, because you declared this entire restaurant off limits after Evil Kurt got a job behind the bar."

Seb's dark eyes went almost comically wide. "Oh, hell, you're right. I totally forgot about that fuckface!" He turned a grin on Ellis. "Evil Kurt and I dated for a hot second before I met Judah. I'd thought I was done with him, but he lingered like toxic waste and got a job almost literally across the street from our apartment."

"More like across the street and five blocks from the apartment." Judah's tone was dry. He'd opted for fried calamari and slipped some crispy battered rings onto Connor's plate as he spoke, knowing Connor would nibble at them. The gesture made Connor smile. "The guy was definitely an asshat, though, and I got why you wanted to avoid him."

Connor frowned. "Does he still work here?"

Seb wrinkled his nose. "Nope. Last I'd heard, Evil Kurt had relocated to Seattle and I was not sad to see the last of his bougie ass."

That got a chuckle from Ellis who, like Connor, had ordered a burger. "What made the guy evil?"

"He was literally incapable of keeping his dick in his pants." Seb made his voice droll. "Now, I appreciate that not everyone is into monogamy, but he knew it was what I wanted at the time and still didn't give a damn. He also blamed *me* for his wandering eye because dating a vers guy was, and I quote, 'way more work than any one man should be expected to do.'"

"What?" Ellis laughed, spluttering into his beer while Judah hid a smile behind his hand. "He actually said that?"

Seb snorted. "He totally did. And what a crock of shit. The least he could have done was admit he wanted to fuck around instead of making it about having to top every once in a while, like it was such a chore."

Jeez.

Connor's face went hot. Even if some part of him had wanted to know how Seb liked to get off (and Connor really, really hadn't), he sure wished he could un-ring that bell. But he never knew how to react when Seb flipped into TMI mode, something the guy did all the damned time, especially when talk turned to sex.

Seb smirked, a wicked gleam in his eye. "Anyway, Evil Kurt didn't last long, but it's not like I cared. I'd already met Judah through friends, see, and was happy to learn he was neither evil nor lazy and just as vers as me."

Fork clattering onto his plate, Judah buried his face in his hands while Seb and Ellis cackled loudly. Connor's smile was frozen on his face, however, and his stomach had gone hard and acid. What the hell was Seb thinking, talking about Judah like that with Connor sitting *right freaking there?*.

Judah's groan sounded pained. "God, Seb. Why are you like this?"

"Because you love it. And hey, no need to be a prude just because you've got a new man in your life."

"I'm not being a prude!"

"Mmm, you kind of are, Jude. You've never been shy about sharing your sexploits before." Seb raised an eyebrow at Connor, the amusement in that one gesture enough to make Connor's blood boil. "Big Con's cheeks are awfully red, though, so maybe he's the reason you've turned over this new leaf? I sometimes forget that he's an old-fashioned guy who likes to play his cards close to his vest."

Squash. Him.

Connor drew a deep breath. "Don't talk about me like I'm not here. Yes, I like to keep my private life to myself. Guard things that are special to me. Not sure why you'd have a problem with that, but if it makes me old-fashioned—"

"It doesn't."

A smiling Judah emerged from behind his hands, dark hair askew, and looked at Connor like he was the best thing he'd ever laid eyes on.

"I've always liked that about you," he said as he wrapped his hand around Connor's. "That you're reserved, but never closed off. Choosy about who you get to know. When you started letting me in, I knew I had to pay attention, because it was already obvious you don't do that for everyone."

The shine in his gray-green eyes instantly loosened the knot in Connor's chest and Connor smiled, ignoring the heat crawling over his cheeks yet again. He didn't care that Seb and Ellis were watching or give a damn what they thought. Judah had proven once again that he really *got* Connor, personality quirks and all, and that was more than enough to cool the fire in Connor's blood.

The heat didn't fade entirely, however, not even after he and Judah bid Seb and Ellis good night. Connor didn't know what to make of that or himself as he strolled through their neighborhood's streets with Judah, their fingers loosely linked. He'd never been a jealous boyfriend. Had never had a rival. And not once felt territorial about the women he'd dated or that he'd needed to work overtime to keep their attention.

Maybe because you didn't love them the way you do Jude.

Connor thought that little voice in his head had a point. He'd never felt like this before. Like he'd been stripped bare and filled up, all at the same time. Humbled. Made whole. And stuffed so full of happy that sometimes he could hardly breathe.

If he were honest, Connor was still falling for his guy and the trip was so utterly wonderful he hoped it never ended. And that helped him see just how much he stood to lose if this thing —this life—he wanted with Judah ever fell apart.

Enter Seb, with his knowing smile and husky laugh, who knew Judah far more intimately than Connor liked to acknowledge. Seb couldn't have been more different from Connor if he'd tried. He was so elegant and urbane, and adventurous in ways Connor couldn't comprehend. Seb wasn't reserved about *anything*, including announcing he'd had sex with Judah in ways Connor hadn't, because not once had Connor imagined Judah might like to be topped. And why?

Connor loved giving himself to Judah. Loved the feeling of surrender that came when Judah slid inside him, and knowing he was wanted and desired. That Judah had chosen him and the connection that thrummed between them, each touch electric in ways Connor still couldn't fathom.

Did Judah want those things too? Crave them the way Connor did but simply never said so? Connor didn't know. He felt sure he needed to pay better attention to his guy, though, and do everything he could to make sure Judah knew Connor had chosen him, too.

Judah ran his thumb over Connor's knuckles and stifled a sigh. His guy had been too quiet tonight, gaze searching as it flicked between Judah and Seb, and watchful in a way that Judah didn't like. He wasn't sure why Connor still seemed uncomfortable around Seb, as if he weren't sure how to act, or why he denied it when asked as his clouded brow told a different story.

The funny thing was that Connor really *tried* with Seb. He didn't balk when the guy turned up early on a weekend and woke them for yoga class, or organized a dinner like the one they'd shared tonight. Connor had even involved himself in the planning this time and offered up one of his favorite pubs as the venue. He'd been friendly if not super chatty during the meal, and his demeanor had only cracked after Seb had started talking sex and cheerfully dragged Judah along.

Not that Judah blamed Connor for being annoyed; no one needed to hear how he and Seb had liked to fuck. Especially in front of Connor who was so private about matters that were close to his heart. Connor seemed uncomfortable even talking about exes, and particularly so when the ex in question was Seb, a man Judah had once loved.

"*I thought we'd make it long term.*" Judah's insides

squirmed as he recalled his own words. *"That we'd get the big, romantic story with the happily ever after."*

He'd said that one night after they'd run into Seb, in fact, back in the very early days of Judah's friendship with Connor. Connor had surprised him by turning surly in the face of Seb's megawatt smile, discomfort rolling off him in almost palpable waves as he'd tried to understand how Judah's ex-boyfriend fit into his life ...

Well, shit.

Did Connor feel insecure about Seb? And why?

Judah's stomach dipped. He'd made it clear he didn't have eyes for anyone else—that Connor was it for him, now and for as long as Connor wanted him around. Which was all well and good, until one considered that Connor had never been with a man before Judah. Had never been in love, either, or exchanged those three powerful little words with anyone outside of his family. Even now, with six months between them, Connor said them to Judah with such reverence that Judah's throat went tight every time. Which could mean that Connor still needed time to understand what Judah loving *him* meant for his own life.

After reaching Judah's building, they climbed the stairs to his apartment, neither speaking as Judah unlocked the door. He leaned against it once they were inside, glad his brother was away with friends so they could talk without interruption.

Despite the somewhat heavy vibe, delight swooped through Judah as he looked at the man before him. Connor was suntanned from being outside this summer during calls on Ambulance P1 and his dark blond beard and hair were tinged with gold. His gaze was intense and almost soulful, though, like he thought he was about to get a truckload of really bad news and Judah couldn't imagine what the hell was going through the big guy's head.

"What is it, Con?"

"Oh. Um." Connor licked his lips. "Jude, do I make you feel good? When we're in bed, I mean."

Judah blinked. "Yes. You make me feel more than good, honestly. Like, I'd use the word 'amazing', if I didn't think it'd go to your head." That got a shy smile. With a chuckle, Judah set his hands on Connor's waist, his tension easing somewhat when Connor looped his arms around Judah's neck. "Is there a reason you asked?"

"I've been thinking about some of the things Seb said during dinner tonight."

"Okay. Things you want to talk about? I'm happy to do that with you, Connor if that's what—"

"I do. Because I couldn't help wondering, you know? If maybe you need more than you're getting from me or want something different. The way you had with Seb."

Oh, hell.

The air in Judah's lungs left him in a whoosh. This was about the vers comment—*had* to be—and all because Seb had run his stupid mouth instead of filling it with food.

"Conner, I—" Judah broke off, throat going thicker than his favorite handknitted socks before he had to look away. There was nothing about their sex life he didn't crave and want and welcome, and knowing Connor doubted that stung. "I love what we have, so much. What you and I do together ... it's everything I need."

"Hey."

Touch gentle, Connor grasped Judah's chin with his fingers and tugged gently until Judah looked his way. But his expression was more worried than ever when their finally gazes met and *man*, Judah was going to strangle Seb the next time he saw him.

"I believe you," Connor said. "And I didn't mean to make you feel bad, Jude, so I'm sorry if I did."

Judah ducked his head and pressed a quick kiss against Connor's fingers. "Don't be. I know you didn't mean anything by it. I *am* concerned about what you might be thinking, however. That you believe I want someone else, or—"

"I don't. I've never thought that even once."

"Well, good. Because there isn't a thing you and I do together that I don't love, Con, every single time."

Connor cupped Judah's cheek. "I know that, Jude. But Seb was telling the truth, right? About you being ...?" His voice rose in pitch a bit as he trailed off, and Judah had to laugh.

"About my being vers? Yeah, that's true. But all that means is that I like to do whatever feels good in the moment when I'm having sex, whether I'm on top or the bottom or no one's getting fucked at all. Sex isn't always about penetration, Con, and you know better than anyone how much fun we can have just with our fingers and mouths." He gave another soft laugh at the shiver that shook Connor's frame.

"I see your point." Eyes heavy-lidded, Connor nuzzled Judah's cheek with the tip of his nose, the invitation in his voice unmistakable. "But if you did want more or even different from what we've had, I'd want that too, for you *and* for me.

"Mmm, okay. I'm happy to do whatever you want, and I'd love it if you wanted to fuck me. I'd also want to know that it was for *us* and not because a certain blue-haired pain in my ass made you think something that isn't true."

Eyes bright and adoring, Connor laughed, his body still shaking with it as he kissed Judah. The heat that sparked between them made Judah groan, and his stomach gave a giddy flip when Connor mashed him against the door.

"This is definitely about us," Connor said between kisses. "Seb got me thinking, sure, but it was all me from there.

Haven't been able to think about much else since we left the pub to come back here."

Judah laughed. "Oh, yeah?"

"Mmm-hmm. I love it when you're inside me. The way you make me feel." Connor pushed his knee between Judah's and smiled at his sigh. "Couldn't help wondering if you'd want that with me. I've never been that way with anyone, because the girls that I dated … well, it just never came up. I know I'd love it with you, though."

Judah had to bite back a groan. Sharing these firsts with his guy—knowing he saw a side of Connor that no one ever had—thrilled him beyond reason. And he felt very smug as he reached down and squeezed Connor's ass, lust leaping inside him at Connor's low noise.

"I know I'd love it with you, too. And like I keep telling you, just do what feels good and you're going to be fine."

They crossed the apartment to Judah's bedroom, kissing and groping as they peeled off each other's clothes. Judah basked in acres of warm muscle as they fell into bed, and he sighed as Connor rolled on top of him, the weight of that big body exactly what he wanted.

God*damn*, he was down with this role reversal.

Spreading his legs, Judah brought his knees up as Connor settled between them, then gently dug his heels into the meat of Connor's ass, insides going liquid at Connor's scorching kiss. They ground against each other slowly, the fire in Judah mounting with each movement. Desire skittered through him like electric sparks as Connor nipped at Judah's jaw, beard bristles rasping the sensitized skin, and Judah hardly recognized his own voice as he groaned.

"How do you want me?" he somehow got out, then smiled at Connor's soft laugh.

"Pretty sure that's a question I should be asking you."

"I love that you would. I'd answer that I want you behind me., Connor, holding me down with both hands while you use lots of lube."

Connor let out a strangled little moan. "God, okay. You'll tell me if I go too rough?"

"Sure, unless it feels good." Judah snickered at Connor's shudder, balls throbbing as turned onto his stomach.

Sitting up, Connor reached for the nightstand while Judah pulled a pillow close and wrapped his arms around it. He pressed his cheek against the cool cotton, eyes slipping shut when the lube bottle clicked behind him, then sank deeper into the bedding as Connor spread Judah's thighs. Heat zig-zagged under Judah's skin like a wildfire running rampant.

Connor was rarely tentative about sex these days, but his touch was light as he fingered Judah's rim. He used a generous amount of lube in his teasing, a gesture Judah would have appreciated if he hadn't been about to lose his mind. Connor's dick was big, just like the rest of him, and it'd been a long time since Judah had bottomed. Judah was having trouble stringing two thoughts together, though, and sweat broke out on his skin as Connor teased a fingertip just inside him.

"Ohhh, fuck. Just like that," Judah mumbled, arching into the touch in a shameless bid for contact. He gasped as Connor went deeper. "More. *Please*. Not gonna break."

"I know. You're so strong." Stretching out beside Judah, Connor cradled him close with his free arm. "I want you to be ready though, and I'm not gonna rush."

Judah relaxed as best he could into the embrace, heeding his body's cues as Connor stretched him open. He held tight to Connor's arm as he panted and groaned, reveling in the sensations pulsing through him and uncaring of how strung out he'd already become. The kisses Connor dropped against Judah's shoulder and face humbled him, so he was trembling by the time Connor slipped a second finger in beside the first.

God, Judah loved this. Connor's skin dragging against his own and being held so tight, the scrape of beard chased by soft lips and wet tongue. The burn in Judah's ass changed, pleasure edging into the ache, and he became aware he was pushing back against the long fingers pumping in and out of him as he rutted mindlessly into the sheets.

"Con. Need more," he whispered, then moaned into Connor's kiss, chest pinching hard when Connor slipped his fingers free.

Biting his lip, Judah buried his face in the pillow, the urge to call Connor back overwhelming. But Connor was already moving, settling onto his heels atop the matress so he could rub circles into Judah's skin with his hands.

Judah pushed up onto his knees, breathless as he lifted his ass high and rested his forehead on his folded arms. His skin pebbled with goosebumps when Connor went still.

"God, Jude. You look amazing. So gorgeous."

The awe in his voice made Judah's cheeks burn but he smiled too, pride buzzing through him like a sugar high. He loved the way Connor looked at him, like Judah was the best thing he could ever have imagined, and a shiver went through him as Connor pressed a kiss against his hip.

He stayed quiet when Connor came up behind him and fisted the sheets as Connor's cock nudged his rim. Expecting more teasing, he gasped when Connor pushed forward instead, exerting steady pressure with his dick as he split Judah open in a long, slow stroke. Judah uttered a broken moan.

"Jesus," Connor whispered, the wonder in that one word going straight to Judah's balls.

The strength in his legs wavered as Connor bottomed out, leaving Judah weak, and he sank onto the mattress with a sigh, grateful for Connor's steadying touch. Covering Judah's body with his own, Connor reached for his hand where it lay on the mattress, then twinted their fingers together. His breath was warm against Judah's cheek as he rocked in and out of Judah, and he groaned softly with each pass, sounding awestruck and overcome.

Eyes closed, Judah held Connor's hand tight, sure that Connor was watching him closely. The ache in his body shifted, a bone deep pleasure building as he reveled in the weight that pinned him to the sheets and the ragged harmony of their breaths. Connor's powerful thighs were caging Judah and squeezing just right, and every nerve in his body fired when Connor pushed especially deep, the motion dragging his cock over Judah's prostate and tearing a yell from Judah's throat.

Connor gasped, the sound so raw and real that Judah lost himself in it, his pleasure sharpening to a point of near pain. His eyes flew open a heartbeat later when Connor suddenly backed off and pulled out, the loss of sensation so total it rocked him to his core.

"What happened?" He struggled onto one elbow, his heart in his throat, though the bolt of near panic fizzled in the wake of another bone-melting kiss.

"Nothing bad," Connor murmured when they finally came back up for air. "Needed to see you, though. Want to watch your eyes while we do this."

Judah huffed a soft laugh. "Okay. We can do that."

He relaxed against the pillows, smiling as Connor laid him out, then quickly wound his arms around Connor's neck after the big guy had settled himself between Judah's thighs once more. Gaze locked on Judah's, Connor pushed back inside, his eyes going big and liquid he moved them over Judah's face.

"Love you," he said, in the low, earnest voice that broke Judah's heart wide open every time he heard it.

"I love you, too."

He drew Connor down, eyes rolling behind his closed lids as they kissed, the heat and pressure of being filled so fucking good. Hooking his heels over the backs of Connor's thighs, he whined as the coil inside him drew tight.

"Fuck, baby. Don't stop."

"I won't." Connor pressed his forehead to Judah's, tendrils of his hair brushing Judah's cheeks as he panted. "And God, you feel so good. So hot and tight, I can't ... *Fuck*."

Yes.

Judah bit his lip. He lived for these moments. Lived to see this big man in his arms come completely undone. Hear him curse and moan, so leveled by pleasure he turned needy and desperate, like he'd never get enough.

Hauling his guy closer, Judah gasped at the pressure Connor's body put on his cock, surrounding the shaft and head with exactly the heat and friction he craved. And God, he was close. Had been for so long, he felt almost like he was floating as he and Connor moved together.

He babbled and swore as Connor snaked a hand between them, but it didn't take more than a couple of pumps to send Judah soaring, and he arched up into Connor, his mouth falling open. Orgasm swamped him, starting in Judah's ass before it took hold of his dick, the huge waves of pleasure turning him inside out. Helpless, he shuddered hard again and again, his cock pulsing over Connor's fist.

Connor moaned. "Fuck, Jude."

Judah held him tight, head spinning like he'd had too many drinks. Reaching up, he grabbed Connor's hair and tugged lightly, smiling when Connor's next thrust stuttered.

"That's it," Judah crooned.

Connor came apart with a cry, face buried tight in Judah's neck, his thrusts going slow and lazy as he rode out his high. He was still panting when he finally rolled off, but he immediately snuggled in, cheek pressed against Judah's chest as they cradled each other close.

They lay wrapped together a while, coasting on endorphins and swapping kisses until Judah started drifting. He bit back a grumble when Connor finally stirred, then clung tighter to keep him close. He hummed in triumph when Connor went back to kissing him, but making out just made Judah feel even more sex-drunk and boneless, and he'd given up fighting it the second time Connor pulled away.

With effort, Judah peeled open an eye. "You coming back?"

"Yes, of course."

"M'kay. Then I'll stay right here."

He curled up on his side, smiling at Connor's soft laughter, and listened as he puttered around, probably picking their clothes up from the floor on his way to the bathroom. The lines of Judah's world grew softer and more hazy with each breath he took, and when the mattress dipped under Connor's weight again, he blinked, knowing from Connor's indulgent expression that he'd drifted off for a bit.

"Sorry." Judah smiled. "Guess I passed out again."

"Only for a minute. I wasn't gone long." Connor held a washcloth against Judah's belly. "Thought you could use this."

"You're such a gentleman." Judah lay still as Connor wiped him down, motions loving as always, if maybe more gentle than usual. "Do you want to stay tonight? I know you're on early tomorrow, but I can be up, too."

"I'd like that." Smiling, Connor set the washcloth on the floor beside the bed, then ran a hand over Judah's ass, patting him softly. "How do you feel?"

"I feel fucking great. Definitely like my guy screwed my

brains out and that I loved every second." Judah grinned wide when Connor ducked his head and laughed, his cheeks that adorable pink. "I'm guessing you loved it, too?"

"Oh, I did. I might use the word 'amazing.'"

"That's my guy. And you'd want to do it again sometime?"

"I would." Climbing back into bed, Connor burrowed in close and pressed a kiss against Judah's shoulder. "I already loved what we were doing, though, and the way you make me feel. I'd never want to lose that."

Judah pressed his nose against Connor's hair and breathed him in. "I don't want to lose that, either. Because you're the only one I want to do this with, Con."

"I know that, Jude. I really do. You're it for me, too." Connor yawned. "And I'm going to apologize now for getting up extra early tomorrow. I have to run home for my uniform before I head for the station."

"Okay. Not like you haven't done that before." Judah closed his eyes. "You could always leave a couple of uniforms here, you know, if that makes your life easier." His eyes flew open again when Connor shifted suddenly, propping himself up on an elbow with a grin so big, Judah had to laugh. "You like that idea?"

"I do. A lot. Although you might be sad when you realize just how many pieces of brown clothing I actually own."

Judah barked out a laugh. "I doubt that very much. And I'll clear out as much space in my closet as you need."

AUTHOR'S NOTE

Thank you for reading! I hope you enjoyed Connor and Judah's story. Please consider adding a short review on Goodreads or Amazon and let me know what you thought—I would love to hear from you.

ACKNOWLEDGMENTS

Lord of the Flies: William Golding
Facebook: Facebook, Inc.
Instagram: Facebook, Inc.
The Lord of the Rings: J. R. R. Tolkien
The Incredible Hulk: Marvel Comics
Jeep: Fiat Chrysler Automobiles
True Detective: Nic Pizzolato
Zoom: Zoom Video Communications
The Mandalorian: Jon Favreau
Yoda: George Lucas

ABOUT THE AUTHOR

K. Evan Coles is a mother and tech pirate by day and a writer by night. She is a dreamer who, with a little hard work and a lot of good coffee, coaxes words out of her head and onto paper.

K. lives in the northeast United States, where she complains bitterly about the winters, but truly loves the region and its diverse, tenacious, and deceptively compassionate people. You'll usually find K. nerding out over books, movies and television with friends and family. She's especially proud to be raising her son as part of a new generation of unabashed geeks.

K.'s books explore LGBTQ+ romance in contemporary settings.

For more books and updates:
https://kevancoles.com/

facebook.com/kevancolesauthor
twitter.com/K_Evan_Coles
instagram.com/k.evan.coles
bookbub.com/profile/k-evan-coles
pinterest.com/kevancoles

ALSO BY K. EVAN COLES

WICKED FINGERS PRESS (SELF-PUBLISHED)

Stealing Hearts

Thief of Hearts (Novella)

Healing Hearts (Novella)

Open Hearts (Novel)

Hooked On You (Novel)

Overexposed (Novella, 2021. Also included in the *Working Stiffs*
COVID-19 Charity Anthology)

A Hometown Holiday (Novella)

Moonlight (Short Story)

PRIDE PUBLISHING (TOTALLY ENTWINED GROUP)

Boston Seasons (Novels)

Third Time's the Charm

Easy For You To Say (TBD)

Tidal Duology w/ Brigham Vaughn (Novels)

Wake

Calm

The Speakeasy w/ Brigham Vaughn (Novels)

With a Twist

Extra Dirty

Behind the Stick

Straight Up

OFF TOPIC PRESS (SELF-PUBLISHED)

Inked in Blood w/ Brigham Vaughn (Short Story)

––––––––

http://www.kevancoles.com

Made in the USA
Monee, IL
26 February 2021